5/18

The
Whispered Kiss

Center Point
Large Print

Also by Marcia Lynn McClure and available from Center Point Large Print:

Dusty Britches
Weathered Too Young
The Windswept Flame
The Visions of Ransom Lake
The Heavenly Surrender
The Light of the Lovers' Moon
Beneath the Honeysuckle Vine

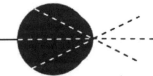

This Large Print Book carries the Seal of Approval of N.A.V.H.

The
Whispered Kiss

Marcia Lynn McClure

CENTER POINT LARGE PRINT
THORNDIKE, MAINE

Library of Congress Cataloging-in-Publication Data

Names: McClure, Marcia Lynn, author.
Title: The whispered kiss / Marcia Lynn McClure.
Description: Center Point large print edition. | Thorndike, Maine :
    Center Point Large Print, 2018.
Identifiers: LCCN 2017057926 | ISBN 9781683247210
    (hardcover : alk. paper)
Subjects: LCSH: Large type books.
Classification: LCC PS3613.C36 W48 2018 | DDC 813/.6—dc23
LC record available at https://lccn.loc.gov/2017057926

To Amanda
Thank you for such beautiful inspiration and
such beautiful, beloved friendship!
To you—"Beauty" personified!

And to Amy, My "Aimes"
Sweet and cherished friend
(who will someday be a spy),
For encouragement, support,
and blessed friendship,
And for uttering my favorite "two-liner" ever . . .
"Let the games begin!
Do we get to see ___ _____?"

My everlasting admiration, gratitude, and love . . .
To my husband, Kevin . . .
For being just enough of a "Bad Boy"
to make life truly exciting!
I Love You!

PROLOGUE

Antoine de Bellamont sat trembling in the presence of the dark Lord of Roanan. How could plucking one bloom from a rose vine have found him thus?

"And what explanation do you offer for your thievery, man?" The dark lord's angry voice boomed, echoing through the grand hall like a violent, threatening storm.

"I-I would hardly call it thievery, milord," Antoine replied. "One bloom from such a rose vine as that on your eastern wall . . . it is merely a trifle."

"You trespassed upon my grounds and stole from me!" the dark lord roared. " 'Tis thievery as the law deems it—plain and simple! And that without reckoning for the trespassing, for which I may take the liberty of killing you!"

"But surely, milord—" Antoine began.

"Silence!" the Lord of Roanan barked.

Antoine swallowed the hard lump of fear in his throat. He fancied his heart had been residing there since the moment he was escorted into Roanan Manor House.

He watched the man sitting in the shadows before him. Enormous in stature, the dark lord's size alone was enough to intimidate. Yet with the angry voice and a character apparently void of any compassion, the Lord of Roanan was no less than terrifying. Antoine wished for a moment he could see the man's face more clearly. Similar intimidation he had never known. Even for his trade as a merchant, he had not known such a threatening presence as now sat before him, half hidden in shadow. Still, in the next moment, Antoine de Bellamont was grateful he could not make out the man's countenance—his features. Better to leave the devil's face a mystery.

"I asked for an explanation, and you have given me none. Only feeble excuses," the dark lord said. "What explanation do you offer, thief? I ask this for the last time, so speak the truth. I will know if you are in earnest . . . or a liar as well as a thief."

Again, Antoine swallowed hard. He reached up with one trembling hand to brush a lock of silver hair from his forehead. Perhaps the truth would set him free.

"I am a merchant, milord—Antoine de Bellamont—from one day's ride south of here, in the port town of Bostchelan," he began. "Do you know it?"

"Of course I know it, you imbecile!" the dark lord growled.

"Forgive me. Of course, sire," Antoine continued. "A merchant I am. However, I have been informed just this morning by a messenger

8

that my ships, all three, have been pirated—all cargo aboard lost as well."

"Pirated," the dark lord mumbled. "Thieves . . . such as yourself."

"No, sire, please. Only wait," Antoine pleaded. "I am penniless, destitute, and must now return to Bostchelan to my four daughters . . . all of whom will now suffer in great impoverishment."

"What has this to do with your own thievery? What has this to do with my rose?" the dark lord demanded.

"I am returning to my daughters, milord," Antoine explained. "Of the four, three are quite spoiled, I am reluctant to admit. I have pampered them, given them anything they required or desired."

"Then you prove yourself an imbecile as well as an appalling parent," the Lord of Roanan said.

Antoine nodded, though he was loath to agree with the angry man. Antoine knew himself to be a good parent. Hadn't he given his daughters everything they had ever desired? What made a good parent if not that? He suspected such a cruel man, as sat cloaked in shadow before him, had no children. What would such a dark lord know of parenting? Still, he was fearful, and agree he must. And yet a vision of Coquette entered his mind then—Coquette, who asked for nothing, expected nothing. Coquette, for whom Antoine had plucked the fateful rose.

He continued his explanation, gazing with pleading eyes into the shadows hiding the man's face, "Yet there is one daughter, my little Coquette . . . she is unlike her sisters. When I asked her what I might bring back for her from my travels to Roanan . . . she asked only for a flower—a rose, that she might gaze upon its beauty in remembrance of her dead mother."

"How touching," the dark lord growled. "I see you put the little one on the same path as the others . . . the road to ruination by way of spoiling her."

"No," Antoine said. "Coquette is not little. I only call her little because she is so very precious to me. Coquette is this month twenty and one."

"Twenty and one and begging for a flower?" the dark lord mumbled. "Is she malformed? Why has she not wed? Why have none of your daughters yet wed? Methinks were they wed, your destitution would not matter so much and your thievery may have been avoided."

"My daughters, all four, are very beautiful, my lord . . . Coquette most of all," Antoine explained. "But I fear I have found no suitor worthy of any of them, particularly Coquette."

The dark lord was silent. Antoine hoped pity for his daughters would keep the man from exacting any punishment for the stolen rose.

"A sad, emotive story indeed, merchant," he said at last.

10

Antoine smiled, relieved. He felt hope rising—hope of being released, of avoidance of peril.

In the next moment, however, the dark lord stood, drew his sword, and slammed it down on the table between them. Antoine gasped, startled and terrified.

"I am not without compassion," the Lord of Roanan growled. "Therefore, I will give you your own choice. Do you know the laws of Roanan pertaining to thievery?" he asked.

Antoine swallowed, the beaded perspiration on his brow beginning to trickle over his temples. Indeed, he knew the laws.

"Amputation, milord. Amputation of . . . of the hands," he stammered. Pain pinched at his wrists as he looked at the steel blade drawn before him.

"That is correct, merchant," the dark lord said. "I may cut off your hands for stealing from me. Here and now, without pause, I may do it, and the law would not question."

"Please, milord!" Antoine began, panic rising in him like a killing fire. "Please! How . . . how would I provide for my daughters? How would I live without my hands?"

"Where were these thoughts before you stole from me, thief?" the Lord of Roanan asked.

"Please, sire, please," Antoine begged, trembling as he watched the man raise his blade. "You . . . you spoke of a choice. You . . . you said you would give me my own choice. What choice did you speak of?"

Sword yet in hand, the dark lord turned his wrist this way and that, the sword, the glint of the steel, catching the dim light. "It is very sharp. An excellent weapon. The cut will be swift and clean, I assure you," he said.

Antoine gulped, terror and fear as he had never imagined rising in him. "What choice do you speak of, milord? Please! I beg your mercy!"

He heard the dark lord inhale deeply, releasing the breath in one long, slow exhale.

"Your hands or your daughter. The one you favor . . . the good one, the unspoiled one. What did you call her?" the dark lord asked.

"Coquette," Antoine whispered.

"Yes, that was it. The only daughter who will not care you are destitute, merchant. The daughter for whom you stole from me. I will take her hand in marriage instead of yours from your arm here at my table. I will wed her, for I am in need of an heir. I will even restore your trade to you. Three ships? Is that what the pirates took from you? Then I will give you three ships and this as well."

Antoine's eyes widened as the dark lord drew a black velvet purse from his coat pocket and tossed it on the table. The sound of the purse landing on the table echoed through the grand hall, and Antoine knew it held a great sum.

"Seventy gold pieces, merchant. Payment

12

for you daughter," the dark lord said. "Or I can take your hands." A triumphant chuckle emanated from within the shadows as the Lord of Roanan continued, "But I am not a monster. Thus the choice is yours. I will cut off only one of your hands here and now—whichever one you choose—and you may seek the aid of the physician in Roanan. I will have you brought to him as soon as the deed is done, in fact. You will surely survive and be able to continue to provide for your daughters—perhaps not in the manner to which they have become accustomed, but provide for them you may all the same. Or . . . you can give me something in return for the thing you stole from me . . . your daughter."

"You . . . you would leave me both hands and restore my ships and trade?" Antoine asked. Perhaps it was good fortune, not bad, that led him to pluck the rose.

"In return for your favorite daughter as wife," the dark lord growled.

"Still, Coquette," Antoine hesitated, "sh-she has done nothing to deserve such—"

"No. She has not," the Lord of Roanan confirmed. "And yet you consider it, do you not, merchant?"

Antoine moistened his lips as he gazed at the velvet purse on the table before him. He must have his hands, both of them! Such a deformity was surely not comely, not to mention the pain of amputation. Further, however would he provide necessity for his daughters without one or the other? And how would he provide necessity for them without his ships? Surely he could not be expected to kneel to hard labor to provide for them. Even yet, hard labor would not provide for their extravagances.

"Still . . . she is my daughter," Antoine whispered, reaching for the purse.

He startled and yelped as the sharp blade of the dark lord's sword bit into the table near his hand.

"Make your choice, merchant, for my patience is wearing far thin," the dark lord growled.

Antoine moistened his lips again. It was not a hard choice to make. Coquette, angel that she was, would never be happy knowing her sisters were not. His ships and trade restored! Why, with seventy gold pieces, he could return to Bostchelan a wealthy man and fill the list his daughters had given him—all but Coquette's request.

"What of the rose, milord?" Antoine asked then. "May I . . . may I retain it and present it to Coquette if I choose to give her over to you?"

There was silence as the dark lord seemed to consider his request.

"Yes," he growled.

"And you will treat her well?" Antoine asked. He would not have Coquette treated poorly—at least, not too poorly.

"No," the Lord of Roanan answered. "I am the Lord of Roanan. I will take from her what I will when I will! She will serve me as I deem she should."

"But she is kind, milord, her spirit as beautiful as her image. I-I—" Antoine stammered, still staring at the purse on the table.

"However," the dark lord interrupted, "she shall want for nothing. Any possession she desires, she shall have. This I promise you."

Antoine grinned. Triumph! His ships and trade restored, his hands still attached to his person. There was no question! He knew the choice Coquette would want him to make. At least, that is what he whispered to his conscience.

"Agreed," Antoine said. "I will keep my hand that I may provide for the three daughters left to me. You have promised to provide for my fourth, and though I am loath to give her over to you, it is the only choice before me."

"Is it?" the dark lord mumbled.

"But of course!" Antoine exclaimed. Oh, how relieved he was! "One daughter that I may keep my hand and provide for the other three?"

"I warn you," the dark lord began, his voice low and resolute, "I will have an heir . . . no matter what manner of treatment it may cost her. And once my heir is born, I will put her off as I would an old dog."

"But Coquette is strong, my lord," Antoine

explained. "The strongest and bravest of my four daughters. She can stand whatever treatment of her you see fit."

The dark Lord of Roanan was silent for a time—such a time that Antoine feared he had only been in jest, feared he did not truly intend to restore his trade and ships to him.

"Bostchelan is one day's ride from Roanan," the dark lord said at last. "If your daughter is not here by the sun's set the day after next . . . then I will ride to Bostchelan myself, cut off your hand, and you shall have no ships nor trade."

"Agreed," Antoine said, fairly leaping to his feet. He moistened his lips once more, nodding toward the purse on the table. "And the purse, milord?"

"Take the damned purse, merchant!" the Lord of Roanan roared. "And watch the port at Bostchelan for three ships to come to you."

Antoine reached out and gathered the purse into his hands. Carefully, eyes wide with excitement, he placed it in the pocket of his breeches.

"Thank you, Lord of Roanan . . . for your mercy," Antoine said, bowing low.

"Thank your daughter for my mercy, you coward!" the dark lord shouted. "Be gone! Be gone, before I change my mind and run you through before me!"

"Yes, at once, milord," Antoine said.

He turned, fleeing from the great hall of Roanan

16

Manor House. As he fled, he smiled. What luck! Surely such luck was not so simply applied. His ships returned! Seventy gold pieces in his pocket!

"Merchant!" the dark lord shouted.

Antoine stopped. He considered his chances of escaping through the open doors before him. Yet they were still twenty or more feet in advance. Two guards stood before them as well. He could not escape, and thus he turned.

"Yes, milord?" he choked.

"The rose," the dark lord said. "The purse you have, but you have neglected the rose."

"The rose?" Antoine asked.

"Godfrey," the dark lord ordered, "give the fool his damnable rose!"

Another man stepped from the shadows. Antoine had not noticed this man before and surmised he must have been standing near to the Lord of Roanan the length of the ordeal.

The man, older yet robust in appearance, lifted the rose from its resting place on the table. In his excitement over the purse of gold pieces, Antoine had completely forgotten the presence of the rose.

With the regiment, rhythm, and timing of one of the king's soldiers, the man named Godfrey strode to Antoine. He stopped short before him, clicking his heels together and extending his hand with the rose.

"I thank you," Antoine said.

"Remember, merchant," the dark lord called as Antoine hurried for the open doors and freedom, "by the sun's set day after next—she will be here or I will come for you."

Godfrey watched the merchant flee down the great steps of Roanan Manor House. Such cowardice! He could not believe he had witnessed it. The merchant had sold his daughter for the price of three ships and a purse of gold pieces. What kind of man valued his own hand and trade over a child?

Turning, Godfrey returned to his master's side.

"And what think you of it all, Godfrey?" his Lord of Roanan asked.

Godfrey shook his head and answered, "An abomination. I could never have imagined such cowardice in a father."

"Oh, there is more there than mere cowardice, Godfrey," the Lord of Roanan growled. He was silent for a moment and then asked, "And what think you of your master who threatened to cut off a man's hand for the sake of a stolen rose? What do you think of your master, who barters for a woman simply to acquire an heir?"

Godfrey was silent. He knew his master well. He knew his master better than his master knew himself. But that knowledge he would keep silent.

"I am in your service, milord," was his response.

"And so you are," the Lord of Roanan said.

Suddenly, the dark Lord of Roanan stood and returned his deadly blade to the scabbard at his hip. The sound of steel being sheathed echoed through the still darkness of the great hall. A moment later, the room echoed again, this time with the triumphant laughter of the dark lord himself.

"What fate has gifted me such sweet reckoning as this, Godfrey, I ask you?" the tall, dark, and fierce lord asked.

Godfrey looked to his lord, glad to be in servitude to Roanan's master and not indebted to him. He thought of Antoine de Bellamont. The merchant's choice was cowardly. Godfrey knew, even as he looked at the powerful, callous man before him, he would have let both his hands be severed rather than see a daughter married to such a man as his lord appeared.

"I ask you, Godfrey," the dark lord said again, stepping from the shadows, "which fate would wink upon me long enough to gift me this?"

"I know not, sire," Godfrey answered. Detestation and amusement blended together in his master's eyes, the result of a fierce flame of loathing.

He considered his lord and the rarity of the smile he now wore. Smiling out from the dim-lit room, the perfect white of his teeth flashed like a lion's. The dark brown waves of his hair framing his face and falling to the vast breadth of his shoulders only further accentuated his intimidating appearance. Large in stature, powerful in body and will, and as hard-hearted as the devil himself, the Lord of Roanan was not to be trifled with, and Godfrey felt ill at ease with no better answer to give his lord.

"That is true, Godfrey," the dark lord chuckled. "I forget myself, for you have no knowledge of the man who has only just sold his daughter to me for the price of a small merchant fleet. No knowledge of the merchant and no knowledge of the daughter."

"No, sire. 'Tis true I do not," Godfrey admitted.

He watched his lord's eyes narrow as he growled, " 'Tis true you do not, Godfrey. Yet I have. I have a knowledge beyond cognition, and I am fated to have my reckoning." His lord fell silent, eyes narrowed, brow puckered into the most scathing of frowns.

Godfrey startled when, in the next moment, his lord slammed one powerful fist upon the table.

"We must make haste, Godfrey," the dark lord commanded. "Two days hence I shall be expecting my bride."

"Yes, sire," Godfrey said with a nod.

The dark lord quirked one eyebrow in Godfrey's direction. "You doubt the merchant will keep his word," he said.

"He seems a coward, milord," Godfrey admitted.

"And a coward he is," his master replied. "And it is why I know he will sacrifice his daughter for wealth, rather than his hand for her sake."

"Yes, milord," Godfrey said, his own wrist aching at the thought of his lord's sharp blade.

"Then let us make haste," the dark lord said again, "for I am to be wed. And thereafter, my heir will be conceived at last."

"Yes, milord." Godfrey nodded, lowering his eyes as his master passed.

He watched his lord determinedly stride from the room, his long legs swiftly carrying him toward the grand staircase.

"Well," Victoria whispered as she stepped from the shadows, "fate indeed. What fate would find us with our lord taking a wife?"

Godfrey released the anxious breath he had been holding. He turned to Victoria, shaking his head in disbelief.

"I know not, madam," he said.

Victoria was the housemistress of Roanan Manor House and had been Godfrey's confidante for near to four years since his arrival. It was often they sat in contemplation of the mystery who was their master.

"I know of seven women who have offered to . . . to bear his heir, legitimate or otherwise, in the course of this past three months alone! And yet he refuses every one. Some know fathers more wealthy even than he is," Victoria offered in a whisper.

"There is yet no remarkable gossip in the village of any wicked dalliance with women where my lord is concerned," Godfrey said. "None other than the common gossip, of course."

"Though I myself have seen many a chambermaid and serving wench near to begging for his applied kiss," Victoria told him.

"That is true," Godfrey agreed. "Still, if he were of the low moral character of other titled men, we would hear of it. Yet the mystery of his anger, his hatred, and constant loathing of others—"

"Of women," Victoria corrected. "One does not serve in this house and yet avoid awareness of his loathing of women."

"His distrust of women, perhaps?" Godfrey offered.

"And yet he would wed a woman of no acquaintance or consequence . . . a merchant's daughter?" Victoria mused.

"A ruined merchant. A cowardly one at that," Godfrey mumbled.

Victoria sighed, shaking her head. "He confounds me." She raised her eyebrows, her eyes widening as she added, "Though I was not at all certain he would not chop the man's hands off right before our eyes!"

"I believe his desire was to do so," Godfrey said.

"I believe it was," Victoria agreed. "But he would not." Godfrey heard Victoria's sigh of relief. "And now?"

"And now," he continued, "now we wait for our new Lady of Roanan to arrive. For our lord will not look back once he has set his path."

"No. Indeed he will not," Victoria whispered.

Godfrey felt his eyes narrow as he gazed out the open doors of Roanan Manor House. How he pitied the girl whose father would sell her. How he worried for the girl who must endure an existence in the clutches of the powerful and apparently heartless Lord of Roanan.

FOR THE WANT
OF A ROSE

"Oh, Father!" Inez exclaimed. "Such perfect stitching and embroidery! Why, I've never seen the like. And the hue of this blue cloth—'tis the most beautiful gown you've ever given me. Thank you, Father! Thank you! Surely Henry Weatherby will propose now! When first he lays eyes upon me in this gown, how could he be anything but my willing servant?"

Antoine de Bellamont smiled, proud and pleased in his daughter's response to his gift of the extravagant gown. Inez was lovely with her dark hair and dark eyes. The gown would more than merely become her.

"And there shall be more gowns of this exquisite quality for all you girls," he said as Elise hugged him once more.

"Oh, Father! We will be envied indeed!" Elise said, brushing a stray strand of auburn hair from her cheek, her green eyes glistening with excitement. "No other woman in Boṭchelan owns such finery as we!" Her fingers caressed the soft pink gown cradled in her own arm.

"None, indeed!" Dominique giggled, holding her gown of green pressed against her bosom and admiring herself in the looking glass. "Will we

24

not be overwhelming to look upon, Coquette?" As she tossed her head and sent ebony ringlets dancing over her shoulders, Dominique's dark eyes burned with vanity.

"Overwhelming, indeed," Coquette said, smiling at her sisters.

A wave of guilt washed over Antoine then as he studied his youngest and loveliest daughter. She was completely resplendent in admiring the rose he had gifted her. Her smile far outshined the smiles of her sisters, even for having received the simplest gift. Still, his trade was restored, gold coins weighted his pockets, and Coquette would soon want for nothing. He further comforted himself in the knowledge she would soon be walking among the beautiful roses at Roanan Manor, to her utter contentment, no doubt. Surely, if one rose—one rose, which would soon wither and die—brought her such great joy, a garden of roses would bring her every happiness.

Yet fleeting as it seemed, the guilt Antoine felt lingered, however thinly residual. He knew he would not be rid of it until he told the tale to Coquette. He suspected he would not be rid of it until the morrow when she was well on her way to Roanan.

Thus, for his own sake, he began, "There is . . . there is something I must speak with you girls about. I am loath to do it, but it must be done. I feel now is the time."

"But, Father, our new dresses!" Inez whined. "I wish to wear my dress now so that you may see how well it enhances my beauty."

"Oh, yes, Father! Let us wear them for you first," Elise begged.

Antoine chuckled, amused by his daughters' excitement. Still, raising a hand, he said, "Only a moment of your day, girls. Only a moment, and then you may be off."

"But, Father, we are weary of talk," Dominique sighed.

"Father has brought you such lovely gifts," Coquette said. "Cannot you give him a few more moments? It is clear he has something important to—"

"Hush, Coquette," Inez interrupted. "Sniff your rose, and be content in it. You did not ask Father for a new dress, so do not be resentful that he did not bring one for you."

"I am not put off, Inez," Coquette said. "It is simply your lack of gratitude I do not understand."

"Now, girls," Antoine intervened. He smiled and took Coquette's hand in one of his. "I've had an adventure, Coquette," he began, "the like one can only dream of." He paused a moment, suddenly awed somehow by her great and unique beauty. Of all his daughters, Coquette resembled her mother most. He smiled at her, proud of her great beauty—her raven hair and emerald eyes

26

shaded by long, dark lashes, her cherry-red lips, her lovely and kind smile. Again, he was awash with guilt. Yet he knew it would pass.

"Have you, Father?" Coquette asked, her emerald eyes flashing with excitement.

"Yes," Antoine said. "And though it is more a nightmare than a dream to tell, tell you all I must—especially you, Coquette."

Coquette smiled. How she longed for adventure! Many were the times she had wished she could accompany her father on his travels—meet the exotic people he met, see the wonders of the world he saw. She gazed at him lovingly, touched he would remember to bring her a rose.

Her sisters had asked for new gowns, naturally. Their desires were ever toward new and exquisite gowns and baubles with which to stroke their own vanity. This kept their lists of wants endless. Yet for her part, Coquette only wished for the happiness of others—even her vain and shallow sisters. Most of all, she wished to see her father kept happy. It was, in fact, the circumstance for which she had sacrificed her own happiness— for her father's sake. She was certain his recent adventure, whatever it may be, had made him happy, for the light of joy was fairly resplendent in his eyes. Coquette was joyous to see him so excited. And so she welcomed her father's tale of adventure.

"Why so, Father?" Coquette asked. "Why should such an adventure be told to me in particular?"

"I was on my way, returning to you lovely girls, my precious jewels . . . by way of Roanan," her father began.

"I've always dreamt of Roanan!" Inez interrupted. "It is said they have the finest jewelers in the country there."

"Hush, Inez," Elise scolded. "Let Father go on with his tale that we may be about our own business."

Coquette sighed. It was weary she was of her sisters' careless behavior, their blatant lack of gratitude. A memory leapt to her mind—a memory, rather a consideration, of what her life might have been had not her father denied . . . but she would not dwell on the past.

"Go on, Father," she encouraged. "I am listening."

She watched as her father seemed to swallow with difficulty. Surely this was a sign of residual excitement. What an adventure he must have had indeed!

"I was passing through Roanan, and on the outer boundaries of the town I came upon the most glorious of estates!" Antoine continued. "Fine stone walls at least ten feet in height, surrounding the gardens and grounds of the most impressive manor house I had ever before seen."

Coquette closed her eyes for a moment, envisioning such grounds, such a wall surrounding them.

"Cached like a secret the house and grounds were, save the beautiful rose vines thriving just inside the front gates—massive iron gates, such craftsmanship I've yet to see elsewhere in this part of the country. And enveloping these massive gates . . . roses!"

"Like the one you brought Coquette?" Dominique asked.

"Yes, exactly," Antoine said. "I thought of my beloved daughters when I saw the beauty of these roses, but especially of you, Coquette, for you had asked me to bring you nothing save a rose to remind you of your mother."

Coquette nodded and smiled. She looked at the rose she held, the beautiful lavender rose her father had gifted her. It did indeed remind her of her sweet mother. How she had missed her mother since her passing! Nearly nine years it had been since her mother fell ill and died, and Coquette missed her every day.

"Did you pluck the rose from the iron gates of the house in Roanan then, Father?" Coquette asked. How she loved to envision it—the enormous gates, embellished with such beauty as she held in her hand.

"I began to," Antoine continued, "yet then I glanced beyond the gates to the gardens of the manor house. Would that I had simply plucked the rose from the gate, but I did not, and fate has intervened."

"What do you mean, Father?" Elise asked.

"I pushed on the iron gates and ventured into the gardens they guarded," Antoine said. "Beautiful were these gardens, I admit. Still, nothing more beautiful grew there than the lavender rose, and as I strolled beneath a rose-laden arbor, I plucked the rose you now hold in your hand, my sweet Coquette. I smiled, thinking of how delighted you would be with its beauty, wondering if I should dig a few roots of the vine and bring them home to you to grow here in Bostchelan."

Coquette smiled and pressed the velvet petals of the rose to her face, inhaling its lovely fragrance.

"Oh, I hope you were not found out, Father," Coquette giggled. "To wander into such a garden, steal such a bloom. You are fortunate you were not caught and reprimanded."

The silence from her father then caused Coquette to glance up at him. He wore an odd expression—that of being entirely startled coupled with some great guilt heaped upon him.

"Coquette, you often unsettle me with your awareness. For indeed, I did not ask permission to take the rose, and therefore . . . therefore I was caught and, consequently, my life threatened!"

"What?" Coquette exclaimed.

"What do you mean, Father?" Inez asked. "What do you mean by telling us your life was threatened? And over this miserable rose you brought to Coquette?"

"It is true," Antoine began. "There is a dark presence dwelling in the place. Roanan Manor, it is called—and the lord of it, the lord dwelling within, is as malevolent a being as ever walked the earth!"

"Father!" Coquette exclaimed. "Your life was threatened?" Suddenly, Coquette trembled with fear and anxiety. Her father's life threatened? Over a rose? "Tell us the tale, Father. Pray, at once!" She must know he was no longer in danger! She must know the rose she had asked for did not yet place him in harm's way.

"A great beast of a man . . ." Antoine began. Yet he paused. Coquette was to go to the beast's dwelling in Roanan Manor House. No need to alarm her further. Antoine knew he must proceed carefully. He did not want to upset his other three daughters. One would be made to pay for her folly in asking for a rose. No need the other three should suffer with worry as well.

"Go on, Father," Coquette said when her father paused. Surely the tale must be told. His life threatened? Over a rose? She still could not fathom it.

31

"A great . . . a great beast of a man came into the garden. On finding me there, he bid I should talk with his master, the dark Lord of Roanan. And so I went. I followed the large man into the great manor house—such wealth you girls have never imagined . . . such furnishings, such exquisite tapestries!"

"Go on, Father," Coquette urged. "We care nothing for furnishings, tapestries, or wealth— only your safety."

"That is right, Father," Dominique said. "First tell us of your adventure. Then you may tell me of the tapestries! You know how deeply I love fine tapestry."

Coquette sighed, unable to fathom the shallow character of her sister.

"Go on, Father. Please," Coquette begged.

"Within the manor house, there was a length . . . a great hall in which sat a large table, partly in shadow, part in light. Behind the table, hidden within the shadows, was a man . . . the dark Lord of Roanan. I could not see his face to witness his sure identity, for he remained in the darkness. I feel it is where he resides. He called me a thief, this dark lord! Called me a thief and told me he would . . . he told me he would take my life as payment for the rose I had stolen!"

"What?" Coquette exclaimed. "Father! No! Surely you cannot be in earnest!"

"But I am!" Antoine assured her. "He drew his

sword upon me, threatened to run me through! I begged for his mercy . . . fell to my knees fairly sobbing, telling him of my dead wife, my four beautiful daughters. Told him, I did, you would all four be lost without me . . . destitute without my money and trade! I begged for his mercy, and in begging, I offered the story of why I had plucked the rose. I told him of my lovely Coquette and her desire to have a rose to remind her of her mother. Still, he cared not, for he was angered at my trespassing and . . . and my thievery, as he called it."

"Thievery?" Inez exclaimed. "A rose? To pluck a rose . . . it is not thieves' business."

"See what you have caused, Coquette? See what danger you have put Father in? The consequences for us all?" Dominique cried.

Coquette was silent. Her request of a rose had not put her father in danger. His own neglect at asking permission to take the rose had caused it. Yet she was guilt-ridden, frightened.

"Father," Coquette began, "Father, I am sorry to have caused you such grief. I . . . I . . ."

"Yet all is well, Coquette," her father told her. "For in listening to my story, in seeing what a good man I am, what a kind and caring father, the Lord of Roanan took mercy on me. He granted me my life . . . granted me my life that I might continue to be father and provider for my daughters. You girls will not linger in loneliness and poverty, for I am saved. And at Coquette's hand."

"What?" Coquette asked. A strange sensation had begun to creep into Coquette's mind and body. The feel of icy fingers at her spine, the hair on her neck seemed to bristle with a strange prickle.

"Well, I do not know what you mean to say, Father," Inez began, "but it was Coquette who brought this on you, so then I am glad it is Coquette's hand that saved you—whatever that means."

"What *do* you mean, Father?" Coquette asked. "How was it I saved you?"

Coquette frowned as her father took her hands in his. She fancied his smile was that of joy but could not fathom why such threats and accusations from this dark Lord of Roanan could end in her father's delight.

"The Lord of Roanan is wealthy, Coquette," he answered. "Wealthy beyond imagination! And he asks only one favor. Only one simple stipulation and I am freed of danger."

"And . . . and what might the stipulation be, Father?" Coquette asked in an apprehensive whisper.

"As I said, he owns great wealth and property," Antoine continued, "but has no wife with whom to share such blessings."

"What?" Coquette exclaimed, pulling her hands

34

from her father's grasp. "Do you mean to say—"

"It is wonderful, in truth, Coquette," Antoine interrupted, "for I have worried so long over your well-being, over seeing you girls cared for before I am old . . . or dead."

"Father," Coquette gasped in a whisper. "You do not mean to say—"

"You will be wife to the Lord of Roanan, Coquette!" he exclaimed. "Your every want, your every need and desire . . . the pure fruition of it all!"

"But I want no things, Father!" Coquette exclaimed. "I want no possessions! I have little need."

"Jewels, Coquette! Gowns, feasts, servants! All of it shall be yours," Antoine told her. "You will want for nothing! You will not ever suffer."

"I want no jewels, no gowns, no feasts! The only want I ever had was lost years ago, Father! Or do you not remember it? When you so easily give me over to a stranger . . . do you not remember my only true want, my only true need? A stranger, Father! You make to give me over to a stranger, a man I have never had any association with, no knowledge of! And yet, three years ago, you—"

"Is my life worth so little to you then, Coquette?" he asked.

Coquette was momentarily struck mute. Of course her father's life was of value to her! How could he ask it? Yet to leave her home, to wed a stranger—a stranger cruel enough to have threatened to take her father's life in payment for a rose. It was madness!

"Of c-course not, Father," Coquette stammered.

"It is all your fault in the first of it, Coquette," Dominique cried. "You and your want of a rose! Would that you were a kind, caring daughter and had asked for a new gown instead of a rose, which now sees Father's life in danger and our security and well-being threatened!"

"Why should Coquette get to marry this wealthy lord, Father?" Inez asked. "I am the eldest! I should be first to wed!"

"And what of Henry Weatherby, Inez?" Coquette asked. Her sister's shallow character yet astonished her.

"Henry Weatherby? Who is Henry Weatherby when the Lord of Roanan seeks a wife?" Inez laughed. "I shall go in Coquette's stay, Father. I shall marry the Lord of Roanan and save your life."

For a moment Coquette was sickeningly relieved. Her sister desired wealth and position. Love and companionship meant little to her. Then let Inez marry this dark lord.

"No," Antoine said. "It must be Coquette. He means the youngest of you four to be wife to him, and I dare not attempt deception. It must be Coquette."

Coquette felt tears filling her eyes. She looked to her father, at once astonished by the happy countenance on his face. How could this be? A stranger? Valor Lionhardt had been no stranger to her. Valor Lionhardt had possessed wealth and position. Valor had stood to inherit greatly, his father being a titled man. Handsome, kind, and strong, Valor Lionhardt had won her love many years before. Further, he had won respect and earned a fine reputation, in spite of his father's antics and low character. Valor Lionhardt had been a gentleman—heroic, courageous, and brave, a man whose very moral fiber was reflected in the definition of his name—*Valor*. Coquette had loved him—loved him more than her own life. And yet when the day had come, when Valor had asked Coquette's father for her hand, her father had flatly refused. Stating the bad character of Valor's father as his reason, Antoine de Bellamont had refused Valor's proposal of Coquette's hand in marriage.

Coquette had been devastated! Her love, her heart, her Valor—refused permission by her father. Coquette's heart broke when Valor hastily quit Bostchelan. Within the hour, he quit it and her. She knew this, for she planned to rebel, ignore her father's word, and run away to Valor. Sobbing, she had packed a small valise and secretly made her way to Valor's family home, only to find Valor Lionhardt had vanished.

For three years, Coquette regretted Valor—regretted not going to him at once, regretted taking the time to pack a valise. Even still, her body ached to be in his arms; even still, her dreams were haunted with visions of his handsome face, his playful manner, his very existence. And now, her father was asking her to wed a stranger?

For a moment, she did not care if her father was run through by the Lord of Roanan's sword. For a moment, she hated her father for stripping her of her true love, whom he deemed unworthy, only to promise her hand to a man who would threaten to take his life over the plucking of a rose.

"You will go, of course, Coquette," Dominique said, "for we need Father! We cannot exist without him. This is your fault! You put us all in danger for the sake of a rose."

Coquette felt the beautiful lavender rose slip from her hand. She sensed it fall to the earth as she looked at her sisters and her father. It was true enough—her vain and shallow sisters were helpless. What would become of them if her father were taken? She looked to her father as well. He valued wealth and position. Valor had not possessed enough of either in her father's eyes. Yet this strange, malevolent Lord of Roanan possessed enough of both? It would see her father happy, proud in the union. No doubt he would brag to all those in Bostchelan of his daughter

Coquette and her wealthy and titled husband. Even for her resentment, her astonishment, Coquette loved her father and her sisters. She could not see her father murdered, her sisters homeless. In the end, she had been the one to ask for the rose.

"Then I will go," Coquette said. Tears spilled from her eyes as her father clapped his hands together with joy. Dominique and Inez breathed relieved sighs. Only Elise did not seem merry.

"You must leave at first light tomorrow," Antoine said. "This is the Lord of Roanan's own stipulation. If you are not there by sun's set tomorrow, he will come for me."

"Tomorrow?" Coquette cried. "But, Father . . . how am I to prepare? What am I to take? I cannot possibly—"

"It is his word. Tomorrow before sun's set," he interrupted. "And fear not, my sweet Coquette," he continued, taking her shoulders between his hands, "there is nothing you must take. The Lord of Roanan will provide for your every need."

"Father," Elise said at last, "surely you cannot mean for Coquette to do this thing!"

"She has chosen it herself," Antoine said. "It has been your choice—has it not, Coquette?"

Coquette stood silent—unable to speak, unable to move, unable to fathom what was before her.

"Take this gown, Father," Elise said, thrusting her new gown into her father's hands. "I do not want it. We will do without. We will run away and hide ourselves from this Lord of Roanan. We will hide from him and Coquette with us."

"Do not be absurd, Elise!" Inez said. "We will not hide. All of this is Coquette's fault! It falls to Coquette to make amends. Poor Father." Inez reached out, linking her arm through her father's.

"Yes! Poor Father," Dominique said, linking her arm through her father's other arm. "How frightened you must have been. How worried for our sake. We are so fortunate to have such a selfless father . . . that he would risk his very life in pursuit of a single rose for his daughter."

"There, there, darlings," Antoine said, smiling first at Inez and then Dominique. "I knew you girls would understand it all."

"Father!" Elise breathed. "Surely you cannot force Coquette to—"

"She has chosen to go," Inez interrupted. "The rose was for her. The Lord of Roanan demanded she come to him. She has chosen this, Elise."

"Coquette?" Elise asked, turning to look at Coquette.

Coquette looked at each sister in turn. Vain, shallow, and diseased with selfishness, she loved them yet. She smiled at Elise. Always it was Elise who walked the blade between vanity and good nature. Of all her sisters, she loved Elise best, for in Elise there was hope—hope in a fine man eventually taking her to wife and drawing out her good nature forever.

If for no one else save Elise, she must go. Coquette knew her sisters would fall into ruination without her father. Closing her eyes for a moment, she tried to push the vision of her lost love from her mind. With the simple request of a rose, her path had been set, and she could not deviate from it without causing death to come to her father and ruination spilling onto her sisters. Inez spoke the truth. Coquette had chosen to go.

"I will go, Elise," she said. "And . . . and all will be well. I am to be a wealthy and titled lady," she added, forcing a smile, even as tears trickled over her lovely cheeks.

"You care nothing for wealth and titles," Elise said, throwing her arms around Coquette's neck.

"I care for you," Coquette whispered.

"Then it is settled," Antoine said. "You leave at daybreak, Coquette. And who is to say . . ." he began, releasing Inez and Dominique and taking Coquette's hands in his own as he smiled at her. "Who is to say this will not be the making of you—you, Coquette de Bellamont, Lady of Roanan? Who is to say this is not meant to be your destiny? "

"Yes, Father," Coquette said, forcing a smile. "Who is to say it is not?"

"There! We are all of us better now. Are we not?" he asked, smiling with utter contentment and joy. "Now, off with you girls. Let me see you in those gowns."

Coquette studied her father, awed at the twinkle and pure delight in his eyes as he watched Inez and Dominique skip off in giggles—as he nodded at Elise as she retrieved her own gown and left.

"There now, Coquette," Antoine said. "Your sisters are happy—happy and safe. And it is all thanks be to you."

"Yes, Father," Coquette mumbled.

"Oh, do not be so fearful, Coquette," Antoine said, embracing her. "You are to be the wealthy Lady of Roanan. What better fortune and future for you I could not fathom!"

"Yes, Father," Coquette said, returning his embrace. She would leave him on the morrow. She hugged him, never wanting to release him, inhaling deeply the scent of him—the scent of tobacco and the sea.

"I must be off to attend your sisters," he said, releasing her and pinching her cheek as if she were merely a child. "I'll leave you to prepare for your trip."

Coquette watched him go. She frowned, allowing herself to release more tears, to sob. Dropping to her knees, she buried her face in her hands as fear and anxiety overwhelmed her.

To travel to an unfamiliar township—to marry a stranger—how could it all be so? After several long moments, she raised her head from her hands, her gaze falling to the lavender rose, which now lay abandoned on the floor.

"I am lost," she whispered. "And all for the want of a rose."

THE LION'S LAIR

Following her father's dreadful revelation, Coquette endured the night with tears and trembling as her only companions. Now, as the rising sun cast brilliant pinks and purples over the horizon, Coquette sat in her father's coach traveling toward Roanan and whatever destiny lay in wait.

The morning air was cool, indicating summer was making ready to leave. Reluctant to further challenge the beauty and glory of impending autumn, summer would soon be gone. Coquette wondered what autumn would bring to Roanan. She could not imagine any place rivaling the beauty of autumn by the sea. Surely, such a place as Roanan could not compare. The colors of autumn sprinkled through the trees and fields of Bostchelan were breathtaking. Coquette was loath to miss the season by the sea. It was yet another motive for her mind to induce anxiety.

The hills and valleys, trees and grasses passed quickly, and all too soon the sun sat low in the sky. Coquette's hands began trembling as the coach rumbled along through a town. Though she had seen no sign declaring it to be so, Coquette felt this was Roanan. Many curious sets of eyes looked after the coach as it passed.

Coquette tried to dislike them. She tried not to think of the rather quaint, cozy appearance of the old buildings, tried not to notice the kind nods to the coachman, the sweet, tiny hands of the children waving to them as they passed. There could be only dark and evil in a place whose titled lord would threaten to kill her father for the sake of a rose. And yet the warm evening sunshine flooding the streets with radiance seemed to be reflected with pure resplendence in the faces of the cheerful passersby.

Billings, the coachman, pulled the team to a halt and called to an elderly man sitting contentedly on a nearby tree stump. "Which way to Roanan Manor House, if you please, sir?" Billings asked.

"Straightaway two mile," the old man answered, smiling.

"Thank you, sir," Billings said as the coach lurched forward.

Coquette's heart began to hammer with such force it caused her pain. Two miles—two miles and she would be at Roanan Manor House. Two miles and might she see the garden from which her father took the rose? Two miles and she would be lost—lost to everyone and everything.

Soon the town was behind them. Trees, grasses, wildflowers, and small animals of every sort embellished the lush, green landscape. There were scents lingering in the air—sweet fragrances Coquette did not recognize. Had she

45

not been so miserable in her anxiety, Coquette would have enjoyed the two miles from Roanan town to Roanan Manor. Yet angst was her only companion, and as the coach traveled, her innards began to twist and turn.

And then, all at once it was there! Roanan Manor was in view, and Coquette felt her own jaw drop in awe, for it was indeed beautiful! The strong stone wall her father spoke of was like a fortress, yet softened by the thick ivy growing over most of it. And there, on the east wall, were the roses—a profusion of lovely lavender—and Coquette fancied she sensed their familiar perfume.

The house was indeed grand—enormous, strong, and built of stone with many, many windows. And then, suddenly, they were before her—the rose-bound iron gates of Roanan Manor.

"It is Roanan Manor, Miss Coquette," Billings shouted.

Coquette could only nod as the coach passed through the gates and into the most elaborate, most exquisite gardens Coquette had ever seen. Roses of every sort and color thrived there—most of all the lavender rose! Trees and flowers of every kind were blended together, creating a world only before seen in the dreams of fairies.

So beautiful were the gardens of Roanan Manor, Coquette experienced a momentary reprieve from her biting anxiety. Still, the respite was fleeting, and Coquette laced her fingers in an effort to still the frightened trembling of her hands.

The coach stopped before a massive work of stone stairs leading to the large oak doors of the manor house. Coquette swallowed hard, feeling as if her heart had been residing in her throat for some time.

All too soon, Billings climbed down from his coachman's seat to open the coach door for her.

"Roanan Manor House, Miss de Bellamont," Billings said, offering her his hand.

Coquette took his hand and, with deep trepidation, stepped out of the conveyance.

As Billings pulled her small trunk from the top of the coach, she glanced to the house to see a man and woman descending the stone steps together. Her heart's already rapid beat only increased as her attention lingered on the man. He bore the straight posture and severe expression of some great battle commander. By his weathered face and graying hair, Coquette judged his age to be near her father's. Her knees began to weaken. She had not considered the age of the man she was to marry. She had tried not to consider the man at all, but to see him now—standing before her so stern and middle-aged—it terrified her all the more.

"You are come from Bostchelan?" the woman asked. She was a mature woman, perhaps of the age Coquette's mother may have been had she lived. She wore her graying blonde hair pulled up high and tight.

"Yes, ma'am," Billings said. "My name is Billings. I have brought the Miss de Bellamont."

The woman came to stand before Coquette, frowning at first, then smiling as if some great wave of relief had only just washed over her.

"Welcome to Roanan Manor House, Miss de Bellamont," the woman greeted. "I am Victoria. I am housemistress here."

"I-I am pleased to meet you, ma'am," Coquette stammered, barely managing a curtsy. She could not help but look from the woman to the older man, a wave of new fear causing her to visibly tremble.

"And this is Godfrey," Victoria said, "the Lord of Roanan's first-man."

The man called Godfrey reached out, taking Coquette's hand in his own. With a rather stiff bow, he bent, placing his forehead to the back of Coquette's hand.

"Your servant, miss," Godfrey said, straightening to his perfect posture once more.

"We will take care of her from here . . . Billings, was it?" Victoria asked, looking to Billings.

"Yes, ma'am," Billings said. "Goodbye then, miss," he added.

"Goodbye, Billings," Coquette managed. Somehow she restrained her tears, kept herself from throwing herself into Billings's arms and begging him not to leave her.

"Milord has arranged for very comfortable lodging and meals for you at the inn in town," Victoria said.

"You will go to the Grassy Glen in Roanan," Godfrey explained to Billings. "There you will ask for Stewart. Tell him the Lord of Roanan has sent you. Give him this, and he will see to your every comfort." Godfrey handed Billings a folded parchment. "And for your trouble," Godfrey added, handing Billings a velvet purse.

"But . . . but I have been paid already," Billings said.

"Milord wishes you to go your own way, sir," Godfrey explained. "Return the coach to Bostchelan, and then use the contents of the purse for your own good pursuits, milord suggests. Perhaps your own stables."

Coquette stared at the man called Godfrey. She was confused. She knew Billings worked well with horses; it was why her father kept him on. Yet why would the Lord of Roanan give him, a stranger, such an amount as the obvious weight of the purse attested to? And who was this Lord of Roanan to make so bold as to suggest Billings quit her father for his own pursuits?

Billings nodded and smiled. He dropped the purse into his coat pocket and turned to Coquette. "All will be well, miss," he said, smiling a greater smile than Coquette had ever before seen him smile. "All will be well."

As quickly as they had arrived, Billings was gone. Coquette watched the coach as it passed through the great rose-covered iron gates of Roanan Manor, leaving her alone and more fearful than she had ever imagined possible.

"I know you must be tired, miss," Victoria said.

Coquette turned to look at Victoria. She and Godfrey seemed to study her quickly from head to toe, but their expressions revealed nothing of their thoughts. "Yes," Coquette said. "I feel a great fatigue overtaking me suddenly."

"I will have Nelson see to the trunk," Godfrey said to Victoria. She nodded.

"There will be enough time only for a short rest," Victoria said, taking Coquette's hand and leading her up the stone steps, "for the ceremony is to take place at exactly eight."

"What?" Coquette asked. "What ceremony?"

"The marriage ceremony," Godfrey answered. "You will be legally wed to milord at eight o'clock this evening."

"What?" Coquette exclaimed. "Surely you cannot be in earnest!" She stopped. She stood at the very threshold of Roanan Manor House, and she fancied she stood on the edge of a deadly precipice.

"Milord is away," Godfrey continued. "I will stand as proxy in his stead."

Coquette found herself simultaneously horrified and relieved. To be wed nearly instantly? And with a proxy in place of the man she was to call husband? It terrified her! And yet the man she was to wed was away. This somehow caused her to experience an odd relief from a bit of anxiety.

"He . . . the Lord of Roanan is away then?" Coquette asked.

"Yes, miss," Godfrey answered.

"When is he expected to return?" she asked. She felt an unusual sort of joy begin to rise within her. Married by proxy, yet still free of body and mind for a time. It may indeed help her to endure.

"He returns at midnight," Victoria said.

As quickly as her hopes had lifted on wings of respite, they plummeted with more force than before.

"I beg your pardon, ma'am," Coquette said. "But if your lord is to return this very night, then why—"

"It must be done by proxy at eight this night," Godfrey interrupted. "Milord has set it to be so; therefore it is incontestable. The reasons matter not to any of us."

"You cannot possibly be in earnest. You cannot possibly be asking me to—" Coquette began.

"I ask nothing of you, miss," Godfrey said. "Incontestable is the will of milord."

Coquette placed a hand to her forehead, for it

began to ache with a devilish sort of fever and pain.

"Come. You need rest," Victoria said, taking Coquette's arm and pulling her over the threshold into Roanan Manor House.

The moment she set foot in Roanan Manor House, Coquette's anxiety increased threefold. Massive it was—rich, elegant, immaculate in every element. Large, intricately woven tapestries lined the walls of the enormous entry hall. At a glance, Coquette immediately thought of Dominique and her fascination with tapestry work, for these tapestries were the finest she had ever seen. Knights battled dragons; princesses stood in waiting at their father's thrones. Such intricate tapestry Coquette had never imagined.

"Your manor house, milady," Godfrey said, bowing low and gesturing Victoria and Coquette should now precede him.

"Your rooms are on the second floor, miss," Victoria explained, lifting her skirts as she began to climb the strong set of stairs to Coquette's right. "You may rest for two hours, and then I will come to help you prepare for the ceremony."

Coquette swallowed hard as she followed the woman up the staircase.

"I have not come prepared to wed," Coquette confessed.

"Were the conditions not explained to you?" Victoria asked, pausing in her ascent of the stairs.

She looked over her shoulder to Coquette and asked, "Yet you knew—"

"I mean to say, my father seemed assured I should travel but lightly. I have only a small trunk and brought no dress so elegant as to be appropriate for a marriage ceremony," Coquette explained. Oh, how she wished in that moment she had argued with her father. How she wished she would have filled her larger trunk with dresses and underthings. To arrive so lacking was humiliating and seemed so entirely assuming.

Victoria smiled and waved her hand in a gesture of trivial concern. "Oh, that has all been taken care of, miss," she said. "New gowns, including one for the ceremony, were delivered this morning, as well as every personal necessity imaginable. Your entire trousseau is arrived and ready for you." She paused, turned back to Coquette, and added in a whisper, "Including a selection of new nightdresses of such delicate elegance as to be envied by the fairies."

Coquette gasped and felt the color drain from her face. She felt her knees threaten to give way beneath her. In fact, she must have visibly weakened, for she felt Godfrey's hand at her elbow as support. To contemplate marrying a man she had never met, a beast of a man who would threaten to kill over a bloom—it terrified her. Yet to contemplate the intimate duties of a wife nearly set her heart to stilling forever.

"Come now," Victoria said, taking Coquette's hand and leading her up the few remaining stairs. "After a little rest, all will not seem so overwhelming as it does now."

But as Victoria opened the doors to the grandest bedchamber Coquette had ever seen, Coquette felt certain consciousness would be lost to her. A stranger! To wed a stranger! To be owned by him, to be at the mercy of his will—in those moments she nearly wished for a faint of death to bring her reprieve from it all.

"Thank you, Godfrey," Victoria said. It was his prompt to leave, and he did, with haste.

"Now then," Victoria said, pulling Coquette into the room and closing the doors behind her, "these are your personal chambers. This is your bedchamber—to the left your sitting room and to the right your bathing chamber."

Coquette stood in horrified awe. The room in which she stood was lavish, drenched in red velvets, silver, and crystal. Along the hearth mantel, candles burned warm and beautiful from within crystal bowls or silver holders, and the soft aroma of lavender scented the room. The bed was large, comfortable in appearance, and covered in red velvet and white linen. It beckoned to Coquette's fatigued mind and body like an elusive dream.

"Here now," Victoria said. "I shall help you to undress, and you may rest awhile. It will do you good." Coquette was tired, astonished, frightened, and overcome with anxiety. She stood, allowing the woman to unfasten her dress.

Once Victoria had helped Coquette out of her traveling clothes and into a light linen nightgown, she gently folded the bed linens back.

"Now, you sleep awhile, miss," she said. "Rest and . . . and try to settle your anxieties. I can see they trouble you."

"I have never even set eyes on your lord, ma'am," Coquette whispered, tears welling in her eyes. "I am frightened, in truth. To marry a man I have never seen? To marry he who threatened my father so—who would demand I succumb to his will as payment for a flower? A flower that has been dying since the moment it was plucked?"

Victoria smiled, and Coquette felt somewhat reassured. The woman had such a maternal look about her countenance. It was comforting in a small measure. She reached out and brushed a lock of hair from Coquette's cheek.

"Would it . . . would it help in the least of it were I to tell you the Lord of Roanan is the handsomest of men? Like a prince from some child's fairy tale, he is that handsome. Does it give you any easement of mind?"

"What good is beauty in a man's features of face when his heart is as black as the devil's?" Coquette asked.

"Then ease your mind," Victoria told her,

taking her hand and leading her to the bed, "for his heart is not so black as that."

Coquette climbed onto the bed. It did feel good to rest her head on a pillow, let her body settle at last. She looked up, her heart momentarily lifted by the elaborate mural on the ceiling. The scene was breathtaking: tree branches heavy-laden with blossoms and birds caused her to sigh as she gazed upon it.

"Rest now, miss," Victoria said. "I will call for you at seven that you may prepare for the ceremony."

"How is it I am expected to sleep with all that is before me?" Coquette asked, even as her eyelids grew too heavy to remain open.

"Rest now, miss. All will be well," Victoria said as she closed the doors behind her.

"What good is a handsome face when the blackest heart is in the bosom?" Coquette mumbled as her eyes closed, her mind drifting into the oblivion of tormented sleep.

"Now, milady," the curate continued, "your name here . . . in your own hand."

Coquette watched as if from a dream as her own hand penned her name on the parchment. The witnesses to the marriage, a Lord Dickerson and his first-man, strangers to Coquette, had already left the room. Godfrey had moved to the back of the great hall the moment the verbal ceremony was ended, and the curate asked that Coquette pen her name on the marriage document. In the brief course of a few moments, Coquette's feet were set on a different path. She was Milady, mistress of the Roanan Manor, legally wedded wife of the dark Lord of Roanan.

"Upon his return, his lordship must pen his name as well," the curate said to Godfrey.

"He returns this night," Godfrey said. "And it will be done before any other thing precedes it."

"Very well," the curate said. "Congratulations, milady. I hope you will feel at ease to call upon me at any time."

"Y-yes, sir."

"I take my leave then," the curate said, nodding first to Coquette, then to Godfrey, and then to Victoria.

"It is legally binding, is it not? Legal and legitimate?" Coquette asked with haste. "Though milord was not present . . . it is still a legal marriage to milord?"

The curate turned, smiling with understanding compassion. "It is, milady. It is incontestable, for his lordship's first-man, who stood as proxy in his lordship's stead, is in possession of his lordship's written will. Even if his lordship should neglect the marriage document, the ceremony is as legally binding as any other—legal in the eyes of God and the land."

"Thank you, sir," Coquette said, lacing her fingers to try and steady her trembling hands.

"Good evening then, milady," the curate said.

Coquette listened to his footsteps echoing through the great hall as he departed. Farther and farther away they sounded, until there was no resonance to tell the curate had ever been there.

Coquette looked to Victoria to find her smiling—a sweet, pleased sort of smile, as if the best union in all the world had only just taken place.

"I feel it is too strange," Coquette said, "to be married to another when it was Godfrey who stood with me."

"Yes," Victoria said. "I will admit it is unconventional, in the least. But as milord's will, it is—"

"Incontestable," Coquette interrupted. "I am beginning to understand—anything milord puts down as his will is incontestable."

"It is true," Victoria said, still smiling the proud smile of a mother who has only just seen her daughter wed.

"You are Lady of Roanan now, milady," Godfrey said. "And I bid you good night."

"Good night, sir," Coquette said. "And . . . and I thank you . . . for your kindness to me."

Coquette watched as a slight frown puckered Godfrey's brow.

"You're welcome, milady," he said with a nod.

"Victoria," he said, nodding at her as well before turning on his heels and taking his leave.

"He is fiercely loyal to milord, is he not?" Coquette thought aloud.

"As we all are," Victoria said. "Now let's spirit you away. You must prepare to meet your husband, for he will come to you this night when he has returned to Roanan Manor."

"Madam, I cannot!" Coquette cried in a whisper as tears filled her eyes. "I cannot possibly . . . I can hardly muster the courage to meet him, let alone allow myself to . . . to succumb to his will. I cannot!"

"You can," Victoria said, taking Coquette's shoulders in her hands. "He is your husband in the eyes of the land and in the eyes of God. It is your duty and his right and as such is—"

"Incontestable," Coquette said. "Yet I do not even know who this man is! How can this have happened? How can it be I am here, a prisoner, my life in ruin? How can this be for me when my father and sisters are safe and happy in Bostchelan? What grievous sin of my own commission finds me in such circumstance?"

"None," Victoria said then. "And yet, wounded as you see your destiny and life to be, perhaps divinity's involvement lands you here."

"Perhaps divinity's abandonment lands me here," Coquette said, brushing the tears from her cheeks.

Victoria sighed the breathy sigh of disappointment, yet Coquette cared not. It was not Victoria who must endure a loveless marriage with a dark and cruel stranger.

"Let us prepare now, milady," Victoria said. "In fewer than four hours, milord will return. You must ready yourself both mind and body."

Taking Coquette's hand, Victoria led her up the staircase. Coquette followed, with visions of being led to the guillotine, of the executioner's ax, foremost in her mind as she was led.

At last, Victoria stopped before two great oak doors across the hall from Coquette's chambers. Coquette tried to still her trembling body as she watched Victoria grasp the latch to the Lord of Roanan's chambers.

"Milord's chambers," she said as she opened the doors. "At times, he has the most unorganized of habits, but I have readied the rooms myself for your wedding night."

Crimson, white, and silver dominated the colors of the linens and furnishings. The large bedposts boasted at least seven feet in height and were hung with heavy, sophisticated draperies. The furniture was heavy, well made of oak, with crimson pillows and elaborate needlework. These chambers belonged to a great man, a titled man. It was further obvious by the enormous hearth, in which burned an orange-flamed fire, and the thick, long-wicked candles on the mantle. The scents of leather, peppermint, and cedar hung in the air, and Coquette was rather surprised at the pleasing fragrance of the blend.

The sun had set long ago, and the fire in the hearth and candles throughout the room cast shadows on the ceiling and walls. Coquette looked up to the ceiling, curious as to whether the Lord of Roanan gazed upon the same serene painted scene she had gazed upon in her own chambers. Yet she was not surprised to see a very different mural embellishing the ceiling of the Lord of Roanan's chamber. There, overhead, was such a sight as she could never have imagined—a meadow, pasture, or some other lovely grassy place spread over the space above her head and in its center a lone lion lounging on a rock. Strong, content, and dominant—that was its countenance, and Coquette wondered, amidst all the beauty of the grasses, where was the lair of such a beautiful and kingly beast?

Slowly, her eyes drifted from the beautiful painting on the ceiling to the massive bed drenched in crimson and then to the hearth where the flames of the fire licked within like a fearsome beast. She realized then, she stood in it—at Victoria's lead, Coquette had stepped into the lion's lair.

"I have chosen the loveliest of your night-dresses for . . . for this occasion," Victoria said. Coquetted startled from her thoughts as Victoria tugged on her hand and led her to the bed. There, spread like a ribbon of sweet cream across the crimson of the bedding, was the most beautiful, delicately ethereal nightdress Coquette had ever seen. As white as winter's first snow, the nightdress dazzled Coquette's imagination—how divine such a gown would feel against her tired flesh! What respite could she find in sleeping in such soft, feathery-light fabric!

Yet in the next breath, fear washed over her as a raging, sea-driven storm. This was to be her wedding night! Oh, how her body trembled with angst and fear—how her mind burned with disbelief and trepidation.

"Isn't it lovely?" Victoria asked. She was smiling at the nightdress, yet her smile faded as she looked to Coquette. "Are you well, milady?"

"Not at all well, I'm afraid," Coquette whispered.

Victoria frowned and then nodded. "There is time to rest, milady," she said. "Milord is nothing if not perpetually prompt. He bid us he would return at midnight; then return at midnight he will—and not a moment before. There is time for you to eat and to rest. I think there would be wisdom in doing both."

"May I . . . may I do so in my own rooms?" Coquette asked, glancing at the mural on the ceiling and feeling as a deer led to the jaws of a predator.

"Yes," Victoria said. "I will away to the kitchens and prepare something for you. And then you should rest, milady. Rest will ease your anxieties perhaps."

As she left the room, as she fairly leapt from the lion's lair, Coquette looked back once—looked back to the deep crimsons and silver; looked back to the ribbon of cream, her nightdress, ribboned across the crimson; looked back, up into the amber-colored eyes of the lion who sat in dominant majesty overlooking his kingdom.

Coquette knew that when next she entered the lair, she would be the lion's prey.

FALLEN PREY

"B-but I cannot possibly appear thus," Coquette whispered as she studied her reflection in the looking glass before her. "Madam, I cannot!" She covered her mouth with her hand, attempting to remain in some control of her emotions. Near panic wracked her body. Tears filled her eyes, and she felt near to fainting.

"You look lovely, milady," Victoria said, gathering the soft ebony tresses of Coquette's long hair in her hands and smoothing it before letting it fall, cascading down her back.

Coquette studied her reflection once more, mortified at the immodesty of her attire. Certainly she was thankful the long, flowing white gown was not entirely gossamer. Still, the manner in which it clung to her form, the sheer capped sleeves revealing her shoulders—how would she endure this night?

"I would not appear thus before my own father," Coquette whispered.

"Of course not," Victoria agreed. "And yet the Lord of Roanan is not your father. Rather, he is your bridegroom, and he will be very pleased in your appearance, I am certain."

"I know nothing of . . . of such things as this," Coquette confided. Spinning around, awash with angst, she pressed her palms together in a prayerful stance as she whispered, "I know nothing of what is expected, how to behave, or . . ."

Victoria reached out, clasping Coquette's hands in her own. The girl was terrified! Obviously, no one had prepared her for marriage—the intimacies of it. Her heart ached for the frightened young woman. Her sympathy fanned at the thought of the master and his apparent hard-heartedness. Still, she knew him yet better than he supposed, and she would use her knowledge of him to try and settle the girl's nerves for a while.

"Though it is said the Lord of Roanan is cruel and heartless, that he kills at a whim, abuses women . . . that he is a beast among men," Victoria began, "though all this is said of him, the Lord of Roanan is ever a gentleman, milady."

"A gentleman?" Coquetted exclaimed. "My own father was threatened at his hand! Further, a gentleman would never demand the price of another man's daughter as compensation for—"

"Sshhh," Victoria soothed, shaking her head. "He is none of it. He is harsh, hard in his ways, yes. But ever he is a gentleman, milady. He bears greatness of character. Even for the immense intimidation that precedes and follows him, he will be . . . temperate."

"I have never even seen him, ma'am—never

met him. How can I allow . . ." Coquette paused. If she pondered her position any further, she would surely faint dead away. Yet what venue was left her? "What manner of man takes a woman's virtue in exchange for her father's life?" she asked.

"Your virtue is not sacrificed, milady . . . when it is given to your husband," Victoria explained. "Further . . . and may I speak plainly, milady?"

Coquette nodded, thoughtful, somehow oddly relieved a bit by Victoria's explanation.

"Further, milady . . . perhaps you should ponder first on what manner of father would sacrifice such a thing for his own sake."

Coquette was silent as her breath caught in her throat a moment. How could this woman imply such selfish atrocities where her father was concerned? Yet Coquette made no sound to reprimand, for in truth—though it pained her, washed her with guilt to admit it—she had secretly wondered the same.

"I chose to come here," she told Victoria, reminding herself aloud as well. "It was my choice."

"Was it, milady?" Victoria asked.

She could not think disloyally toward her father. He had raised her, cared for her, protected her, and she would be no traitor to him.

Shaking her head and pulling her hands from the woman's, she mumbled, "I chose this. I chose this freely. And in choosing, I must endure."

"Then I will leave you now, milady," Victoria said.

"Must you?" Coquette asked, her voice barely a whisper. "Could not you linger . . . just a moment more?" She felt ill. Her stomach twisted in agony, and she was not entirely certain her husband would not enter to find its contents drenching the fabulous carpets of his bedchamber. Her knees shook, her hands violent in their trembling. *How could this be?* she wondered. *What fate has found me here?*

"I must go, milady," Victoria said. Still, with a nod she smiled, offering reassurance as she added, "You have nothing to fear, milady. The dark Lord of Roanan will not harm *you*." Taking hold of Coquette's shoulders, the woman turned her toward the hearth and the warmth of the fire. "Warm yourself as you wait, milady," Victoria said. "You are chilled, and the fire will help rest you somewhat." She left, quietly closing the door behind her.

Coquette gazed into the fire for a moment, watching as the orange hot flames licked the logs they slowly devoured. The warmth did soothe her flesh but not her mind—not her soul. She buried her face in her hands for a moment, willing her tears to stay at bay. She could not show weakness—not before the dark Lord of Roanan.

She raised her head, straightened her posture,

closed her eyes, and envisioned her father, her sisters, the waves of the sea as they spread over the sands. Inhaling deeply, she endeavored to calm herself, to prepare as best she could for the inevitability of the night stretching out before her. She knew little about the intimacies of marriage. What she did know frightened her beyond imagination. She sickened, thinking of enduring the night and every night thereafter in the presence, in the clutches, of a stranger. She imagined the lion in the mural overhead seizing her throat in its powerful jaws; she imagined the crimson of the draperies and coverlets on the bed were her own life's blood draining from her.

Her dark thoughts were interrupted, and she stiffened when she heard the door to the bedchamber open at her back. The hair prickled at the back of her neck as she sensed his presence in the room—her husband. Lacing her fingers, hands at her waist, she waited—waited for him to approach, to seize her like the fierce, hungry lion would seize an innocent deer.

The dark Lord of Roanan stood silent, studying his newly acquired bride. Removing his coat and tossing it to the nearby chair, he grinned as he unbuttoned the cuffs of his shirt, then his vest. From the back she was more than comely—she was exquisite! He pulled his vest from his torso, carelessly tossing it to join his coat on the chair.

Loosening his cravat, he pulled it from his neck, freeing his collar and first three buttons of his shirt.

Striding toward her, he paused a moment, a frown puckering his brow. What must this beauty think of the Lord of Roanan? What must she think of a man who would threaten to take her father's hands and then accept a woman's life in exchange?

Inhaling deeply, he straightened to his full, intimidating height, his eyes narrowing as he looked at her. He was Lord of Roanan! He had not time for compassion or thoughtfulness. He would have the chit! She was legally his, and he would have her.

Coquette sensed the Lord of Roanan was near. She heard his boot steps as he moved to her, yet she could not turn—she could not face the man who was now her husband. She grimaced, her determination wavering as she felt him take her hair in his hand, lift it to his face, and inhale its fragrance. Tears welled in her eyes, and she thought of all the young women in the world who had known her fate—given to a man she knew nothing of and expected to endure lifelong. Her breath caught in her throat as a vision of her beloved Valor entered her mind. How she had loved him! How she loved him still! But she must put his memory away, for he was only that—a memory—and true life would not be so beautiful as Valor's memory.

She startled when warm fingers touched her neck from behind, slowly sliding down over her shoulder to her arm. Without turning her head, she yet ventured to glance at the hand resting on her arm. It was large, sun-bronzed, with the look of strength and power. She frowned, curious as to the rather rough condition of the hand and fingers; clean though they were, the remains of a small wound on the back of the hand near the palm surprised her with its presence. Likewise, these fingernails, although unsoiled and trimmed, were quite lacking in pampered care. Had the sheer power and intimidation hanging thick in the air not told her otherwise, she mused this might be the hand of a field laborer and not a great lord.

Coquette held her breath as she felt the Lord of Roanan's free hand brush her hair to one side. She winced, trying not to cry out as she felt moist lips press against the flesh of her shoulder. She could not endure. She could not!

"I am the Lord of Roanan," the man mumbled, his lips lingering near her shoulder.

"I-I am Coquette de Bellamont," Coquette stammered—breathless, terrified, close to panic.

"You are now the Lady of Roanan," the man said, and she bit her lip as she felt a strong hand slip beneath her hair at the back of her neck. "And you will respectfully turn to face me, for I will take no woman to my bed save she greets me thus first."

For a brief instant, Coquette considered casting off his demand, refusing to face him, hoping to prolong avoiding what must be. Still, the powerful intonation of his voice frightened her. She thought of the dark lord's threat to take her father's life, and though her virtue was paramount, the dark Lord of Roanan was her husband. Better to sacrifice her virtue to he who legally owned it than to sacrifice her life and her father's for fear's sake.

Swallowing hard and casting her gaze to the floor, Coquette slowly turned to face the dark lord. Her eyes first caught sight of his boots. Large they were, and she looked from the rather dusty black tips of them to the red leather cuff just below his knee. His breeches were black as well, and she shuddered at the pure size and apparent power of his long legs. Slowly, for her courage was shallow, she began to raise her head, studying the broad expanse of his torso and shoulders, the length of his arms covered in the billowy white of a gentleman's shirt. He'd stripped himself of his coat and vest and released the upper half of the buttons of his shirt. The solid contours and muscular definition of his exposed chest and flesh further unsettled Coquette, and she tightened the lacing of her fingers at her waist.

By the time her gaze traveled the length of him to his throat, her courage abandoned her. She could not look to his face. Indeed, he was a beast of a man from the neck down—tall, muscular, profound in his physical perfection. Still, she paused before witnessing his face. Such a form could only belong to the handsomest of men, and yet it mattered not to Coquette. Handsome or vile in appearance, her body and soul were abhorrent to know him.

"I will not devour you, milady," he said, "no matter what stories have been told you about me."

Coquette swallowed hard once more, struggling to find more courage as he continued.

"Look then. Look to he who now owns you as wife."

She raised her gaze to see, for the first time, the face and features of the Lord of Roanan.

Her breathing stopped, her breath dying as she gazed on his perfect face, intense amber eyes, narrow and straight nose, square jaw, and strong chin. The brown of his hair, windblown, gave him the look of some wild predator. Still she did not breathe.

"Draw breath, girl, before you expire," he demanded.

She gasped then, at the sound of his voice, teetering backward as recognition struck as fiercely as a thunderclap.

He reached out, taking hold of her arm and steadying her as she breathed, "Valor!"

As her knees gave way, he ably caught her, growling, "Do not faint, girl! We have business to be about this night, you and I." Cradling her in one arm, for her legs still refused to support her, he took her chin in hand and said, "And do not call me by that name again. You may address me as milord, sire, Lord of Roanan, Lord Lionhardt, or even the name given me by the population of Roanan, Lionhardt the Heartless—but never again by that name. Do you understand?"

"B-but, Valor . . . I—" She was silenced as his hand covered her mouth.

"Master will do as well," he growled, glaring down at her. "Now gather yourself that we may be about the task at hand."

He pushed her to her feet, steadying her shoulders. Her mind reeled with confusion. Valor! How could it be? How could it be Valor was Lord of Roanan? Valor Lionhardt was no beast as the Lord of Roanan was rumored! Yet this man before her—this man was not the Valor Lionhardt she knew, the Valor her heart yet loved and longed for.

As she looked into the lion-amber of his eyes, she saw no warmth, love, nor kindness—only the flame of anger and loathing. There was no dazzling smile to make her heart merry—only the wrinkled brow of a frown, the countenance of antipathy as he glared at her.

"B-but how can this be? You cannot possibly—"

"I am Lord of Roanan, as was my uncle, my mother's brother, before me. I inherited the title, the lands, everything, when I was but eighteen. Yet I had no need of it until I had need of it," he said. "But you need no explanation. You deserve none. Know only this: I am the Lord of Roanan, and I have taken you as a wife in order to fulfill my need to produce an heir. My uncle had no heir. Thus I am lord. However, I am desirous of my own heir—someone to whom I can bequeath this grand and glorious opulence when I at last leave this loathsome existence," he said, looking about the room. "Therefore, I find myself in need . . . which in itself is a foreign concept to me. However, in need I am. In need of a vessel . . . rather a woman to carry my child to maturity, thereby producing an heir. Thus, know this: I shall have my heir . . . the venue and vessel being you."

His manner was so hateful, so cruel, so unfeeling. In those moments, Coquette realized she did not know this Lord of Roanan. In those moments, she understood Valor was lost to her. Valor Lionhardt had ceased to exist, and in his place stood a cruel, heartless, unfeeling beast.

Hot tears—tears of anger, hurt, disappointment, horror, heartbreak, and every manner of anxious and fearful emotion—brimmed in Coquette's eyes, yet she willed them to restraint. The terseness of his manner of speaking of such things—it allied with vulgarity.

"And you," she began, finding a different kind of courage than that which had abandoned her only moments before, "expect me to be this . . . this vessel. This receptacle . . . this cauldron in which to brew and birth your heir."

"Naturally," he told her, his voice void of any emotion, save dominance. "You are, after all," he said through clenched teeth, "my wife."

"And if I refuse?" she asked. "If I refuse to be the repository for . . . if I refuse to allow you to—"

"You will not refuse," he said, stripping his shirt from his body and tossing it into the nearby chair. "For, imbecilic as your father is," he added, "he has your undying devotion." Unexpectedly, he reached out and took her chin firmly in one hand. His eyes smoldered with anger, fury, and barely restrained rage as he glared at her. "Which is more than any other man on earth can say, is it not?"

His face was mere inches from hers. The heat of his angry breath warmed her like a fever as his mouth hovered over her own. For a long moment, she was lost—lost in the memory of Valor, of his strength, passion, and character— lost in the long-buried desire for his kiss, to feel his arms bind her to him. The sudden memory of the sensation of his kiss caused excess moisture to spring to her mouth. But the anger in his eyes quickly vanquished the wistful reminiscence. This was not Valor. This man before her was a stranger—an angry, hateful, careless stranger.

She knew then her anxiety had been founded. She had waited—waited dressed in the intimate apparel of a new bride—waited for her bridegroom, a stranger, to arrive and change the very course of her life. And so a stranger had arrived. In her soul she wondered if it would have been better to be found waiting by someone she had never laid eyes upon rather than a man who was the mirror image of Valor in body but void of anything like him in heart. The Lord of Roanan was a monster, a beast! It appeared nothing remained of the man Coquette so desperately loved. Every breath of the lover she had longed for had vanished.

She returned his heated glare, suddenly angry with him for becoming what he had become. His face and form both combined to create the most alluring, most attractive man the earth had ever witnessed. It was ever undeniable, his physical appeal. And yet the black sludge of his soul was apparent in the harsh hatred in his eyes.

She wondered then—did she perhaps have some hand in this loathsome transformation? Had Valor turned into this dark demon as a result of what had taken place, or rather what had not taken place, between them? She was further sickened with guilt at the notion. She must know—she must know if the beast standing before her was of her own making.

"I-I was bewildered. I feared disappointing my father, Valor," she began. "When he refused you, I only—"

"Milord!" he interrupted. The frown, something akin to a wince, furrowing his brow told her he would allow nothing, no stray from what he had ordered. His will was incontestable. Growling through clenched teeth, he said, "You will call me milord, and you will never refuse me. It is me you will fear disappointing now!" He released her, straightening his posture in an air of defiance. "I will have my heir, and you will accept me willingly, else your father pays the price."

"You would kill my father if I do not—" she began.

"Kill him?" Valor growled. Unexpectedly, he chuckled, shaking his head. Glaring at her once more, he said, "He has told you I will kill him if you refuse to submit to me? Then kill him I will."

Animal, she thought. *Beast!* And yet she had agreed and was wed to him. She had agreed to wed a stranger—a coward who had remained hidden in shadow even as he delivered a murderous threat to her father. Her father did not know the Lord of Roanan was Valor, and she who had thought to give herself to a stranger now endeavored to convince herself she would be more willing to do so. Yet as the nausea lingering in her stomach before Valor arrived diminished, giving over to something akin to an odd titillation, she knew her mind was endeavoring to lie to her heart. Better to endure what must be endured in the arms of the handsome man she once loved than in the arms of a stranger.

"Then I will not refuse you," she whispered, looking away and to the fire still burning warm in the hearth.

"No. You will not," he confirmed.

Coquette startled as a soft knock echoed through the quiet room.

"That would be Victoria," Valor said. "She is irritatingly thoughtful on your behalf and has brought you warm milk and nutmeg to soothe your tender, innocent nerves."

Striding to the door, he opened it. Coquette watched as Victoria handed him a silver tray carrying two silver chalices.

He nodded at Victoria, mumbling, "Thank you," and closed the door.

Lifting one of the chalices from the tray, he drank from it as he approached. "This is a good thing she gives me now and again," he said, holding the tray out to her. "You will drink it. I will not have Victoria's efforts unappreciated."

"I would never be so discourteous," Coquette said, taking the chalice.

As Valor tossed the silver tray to join his discarded clothing on the chair, Coquette sipped the warmed milk. The scent of nutmeg did serve to soothe her slightly, and the milk was calming to her stomach.

Valor finished his drink, setting the chalice on the mantel as he watched the fire.

"I am not a patient man," he said, folding his powerful arms across his broad chest and glaring at her.

Coquette hurriedly finished her milk, handing the chalice to him when he held out a hand to her. He set the chalice on the hearth next to his and then reached out, taking her shoulders between powerful hands.

"Would you prefer I play the attentive lover for a time?" he asked. "Or does your preference run toward simple, quick endurance of what must take place between us?"

"I know nothing of either manner," Coquette told him. She felt strangely warm suddenly, more relaxed than a moment before, even for the line of conversation between them.

"Nothing?" he questioned. She fancied an expression of concern briefly crossed his handsome face. However, had it been concern, it passed as quickly as it had begun.

"No. Nothing," she assured him, feeling nearly

dizzy. "I then leave . . . leave the manner to you . . . milord."

His eyes narrowed as he looked at her. "Very well," he said. "You are prepared then to submit?"

"I am," she said. She felt as if her speech was slow, slurred, and unclear. She wondered for a moment why she had agreed so easily when only a moment ago she had been terrified, anxious, and despairing.

She shook her head, dizzy again as she watched him go to the bed and pull back the coverings. He returned to her, scooping her up in his arms and carrying her to the bed. As he laid her down, she could not stop her head from relaxing onto the soft down pillow beneath it. Her eyelids felt heavy, as did her arms and legs, and there was no fear left in her, even as her gaze moved to the lion of the lair waiting on the ceiling above.

"We begin then, wife," he said as he braced himself on powerful arms above her. "You will bear my child," he said. "You will." As his head descended toward hers, as she felt his hot breath on the flesh of her neck, all else was lost to her in the darkness of unconscious oblivion.

THE HEARTLESS NIGHT

Coquette slowly opened her eyes. Bright sunlight streamed through the eastern windows, and she smiled, pleased by its cheery warmth. Inhaling deeply, she stretched, feeling as if she had not moved a whit during the night. She wondered that she had slept so long. If the brightness of the sun were any indication, even Inez would have risen by now. Closing her eyes a moment more, she let her head linger on the downy softness beneath it. Never had her bed felt so comfortable. Never had she been so unwilling to fully awaken and leave its warm comfort. Yet the day had begun, and she had far overslept. Opening her eyes, she gazed for a moment on the vision overhead—the lion, his stone throne.

Gasping, she sat upright as memory and realization washed over her. She was not in her father's house in Bostchelan! The white linens and fine crimson coverlet enveloping her were not hers, nor was the bed they donned! Visions began to burst about in her mind as it lingered on the events of the previous day—and night. Suddenly her anxieties began to return as memories flooded her consciousness—her travel to Roanan in the coach, the unconventional wedding ceremony. She glanced down to see she still wore the lovely nightdress Victoria had chosen for her. Quickly, she glanced about the room, afraid Valor might be sitting in a chair watching her, as fretfulness entered her mind in the wake of confusion. She was alone, save the lion staring at her from overhead. Closing her eyes, she put her hands to her temples, pressing on them none too gently. She could remember nothing after Valor had entered his bedchamber, informed her of his desire for an heir, and handed her a chalice of warm milk and nutmeg. She strained her memory, begging it to release information to her. Yes. She could see him, handsome, alluring, hard-hearted Valor—the Lord of Roanan. She could see him taking the chalice from her hand once she had consumed the milk and nutmeg within. She could feel her body, lifted in his arms, carried to their marriage bed, and she could see him—his fine features, powerful body hovering above her— and then nothing! She could remember nothing further.

Yet here I sit, she thought, *in his bed in the morning light.* She glanced to the chair by the hearth, where still remained his cast-off coat, vest, and cravat, the silver serving tray Victoria had brought as well. There, on the mantel, two silver chalices. She swallowed hard as she noted the pair of tall boots on the floor near the chair, black breeches, and white shirt abandoned beside them.

Still, she frowned, for she remembered nothing else. How could a person not recall the events of their own wedding night? Had it been so frightful, so terrifying, so unendurable that her mind had simply shut it out?

"Ah. You're awake."

The deep, resonate sound of his voice startled Coquette. Quickly pulling the crimson coverlet up to her throat, her eyes widened as she turned to see Valor entering from an adjoining room. She frowned, puzzled at how less intimidating he appeared in the bright light of morning. His hair hung in dark, damp waves about his face and neck. He wore black breeches and was working at tucking a fresh white billowing shirt into the waist of them.

He strode to the enormous wardrobe against the eastern wall and removed a vest, coat, and stockings.

"You are a sound enough sleeper," he said, retrieving his boots and sitting down on one side of the bed. "I assume, therefore, I did not disturb you."

Coquette's mind spun, attempting to find a response. She remembered nothing of the evening following Valor's carrying her to their marriage bed. How could she possibly respond in earnest? It occurred to her that was exactly what she would do—respond with the utmost honesty.

"You did not, sire," she said. For it was the

truth—she had slept completely undisturbed.

"That is as it should be," he said, pulling on one thick stocking and then the other.

Coquette watched, her attention transfixed by his very presence. How handsome he was! Her heart fluttered, her breath quickened. How could it be Valor sat near to her, pulling on his boots? She wished—oh, how she wished—it was her beloved of the past before her—the strong, kind, compassionate, romantic lover she had known. In those moments, she could almost imagine he was such. And yet, as he glanced at her, the lion-amber of his eyes burning with pride, triumph, and smoldering anger, she winced at the change in him. Though outwardly he was even more handsome than ever he had been, inwardly he had transformed, transfigured into something dark and cruel.

"Victoria will have instructed the maids to prepare your bath," he said, standing and buttoning the upper buttons of his shirt. "When you are finished and have had your morning meal, you will go to the stables. You must choose a mount, for I am considering allowing you the freedom of riding now and again."

She was somewhat puzzled at his composed demeanor. Though she still sensed the heated blush on her own cheeks at his viewing her, addressing her as she sat so casually clothed in his bed, yet he seemed unaffected. The part of her mind tainted by worldly gossip wondered. *Perhaps it is commonplace for him—speaking to a woman as she sits amid his linens.* She swallowed hard, attempting to dispel the need her stomach felt to wretch at the thought. Could it be her father had been correct in his assumption of what Valor Lionhardt would become? Had he indeed taken on the low character of his father?

"Now, I am away to Roanan," he told her as he put on his vest and coat. She watched as he strode to the large looking glass and began struggling to tie his cravat. "I will return this evening, and you will dine with me at six. I will give you this day to yourself, for I am certain you are fatigued after such events as occurred yesterday . . . and last evening."

Coquette felt her blush deepen, suddenly angry she could not remember the night that had passed between them.

"Most of what you require can be attended to by Victoria or the maids. Godfrey will be at your service as well." He growled and stripped the cravat from around his collar and replaced it, beginning again. "Further, I will allow you respite from your duties as my wife this night. You may sleep in your own chambers." Again, he growled and stripped the cravat from his neck. "Damnable thing this is!" he mumbled.

Coquette needed escape! She was overwhelmed with torment in his presence. Suddenly, her need to self-preserve found her rising from the bed and going to the place he stood before the looking glass.

"Would you allow me, milord?" she asked him.

His eyes narrowed with suspicion as he looked at her. "It might be you would tighten it too much—attempt to strangle your way to freedom," he said.

Coquette was vexed he would think so low of her. After all, she had not turned her heart to stone, to violence, the way he had. "I only endeavor to assist you, sire," she said. He studied her for a moment more and then handed her the cravat. With trembling hands, Coquette wrapped the white length of silk around his neck, under his collar. She had become quite adept at forming a well-fashioned cravat, having tied her father's for years.

"There," she said, gesturing he should turn and view her effort in the looking glass. She watched as his eyebrows arched for a moment in approval.

"Were I in the habit of offering compliments," he began, "I should grant one to you for such a well-fashioned presentation."

She frowned, noting he had managed somehow to compliment her without literally doing so. She cast her gaze to the floor then as he slowly studied her from head to toe, smiling as if pleased at what his eyes beheld.

"Milady," he began, "it might serve you to quit

my chambers in favor of your own just now—lest I rescind my own word and demand you spend this evening with me as well."

Coquette gasped at his inference.

He chuckled, obviously amused by her discomfort. "You have to my count of five to make for the door and escape, milady," he chuckled, "else I will cancel my engagements in Roanan in opt to stay here with you and—"

She was off then, before he could begin to count, dashing toward the door to his chamber. Pulling on the great iron latch, she struggled to twist it as he added, "You offend me, milady. No offer of a kiss to bid me good morning?"

Coquette's cheeks blazed crimson as she dashed out of the lion's lair, across the hall, and into her own chambers. Valor's amused laughter echoed behind her. Closing the doors to her chambers, she stood breathless, feeling as if she had only just outleapt a blood-thirsty predator.

She jumped, gasping, entirely startled as almost instantly there came a knocking at the door. Coquette held her breath. It was he! Valor! He had followed her! He did not mean to let her escape. Again the knock and Coquette surmised then it was not Valor, for indeed he would have pounded on the door rather than this light knocking. Indeed, she surmised he may not have knocked at all—simply opened the door and let himself into her chambers.

"Yes?" Coquette called. "Come in, please." She could not stop the heavy, relieved sigh that escaped her lungs as the door opened to reveal Victoria.

"The maids have prepared your bath, milady," Victoria said. "And I have brought fresh towels for you."

"Th-thank you, madam."

"It would please me if you would call me simply Victoria, milady," Victoria said.

Still unsettled by Valor's toying with her, Coquette nodded. "As you wish, madam."

"A morning bath is the best refreshment there is, milady," Victoria said. "Soothing it is to the nerves. Calming."

"Yes. I suppose," Coquette mumbled.

"Victoria. Come at once, Victoria!" The sound of Valor's commanding voice echoing from across the hall sent Coquette's limbs to trembling once more. Yet she smiled, nearly giggling as she saw Victoria roll her eyes with exasperation.

"What? He's in a temper already this morning?" Victoria said, smiling at Coquette. She winked and whispered, "You enjoy that bath, milady. It will do you good, and today will not be so demanding as was yesterday. I promise."

Coquette smiled. She did feel somewhat comforted by the woman's reassurance. "Thank you, Victoria," she said.

She felt warmed by another wink gifted her by

the woman as she closed the door behind her. The smallest spark of hope flickered in her bosom. Perhaps she would find a friend in Victoria. And if nights spent in Valor's chamber had no more effect on her than to find her oversleeping into late daylight, perhaps she could endure. Perhaps.

"The stables, milady," Godfrey said. He clicked his heels together and bowed. With a nod he turned and left. Such stables Coquette had never envisioned! Exquisite, obviously well-bred horses pranced about within a nearby fenced area, and the stable buildings were vast and well cared for.

Coquette had always dreamed of owning her own mount. Her father had never allowed his daughters to ride often or to own their own horses. He feared the freedom of riding would find them lost or injured. Therefore, at the sudden realization she might be allowed to ride occasionally, Coquette's heart leapt with delicious anticipation.

"Milady?" a young man greeted as he approached. "How may I serve you?"

"I was told to . . . his lordship instructed me to choose a mount," she explained, feeling awkward. The young man before her seemed hardly older than herself. Yet the expression on his face told her he saw her as some great lady, not a mere merchant's daughter recently arrived from Bostchelan.

"Yes," the young man said. "Milord had informed Richins of the need to choose a mount for you. I am William and will serve you however I might, milady. However, Richins is just inside. I will take you to him. He and the master are discussing matters with his stableboy."

"The master?" Coquette gasped. She was certain Valor would have been away to Roanan by now.

"Yes," William said. "He is riding to Roanan but wanted to inspect the new stableboy before leaving. If you would be so kind as to follow me, milady."

Coquette laced her fingers together, bracing them against her waist. Her hands had begun to tremble at the knowledge Valor was still about. It seemed she would have to face him yet again, and she wondered whether she would ever find easement in doing so.

Entering the stables, Coquette drew in her breath at the sight of Valor. He stood instructing the new stableboy in the caring of his mount. Taking a currycomb from a nearby shelf, he demonstrated the manner in which he wished the boy to curry the enormous black horse.

Coquette mused that at a distance he again appeared as if little in him were altered. His shoulders were broader perhaps, his hair a bit longer. Still, for all the world he looked like Valor

Lionhardt, the man Coquette loved so desperately and had loved for so long.

In truth, he was ever more the most beautiful man to walk amidst Mother Nature's finery. The straight slope of his perfectly formed nose gave him an instant look of nobility. His squared jaw and his chin boasting the slightest cleft also spoke of a bloodline bold with handsome men and beautiful women. His hair was still the same dark, soft brown, chestnut waves still framing his face to meet his broad shoulders. Would she ever become accustomed to seeing him without being startled by his familiar, yet stranger's, beauty?

Coquette held her breath as Valor suddenly glanced at her. For a moment, she feared he had somehow read her thoughts—heard her musing of his overpoweringly handsome, lethally alluring physical form. The amber of his eyes, once as warm and bewitching as some sweet fairy's potion, narrowed, seeming to study her with disdain. Suddenly she felt oddly light-headed and realized she had been holding her breath far too long. She inhaled then exhaled, yet the dizziness remained.

"Richins," he called. "Milady has arrived."

He returned his attention to the horse and stableboy, and Coquette endeavored to breathe normally once more. Still, she found herself incapable of looking away from him, longing to gaze on him at a distance forever.

She closed her eyes a moment to break the spell. It was an aid she had discovered long ago—long ago when Valor had loved her—when, at times, his emotional and physical allure had been overwhelming to her. Many were the occasions in those beloved years past when Coquette had found herself weakened in his arms, gazing into the soft amber of his eyes and uncertain she could deny him anything he might ask of her. Never did he ask for anything beyond what virtue would allow. Yet she often felt, in those long-ago days, that had he asked, her resistance would have been sorely tried. It was then she had learned to close her eyes against the powerful magnetism of his perfect masculine beauty, against the pure and obsessive love for him searing within her.

Suddenly, she felt entirely besieged, thoroughly overcome, with the knowledge she had been led to her lost love Valor, only to find him so comprehensively altered. She was overly dizzy suddenly, weak, and, though she fought to deter it, she knew she would swoon.

She felt her breath give way, felt her body crumble to lie on the dirt of the stable floor. Nearly as soon as she had fallen, her breath returned to her, and she endeavored to right herself.

"William! Richins! Assist me!" she heard Valor shout. In the next moment, he was beside her, kneeling on one knee, her face in one powerful hand, forcing her to look at him.

"Milady has fainted," he said as William, the stableboy, and another man hovered over her.

"I am well," she whispered, humiliated at the realization she had succumbed to swooning before the men. How weak they would ever think her now. "I am well, milord."

Still, as she looked into the frowning face of the Lord of Roanan, she knew he was not convinced.

"Richins," he said as he stood, swooping her into his arms. "You will finish instructing Latimer where Goliath is concerned. Have the boy unsaddle Goliath as well. I will not ride to Roanan today."

"I am well enough, milord," Coquette said, yet feeling light-headed still. "You may away."

"William, go before us and tell Victoria what has happened. Make haste," he said. The man had to trot to stay ahead of Valor's long stride as he carried Coquette toward the manor house.

"I am able, sire," she told him, though in truth light-headedness still threatened her consciousness. "Truly."

"Able women do not faint in stables," he grumbled.

Oh, how desperately she wanted to cling to him, to slip her arms around his neck and lay her head on his shoulder. Yet the tense power of his body, the knowledge of his being Lord of Roanan and not simply Valor, kept her from it.

It seemed mere moments had passed when Valor carried her into the house and laid her on a chaise lounge in a parlor near the kitchens. Victoria was at her side, helping her to drink cool water from a silver chalice while Valor paced back and forth nearby.

"I have sent William for the physician," Valor told Victoria.

"Are you certain it was wise, sire?" Victoria asked.

"Wise? She lost consciousness in the stable, Victoria!" he shouted. "To my knowledge it is not the everyday occurrence!"

"Yes, sire," Victoria said, helping Coquette to sit upright.

"I am well, I assure you, sire," Coquette said. "I only felt light of head for a moment. Perhaps I was simply . . ." She was desperate to find an excuse for him, to settle his angry, worried expression—to alleviate Victoria bearing the brunt of his anger. "I-I did neglect to breakfast this morning," she admitted.

In truth, her stomach had been such a bundle of knotted nerves, she had been afraid to attempt to eat anything. She wondered whether it was her breathlessness in the stable at seeing Valor that had caused her faint. Yet she knew neglecting breakfast had likewise been an unwise choice. She had endured too much physical and emotional duress over the past few days, been rendered breathless in Valor's presence too often, for skipping meals to bode well.

"You did not eat?" he asked her. "Why would you begin the day with no breakfast? Especially after . . ." He paused, glancing to Victoria, whose eyes quickly widened as if in warning he should not continue his planned speech. "After such a night as last?" he finished.

"I did not think of eating, sire," Coquette said. "Pray, forgive me my folly. I did not expect it would affect me so."

"Send Godfrey to stay William and the physician, milord," Victoria said.

"Yes. Yes. Godfrey!" Valor shouted.

As she watched Godfrey arrive, as she watched Valor tell him to ride after William and tell him milady was fine and not to bring the physician, suspicion began to burn in her mind. Why? Why not summon the physician as a precaution?

"Hereafter you are not to leave the manor house without first having eaten," Valor ordered.

Coquette fancied his index finger trembled as he shook it at her. Indeed, she noted beads of perspiration on his forehead, the amber of his eyes bright with more concern than anger.

"Yes, milord," she replied as she watched him briefly place a fist to his mouth.

This was his fault! Valor struggled to remain calm, to rein his emotions into careful lines.

Still, it was his fault, and he knew it. Guilt began to creep over him, and he fought to keep it at bay.

When fate had gifted him Antoine de Bellamont as a thief and trespasser, he had thought only of revenge—of revenge and of at last owning the only woman he had ever wanted. Vowing he would not love her, he had convinced himself owning her would gift him infinite satisfaction. Yet when he'd entered his bedchamber the night before to see Coquette standing before him, his conscience had endeavored to return. More beautiful than even he had remembered, more inherently good and innocent, he knew at once he would have to draw upon every black emotion within him were he to resist her. Even though he held rights as her husband, he had vowed to resist her. And resist her he had, with Victoria's aid and knowledge.

When he had turned to see her collapse, he doubted what he had done—feared it had somehow harmed her. Fear was not an emotion with which he was any longer acquainted. He loathed fear and the weakness it stirred in him. He despised Coquette and the weakness she stirred in him.

"Such a long trip yesterday, milord," Victoria told him. "Such a very long trip and then the ceremony and . . . and beyond. Nothing to eat has simply worn her down."

• • •

"Then make certain she eats when first she rises from here forward," Valor growled.

Coquette looked away as the fire of his narrowed, angry eyes burned upon her.

"My day is in ruination for all this! See to her, Victoria. And put her abed earlier than would be expected," he said, storming from the room.

"Yes, milord," Victoria said.

Inside, Coquette trembled. Something was about that she did not understand. Something had passed between Valor and Victoria, causing her to reconsider the trust she had begun to place in the woman.

"Truly, Victoria," Coquette began, "am I well? Is something amiss with me, do you know?"

Victoria smiled, patting her cheek with reassurance. "I'm afraid you have been overly taxed, milady," Victoria said, "and quite underfed today."

"Would you deceive me now to protect your master?" Coquette asked plainly.

Victoria inhaled long and deep before answering, "Yes, milady. I would. But I am telling you the truth in these moments. You are simply overly taxed."

Though Victoria's truthfulness unnerved her greatly, she somehow felt relieved by it.

"Then I will eat something and wander through the gardens awhile," Coquette said.

"Both will do you good, milady," Victoria agreed.

Yet Coquette felt ill at ease. Something was amiss, she was certain. Valor, appearing so terrifying, confident, and commanding since she arrived, had seemed entirely unsettled for some time after her faint. The manner in which Victoria calmed him was also unusual—a housemistress instructing the master on matters of whether a physician was needed? It was, all of it, strange. Yet something in Valor's eyes, however fleeting, had been familiar. Concern? Worry? For an instant, Coquette's mind mused. Perhaps her true Valor still resided somewhere deep inside the beast-self he had become. Perhaps not all of him was lost. Perhaps she would find him one day, draw him out to their mutual happiness.

Still, as she thought again of his threat to her father's life, of his insensitivity to her the night before, she abandoned the hope of it. Her Valor would have sent for the physician, no matter what Victoria's assurances had been. Her Valor would have worried over her well-being to greater length. No. The Lord of Roanan was not her Valor. The Lord of Roanan was cruel and heartless, and Coquette must accept.

The gardens at Roanan Manor were of a heavenly beauty. After enjoying a light meal of poached eggs and a muffin, Coquette left the manor house in search of some resemblance of serenity and peace. She found the gardens provided both. Lush with green and bright color, she knew autumn was at summer's gate and would strip the gardens of their purples and pinks. Yet as she walked beneath grand oaks, gazed at the rosehips along certain paths, she knew autumn would bring more brilliance to Roanan Manor's gardens even than summer.

Amid a grove of trees, Coquette came upon a pond. Large fish of the brightest orange and pearl swam lazily in the sun-warmed water. A bench sat at its bank on one side, a bench made of small tree limbs and leather, and Coquette sat upon it, considering the fish as they swam back and forth in the water.

Warm breezes through the leaves overhead breathed soothing whispers through Coquette's hair. The bright sun on her face warmed her, and she sighed with momentary contentment as she watched a tiny bluebird bathing in the water.

"You are recovered then?"

The voice startled her. She turned to see Valor standing behind her. She wondered how long he had been there. Had he followed her out of the house? How long had he been watching her as she sat in ignorant serenity?

"Yes, sire," she answered. "I am not normally so weak, yet I suppose the events of the past few days would weigh very heavily on anyone."

"Hmm. I suppose," he mumbled. "I will expect you at dinner, in any event," he said.

"At six. Yes, milord," she said.

"There is a box beneath the bench," he said. "In it, you will find a pair of gloves and bits of stale biscuits. You may feed the fish if you wish."

She realized she might have intruded, however unknowingly, on Valor's own sanctuary of peace.

"Forgive me, milord. I do not mean to intrude here," she said.

"You may feed them when you wish," was all he said as he turned and left.

Coquette closed her eyes against the vision of his walking away. It suddenly reminded her of the day he'd left her father's study—of the last time she had seen him as Valor Lionhardt, her true beloved, instead of Lord Lionhardt, the dark Lord of Roanan. Would that he could be both. Yet she knew he could not. The tide had taken Valor and washed ashore a stranger to her.

Valor's breathing increased as his emotions threatened to surface. Was he to have no privacy now? As he stormed down the garden path toward the house, he determined, though he would keep from Roanan, he would have Latimer saddle Goliath all the same. He needed to ride. Hang it all! He would saddle Goliath himself! Goliath would carry him into oblivion—where the past could not haunt him and the beauty presently sitting at his fishpond could no more distract him.

He must hold firm! He must keep his presence of mind! Revenge—revenge and triumph—it was all that mattered. He must hold to bitterness and loathing. He paused as he approached the stables. Yet how would he keep himself from her? He closed his eyes, trying to dispel the vision of her as she had looked last evening—soft, beautiful, innocent, seemingly so unaffected as he had been by her father's refusal three years before. He thought then no emeralds held the flash her eyes did; no woman on the earth could cause such a fire to flare within him.

He grimaced, forcing a vision of her cowardly father to the forefront of his mind—Antoine de Bellamont, the coward. And yet what was Valor Lionhardt but a different sort of coward?

Growling, he opened his eyes, running an angry hand through his mane. Hold to the stone heart within. It was what he wanted. It was who he had become—Lionhardt the Heartless. He chuckled, fancying the byname bestowed upon him by the townsfolk of Roanan sounded as one of Arthur's very knights of the round.

"The Heartless Knight," he fancied aloud. But his musing was to his own detriment, for in the next thought his mind whispered to him— what of the night spent with Coquette? What of his first night with his wedded wife? Was it not also heartless of a different sort—void of desire, passion, love? What might have passed between them three years past had Antoine de Bellamont not refused the hand of his daughter? For certain, it would not have found Coquette instantly induced to deep and wakeless slumber by way of Victoria's unusual nutmegged milk. It would not have been such a heartless night between Valor and Coquette had Antoine not stripped love and happiness from him. But he had, and Valor determined there would be many a heartless night in his future. And so be it!

He strode to the stables, saddled Goliath, and rode—rode the day to the ground, until his body was worn and his mind again intent on his resolve. He had not brought Coquette to Roanan to woo and win her once more. He had brought her to Roanan to triumph! To defeat her merchant father!

Yet as he entered the dining hall at six to see her sitting clothed in the softest of blue gown, her ebony hair cascading over bare shoulders, Lionhardt the Heartless worried for the strength of the darkness within him. Many a beast had been brought to ruin and domesticity at the hand of beauty. Still, his resolve was strong, and he would not bend. He prepared himself then—another heartless night would proceed.

A LETTER TO CONTEMPLATE

A week passed, and with it, somehow Coquette's strength of mind grew. Rest and conscious acceptance of her circumstance led her to determination—determination to keep herself. As each day passed, Coquette was determined she would not be lost to resentment and bitterness the way Valor had been. In truth, Valor himself had unknowingly given her strength. Each morning as she awoke—each time in her own chambers, for Valor had not demanded she attend him again since their wedding night—she was struck by his lack of pleasure in a new day. In being ever angry, ever walking the halls of Roanan Manor House wearing a perpetual frown, Valor seemed to find no easy delight. Coquette was not surprised, for a blackened heart did not allow gladness to easily enter a dark soul. Still, it caused her further awareness of her own—awareness of the need to cling to a light heart, a bright soul. This she endeavored to do.

Each morning, after a rather hearty breakfast prepared for her at Valor's demand, she meandered through the breathtaking gardens of Roanan Manor. Fresh air, lovely colors, and a pause at the pond to feed the fish filled her soul with moments of respite. Further, Valor had chosen a mount for her and had indeed allowed her to ride most every day. Naturally, William, Richins, or even Godfrey must accompany her, for Valor had not condoned her riding alone, the reason being she was not familiar with the countryside and might easily become lost. Silently she mused he was afraid she would ride away from him. But fear did not seem part of his character, nor desire for her company in any aspect, with the exception of dinner. Always he demanded she dine with him, and oddly enough, Coquette had begun to somehow look forward to it.

Though their conversation was always stiff, lacking any depth and true merit, she had begun to revel in the knowledge it was the only time Valor seemed the least bit unsettled. At first she had taken his attempts at disorganized conversation as the result of bored irritation. However, she had begun to realize that for some reason, their dinner hour unsettled him. Perhaps it was irritation of some sort still. Yet it seemed he was never quite as completely gathered as he appeared any other time, and it caused Coquette curiosity.

And then one night, over a week after her arrival, Valor entered the dining hall as the clock struck six, a deep frown furrowing his brow. Coquette had taken to arriving early to ensure she would be waiting when he arrived and sat straight and at the ready.

"This was delivered for you," Valor fairly growled, tossing an article of post to the table before her. "Mind you, it is simply my good nature today that allows you to know it has come." He rather slammed himself into his chair, his chest rising and falling with the labored breathing of restrained anger.

"It is a letter," Coquette said, retrieving the post from the table and looking at it, "written in Elise's hand."

"It is why I chose to allow you to have it," Valor growled, "for it is not a man's script. Therefore, I assume it is not from your father."

Coquette frowned, wondering whether her father had attempted to write her. Perhaps he had and Valor had simply not allowed her to have the letters.

She was somewhat unsettled as he seemed to have read her thoughts when he said, "You have received no other letters from Bostchelan. This is but the first, if you are thinking I have kept others from you."

"Thank you, milord," Coquette said, placing the letter in her lap. She would relish the news from her sister after dinner when she was alone.

"Read it then," Valor demanded, "unless you are afraid to let me hear what news your sister has sent to you."

Afraid to let him hear Elise's news? Of course she was afraid to let him hear it! He sat relaxed in his chair, one elbow crooked over the back of it, while his free hand toyed with the napkin at his place setting. She knew he would not be deterred; yet she must try.

"I-I am certain there is no information of consequence, sire," she stammered.

"But I am certain there is," he said, his eyes narrowing as he looked at her.

As ever was the case, the speed with which Coquette's heart beat increased as he looked at her. Silently scolding herself for allowing his profound attractiveness and allure to affect her so, she determined she would attempt to read the letter aloud while brushing over anything her eyes beheld that might give Valor cause for scorn.

"Very well, milord," she said. Over the past week, Coquette had begun to learn the importance of standing firm in Valor's presence—not firm in denying him, but firm in not displaying the profound effect his intimidation had on her. She was becoming quite adept at pretending confidence.

Carefully, she broke the seal of the parchment and unfolded it.

"My dearest Coquette," she began. She could feel his gaze burning into the side of her face yet resolved to seem impervious. *"It is well I hope this finds you. Dominique bids I ask you*

concerning the tapestries Father mentioned. Are they as wonderful as she dreams?"

"Are they?" Valor asked.

"Yes, sire," Coquette answered. "They are."

He nodded, proud and pleased by her answer.

"Continue then," he ordered.

"So much has transpired in the few short days since you quit Bostchelan. There is so much to tell," she read on. She paused, feeling a frown at her own brow. She did not quit Bostchelan—she was pressed to leave!

"It vexes you," Valor said, "the fact she implies you chose to leave."

"No," Coquette lied, entirely unsettled by his uncanny ability to sense her thoughts. "I . . . I only wonder what so much has transpired. I have been gone but ten days."

"You're counting them, I see," he said. A mischievous, knowing grin spread across his face.

"I will continue," Coquette said, angry with the blush rising to her cheeks.

"Yes. Do," he said.

"Two days ago, Father's three new ships arrived heavy-laden with such wealth of commodities you can not imagine it—every conceivable textile, silver, gold, spice, antiquities! And you should see the gowns brought over for the three of us sisters you have left behind you. Father is happier than I ever remember him being, Coquette! And his

107

happiness is our own. We are moving, as well! I cannot tell you where yet. It will be such a surprise when you visit us for you to see where we will be living. Father is more wealthy than ever any of us have imagined!" Coquette paused, hurt by Elise's lightheartedness, by her father's utter happiness while she lived under the roof of intimidation and disdain. Distracted by her own miserable reaction to the contents of the letter, she entirely forgot to not share it fully aloud to Valor.

She continued to read. *"Henry Weatherby has asked for Inez's hand only this morning! Father has given his permission, of course. Though Henry is not so wealthy and titled even as your Valor was, I believe Father is content enough in his own wealth now and in seeing you so rightly settled that his heart is softened toward Henry. Further, I think he has begun to worry none of the rest of us will marry, and he will not be rid of us! I do worry for you, Coquette. Yet Father assures me your Lord of Roanan is not so dark as his reputation attests and that you will be well cared for and happy. He says you will be a great lady, and though this seems to irritate Inez and Dominique somewhat, it eases my heart on your behalf. I do wonder though . . . how could your lord, that is to say, your husband—for it reaches our ears you are already wed—how could he threaten to murder our father on one day, yet earn Father's praise in the next? It is a mystery I am certain you have solved by now, and so I will sit here at the side of the sea of Bostchelan and imagine you happy and as the beautiful, grand Lady of Roanan. It is the only way to ease my mind on your behalf, Coquette. I send my love to you in this letter and hope to see you again one day soon. I miss you so! Lovingly Yours, Elise."*

Coquette swallowed the emotion in her throat. It was true Elise cared for her. Had she not cared enough to write the letter? Still, the shallow nature of her father and sisters was painfully evident in its contents. She was hurt by the lighthearted tone of the letter, humiliated when she then realized she had read it fully to Valor.

"A letter to contemplate, indeed," Valor said then. "Henry Weatherby, is it?" Valor asked. "For Inez, the eldest? Henry, who has no title and little wealth to speak of, is worthy of Inez. The oldest sister chooses who she may, and your father consents, while the youngest was given no choice even for the wealthy and soon-to-be titled man who asked for her hand."

"Henry . . . Henry cares for Inez," Coquette quietly insisted. Still, his words rang too true in her ears.

"Henry? Care for Inez?" Valor exclaimed. "Henry Weatherby is a puff! A puff who cared only for you, if memory serves. And yet he is worthy of Inez, the eldest, when I, wealthy and

109

soon to inherit my father's title, was not worthy of the younger?"

"Father's heart has softened. Perhaps because of my own unhappiness at his refusing you." Coquette ventured to defend her father, though in the moment she felt little like doing so.

"His heart is not softened!" Valor fairly roared. "He as much as sold you to me! To a stranger, he thinks!"

Coquette stood, glaring at him as tears filled her eyes. "You threatened his life, and I chose to come!" she told him. She watched as Valor's jaw clenched tight with fury. He was withholding words, she knew. He was considering what he would say next rather than roaring what his temper urged him to say.

"And there it is before you," he said. "You claim your own unhappiness at your father's refusing me—claim he is softened because of it. And yet I will tell you this of it—your father does not know I am Lord of Roanan, and with my own mouth I assured him I would treat you badly. Yet he bid you come to me—your life for his—and he gives Henry Weatherby Inez's hand! And there, still, you long for his company? Your sisters bathe in luxury and wealth, happiness and home, while you endure Roanan, and still you long for them instead of . . ." He paused, his teeth grinding with rage. He tugged at his cravat, loosening its knot and stripping it from his neck as he unbuttoned several buttons of his shirt. He breathed a heavy sigh and said, "Yet in truth, I had no siblings on which to slather unconditional adoration. I had no father worthy of admiration. You have no father to be admired as well. Yet you are a woman, and women are softhearted. Still . . ." He stood then, slamming one powerful fist on the table before him. "Are you so blind as this? Your father values wealth beyond any-thing—even beyond you!"

"You are wrong! He values his children!" Coquette cried. "You would have killed him! My sisters and I would have fallen into ruin! Does he not deserve happiness and wealth for being willing to give his life for us?"

"But that is where you are mistaken, my beauty," he growled. "He was not willing to give his life for you. He was not willing to give even less."

Coquette covered her ears with her hands. Yet the gesture did not stop the truth of his words from echoing in her mind. "What kind of daughter would allow her father to be killed for her sake?" she whispered.

"It was for the sake of thievery, not for the sake of you," he said.

"It was a rose, Valor!" she cried at him. "He only took a rose!"

"Did he?" he asked, infuriated still. "What did he take from me—a rose? Nay. He took my life when he refused me you! And you were content in it! Better I am the beast I am now in your eyes than should your father be disappointed in rebellion from you then!" His eyes narrowed as he glared at her. "And you will not call me by that name again!"

"I was not content in it!" she cried, ignoring his last command. "I was not!"

"You *were* content in it!" he shouted. "Standing so wilted, so bewildered as I lowered myself to beg you away with me! It is well I remember it."

"Do not speak to me of contentment," she cried, "for you do not know it by sight, it is sadly obvious. Yet I will speak to you of choice—of the choice to remain true to myself, for I became no hateful beast who would threaten lives over one fading rose!"

He continued to glare at her yet remained silent. She fancied there was confusion in his eyes. Had her words touched him somehow? In the next moment, she was assured they had not.

Angrily sweeping his arms across the table before him, he sent silver spattering to the floor, china splintering into shards. Striding to her, he took her chin none too gently in hand and said, "Tomorrow you will ride with me to Roanan to set the tongues of gossips to wagging their wild ways. And then—sleep well this night, woman. For the next will be spent in my company!" Picking up the china plate on the table before her, he hurled it across the room, watching as it shattered against a wall. "Victoria!" he shouted. "Victoria!"

Coquette brushed the tears from her cheek, trembling as she stood in the presence of his rage.

"It was once you trembled with joy and desire when I was near. You may thank your father for the reason you tremble now," he said, his voice still angry but void of the roar it held only moments before.

"You have chosen the reason I tremble now, milord," Coquette said. "Place the blame where you will—yet you have chosen it."

He said nothing, only continued to breathe heavy, angry breaths.

"Yes, milord?" Victoria said, entering the dining hall. Her eyes widened as she looked at the smashed china and scattered silver.

"I have . . . I have found myself in a fit of temper," he said, attempting to steady his breathing. "See that milady is well fed and found comfortable in her bed."

"Yes, sire," Victoria said. "Will you not take dinner then, milord?"

"I have no appetite for dinner," he said. Then speaking to Victoria yet glaring at Coquette, he added, "My appetite runs to merchants' daughters, and it seems I cannot escape it." He stormed from the room, leaving fury, rage, and loathing in his wake.

"Are you well, milady?" Victoria asked.

"I am," Coquette said.

She was surprised in it herself, for Valor had become an entirely menacing apparition. And yet something in her could not wholly release the memory of the man she had known and loved. Something in her desired to battle with him, as if battling the demon he had become would unearth who he once had been. Further, her very soul knew he would not harm her being, even for his display of angry temper.

"How you are well and so utterly composed I cannot fathom, milady," Victoria said, stooping to retrieve the scattered silver. "Such an unruly boy's tantrum is in him at times. Godfrey and I can but wonder what has made him thus."

"You do not know?" Coquette asked. She had assumed Godfrey and Victoria both knew Valor's history—Valor's and her own.

"No, milady. It was three years past milord arrived to claim the title and wealth of Roanan. Though his anger and darkness have steadily increased, he has never spoken of what reason was given to it."

"Yet you serve him faithfully," Coquette said. "And I sense there is more to your loyalty than mere price."

Victoria looked to Coquette. She seemed to study her, weigh her trustworthiness a moment before speaking. "Forgive me, milady—but I sense there is more to your enduring than is evident as well. Perhaps it is we, all of us, know there is more than the dark beast in him," she said.

"Still, his temper is far too violent," Coquette said, skirting agreement. "His indulgence toward violence frightens me."

"Has he harmed you?" Victoria asked.

Coquette looked to her, seeing an expression of rather daring on her face. "No. Never," Coquette said. "But he threatened my father. Even his life."

"Threatening is far different than acting, milady," Victoria told her. "You need not fear him."

"I know it," Coquette admitted.

"Now, let us away to the kitchen. You need a good meal," Victoria said, placing a comforting arm about Coquette's shoulders.

Sleep did not come easily to Coquette that night. As she lay in bed into the latest hours, her mind was alive with contemplation. She had read Elise's letter again. Over and over she had read it, Valor's words echoing in her thoughts each time she did. Yet her father loved her, she was certain. And still, Valor's judgments rang true in her mind. Her father had chosen to give Coquette's life in place of his own—and that being *if* Valor truly intended to kill him. Something in the back of Coquette's mind had begun to question whether Valor was capable of killing her father.

Threatening is far different than acting, milady. Victoria's words reflected truth. Yet Coquette could not believe her father would send her to wed he whom he believed to be a stranger if anything less than his very life were at stake.

She tossed in her bed, determined to contemplate other venues—her father's willingness to give Henry Weatherby Inez's hand in marriage, for instance. Flatly he had refused Valor Coquette's hand three years previous. What now made him so willing to accept such as Henry Weatherby? Perhaps it was simply as Elise had implied in her letter; perhaps her father worried his daughters would not marry if he did not lessen his standard or expectation in sons-in-law.

Coquette shook her head, trying to think of something else. And then—then it began— the moisture in her mouth increasing as she thought of Valor. For all his cruel fury, for all his apparently wicked ways, she could not chase the handsome vision of him from her mind.

"He is a beast!" she whispered aloud to herself, trying to evoke visions of his anger. Yet the vision most prevalent in her mind was that as he had appeared the morning after their wedding. He had emerged from his bathing rooms, damp-haired, loose-shirted, bootless, and the memory gave her cause to sigh with admiration.

She closed her eyes, reminiscing likewise the last time she had seen him before her father had refused to bestow him her hand.

Valor had come upon her in the gardens of her father's house in Bostchelan. Taking her in his strong arms, he smiled down at her, loving desire apparent in the warm amber of his eyes. Gently pressing his mouth to her own, he had whispered, "I love you, Coquette de Bellamont. And I will have you—at any cost."

Now, lying in her bed at Roanan, Coquette's heart beat more rapidly as her memory lingered on Valor's whispered kiss—the light touch of his tongue to her lips as he spoke the words, the feel of his breath warm in her mouth.

"He is a beast!" she told herself again. "Cruel, void of feeling save hate and anger!"

Yet as she at last began to drift into much-needed slumber, it was the vision, the memory of Valor's kiss, whispered with such adoration and love—it became the fabric of her dreams.

THE ATTENTIVE LOVER

The cool air of morning was refreshing, invigorating in its promise of the change of season. Coquette could not help but smile at the sight of squirrels gathering food for their winter stores, the first few splashes of crimson high in the tops of the oaks. Her mount was lovely, a strong bay mare called Meg, and she kept pace perfectly with Valor's black Goliath. She loved the sound of the leather of the saddles and cinches as they rode.

Valor had said little since they rode out from the manor house for Roanan. He seemed thoughtful, somewhat anxious, but Coquette was determined to enjoy the day. Lingering in the back of her mind, however, was Valor's threat of the evening before—that she would spend this night in his company rather than in her own chamber. Still, she would face whatever night brought when night did bring it. For now she was away to Roanan, and she was happy in the knowledge.

"As do I, you will bear the brunt of gossip," Valor suddenly said, "much of it cruel, highly embellished—malicious even. You must grow a thick skin to it."

"What sort of gossip, milord?" she asked.

She could well imagine, for she knew the

gossip that had widely circulated in Bostchelan concerning Valor's father. Still, was it gossip when so much was truth? So she felt obliged to ask him, for she wondered what gossip was spread regarding her own husband.

"The sort that makes for immoral accusations and lends excuses to those unwilling to own to their mistakes," he said.

She looked to him, fancying he was uncomfortable in speaking to her about the venues of the gossip he anticipated.

"Are you similarly accused as was your father?" she asked, with thinly veiled impertinence. A vision of his being so obviously comfortable in addressing her as she sat amid his bed linens entered her mind. He seemed little disconcerted speaking to her as she sat wearing only her nightdress. Her father's low expectations of Valor entered her mind, as did the immorality of Valor's own father. Yet she battled such thoughts, for was she not questioning her own father's character of late?

"I am similarly accused," he stated. "And often."

"There was truth in the gossip regarding your father," she ventured, her hands suddenly trembling with trepidation. She would not believe Valor had taken on his father's low character and immoral habits. She would not! Yet he was so much changed; she feared his answer in that moment.

"You've no need to remind me of the low character of my father," he said.

"I meant but to ask you . . . to inquire if . . ." she stumbled.

"You want to know if the gossip is as true of me as it was of my father," he finished for her. He looked at her, the angry amber of his eyes flaming with indignation.

"I did not mean to offend you, milord," she mumbled, ashamed at her own implication.

"They may say you will quit me in two months in favor of some other lover," he said. "They may even name him for you. Perhaps they will name my man, Godfrey, as your lover. Will that make it truth—that they have named it to be so?"

"Of course not!" Coquette exclaimed, blushing to the very tips of her toes. What an inference! How could he even concoct such wild ideas in his thinking?

"Then in that you have your answer to the truth of my character," he said, "for albeit your father insisted my father's nature would come to full fruition in me, it has not." With one more glaring look at her, he growled, "On, Goliath!" The enormous black horse took to an immediate gallop, leaving Coquette and her mare far behind.

After a time, however, Valor reined in, waiting for Coquette to join him.

"Prepare yourself, little beauty," he said as they

approached Roanan, "for I feed you to the wolves this moment."

As they entered the streets of Roanan, Coquette was astonished at the multitude of inquisitive stares and accompanying whispers.

"Milord," one man greeted, tipping his hat to Valor.

"Good morning, Eaves," Valor said. "Have you met Milady of Roanan as yet?"

"No, sire. I have not yet had the pleasure," the man said.

Valor reached over, taking hold of the reins in Coquette's hands and pulling her mount flush to his.

"This is Lady Lionhardt, Eaves, your Lady of Roanan," he said as the man removed his hat and nodded to Coquette.

Coquette smiled and returned his nod of greeting.

"This is Eaves, milady," Valor said to her. "He is the greatest blacksmith in the country. By far."

"Thank you, milord," Eaves said, smiling at Coquette.

"I am pleased to meet you, Eaves," Coquette said.

"And I you, milady," Eaves said, smiling. "We were hearing his lordship's new bride was as pretty as any princess, milady. And may I say, your ladyship is far more than that."

"You are far too kind and flattering, I am

certain, sir," Coquette said, silently commanding her blush to cool.

"What news of Roanan?" Valor asked.

"Oh, not so much of late, milord," Eaves said. "Yet old Mathilde died three days past."

"Mathilde?" Valor asked, dismounting then. "A good soul was she. I hate to hear she has left us."

Coquette frowned, confused by Valor's suddenly polite demeanor. She watched as he handed Goliath's reins to Eaves.

"I will have a basket sent to her daughter. Perhaps a new sapling as well," Valor said. He held his hands out to Coquette. By reflex, she placed her hands on his broad shoulders, allowing him to lift her down from her own mount.

"Thank you for telling me of Mathilde, Eaves," Valor said, linking Coquette's arm through his own. "And would you see to Goliath and Meg for me? I am not so certain Goliath was not having some discomfort on the ride here."

"Yes, milord. Of course," Eaves said. "Milady," he added with a bow before replacing his hat.

"Come, milady," Valor said. "Let us walk in Roanan."

Coquette looked to him, inquisitive. He was so altered. His presence still commanding, thoroughly intimidating, yet his brief conversation was somehow void of the familiar arrogance normally radiating from him.

Each person who passed them on the streets of Roanan offered kind greetings, Valor instantly responding with a polite greeting in return. Coquette simply smiled, wondering which of these kind-seeming people were the vessels to carry malicious gossip and which were truly the Lord of Roanan's allies in spirit.

They walked without haste for a space, until Valor led her to a shop filled with books, sweet pastries, and trinkets of every sort. He purchased a book—a book that she was certain she had seen already on a shelf of the vast library at Roanan Manor. Likewise, he purchased three pieces of hard, golden confection, depositing one in his mouth and two in his pocket. Lastly, he purchased a fine set of lace gloves for Coquette, pleasing the shopkeeper with an extra silver coin for her trouble.

Within the hour, Meg walked abreast of Goliath, and Coquette rode in wonder at the polite Lord of Roanan she had witnessed in town.

"It will begin at once," he said suddenly. "It already has."

"The gossip, you mean?" she asked. Surely such kind people as she had only just met would say nothing against Valor and especially herself. "But surely, sire—they all . . . they all seem so . . . so very fond of you."

At once, Valor broke into amused laughter, and Coquette could not help but smile at the sight of his merriment. How much more handsome he was happy than ever brooding!

"You say it as if it is inconceivable to you," he said. "Yet once you too found me of a quality to admire."

Coquette was uncomfortable. Somehow, the appearance of his dazzling smile had unsettled her, causing her to feel fondly toward him. "I meant only to ask what malicious gossip can thrive when everyone there seems to see you as—" she began.

"You did not meet them all," he said. "Not all the inhabitants of Roanan greeted us this day. You met the few who think of me as contributing to their livelihood—the blacksmith whom I paid for service to Goliath that was not needed, the shopkeeper whose books and sweets I buy each time I visit."

"Surely they do not admire you simply for the sake of your purse, milord," she said. She had seen the way these people greeted Valor, the true admiration in their eyes. He himself did not see they admired him for himself, not simply his purse.

"The gossip has begun, milady," he said. "As I said, thicken your pretty skin against it."

Suddenly, she desired to hear her name drop from his lips. She did not want to be *milady*. She wanted to hear his voice speak *Coquette* as it once had. She tried not to think of the way he had referred to her as Kitty in the past. When first they had become sweethearts, he had taken to calling her the more familiar *Quettie,* which he quickly smoothed into *Kitty.* How she wished he would name her that instead of milady.

Shaking her head to dispel the sweet memory of the Valor she once knew, she looked to him and said, "My skin is thicker than you think, milord."

"Such soft skin as yours could not be too thick, milady," he said, causing her to quickly look to him. For an instant, she thought she saw a familiar, teasing merriment in his eyes. But it vanished quickly as he added, "I am impatient to find you in my chambers this evening—as I know you are impatient to find yourself there as well."

"You obviously do not know the nature of my skin or the vast length of my patience, milord," she said, cropping Meg to a canter. She must escape him, for the blush on her cheeks was blazon, she knew. How dare he utter such insinuations! How dare he? Yet Coquette was greatly unsettled by the sudden and brutal hammering of her heart.

"Beast!" she muttered to herself as she rode on toward Roanan Manor.

Valor smiled and chuckled. Immediately, however, he endeavored to rein in his amusement. He would have to be careful in teasing her, for it could be his undoing. She evoked some long-lost desire toward jest from within him, and he must mask it, beat it down lest it weaken his resolve.

The little vixen, he thought, summoning indignation. How dare she imply she would have long patience in resisting him? Why, Valor knew full well that if he were a mind to have her do so, she would be willingly in his arms in a hair's breadth!

Perhaps it was time the merchant's daughter was taught her lessons in humility. Perhaps it was time he championed less chivalry and more virility! *Hmph,* he thought. *We shall see how her prudence defends the advances of the Lord of Roanan this night!*

"You seem overanxious this evening, milady," Victoria said as she brushed Coquette's long hair. Sitting before the looking glass in her own chambers, Coquette's heart pounded with angst. The standing clock read one quarter of an hour before eight, and she was a knot of nerves and worry.

"I suppose I am only tired from the trip to Roanan today," Coquette said.

"Well, I am certain there were many sets of curious eyes upon you there," Victoria said, smiling. "No doubt the silvered tongues of the old gossips are weaving tales as we speak."

"No doubt," Coquette breathed.

"I will bring you some warmed milk with nutmeg this evening, milady," Victoria said. "It will quiet you and send you to sleep much soothed."

"I have not had your spiced milk since the first night I arrived," Coquette said.

"You have had no need of it since that first night, I do not think," Victoria said.

Coquette blushed crimson, as crimson, she fancied, as the coverlet on Valor's bed.

"Yet tonight . . . it will be good for you to have it," Victoria added.

"I have been here nearly two weeks, Victoria," Coquette said. "Milord . . . he does not seem to be as . . . as demanding that I away to him as I imagined a husband would be."

Victoria held her breath for a moment, entirely irritated with her lord. Did he not realize milady's complete innocence? Did he not yet admit the true desires of his own heart? Yet she must be careful, for there was much she felt she did not know—something keeping the Lord of Roanan from his wife and all he desired of her.

"I will bring your drink promptly," Victoria said, setting the brush on the vanity and taking Coquette's elbow in urgency she should stand. "For now, you should away to his chamber, lest he arrive early and be vexed to find you absent."

Coquette did not miss the manner in which Victoria had so demurely skirted her questions. Perhaps she was simply uncomfortable discussing the intimacies of her lordship's marriage. Therefore, Coquette chose to urge her no further and simply allowed Victoria to escort her across the hall to Valor's chambers.

Once inside and alone, she began to tremble. With no memory of what had transpired on her wedding night, she was as unsettled as ever before.

She must distract herself—give her mind and body respite from worry. Thus, she glanced up at the lion overhead. Turning her head this way and that, she decided the nature of the mural was much better viewed from the bed. Carefully, for she was every inch disconcerted, she lay on Valor's bed, gazing up at the lion. She glanced at the clock. Yet ten minutes were to pass before he would arrive. So she stared at the lion above her. There were attributes of the lion she had not noticed on her first night in the room. Its eyes were so like Valor's she was surprised she had not noticed the resemblance before. The same color and shape, she fancied the lion had been painted while the artist gazed into Valor's very eyes.

"You come to me early? How flattering, milady."

Instantly, Coquette leapt from the bed. Valor had entered by way of his bathing rooms once

128

again. Coquette put a hand to her bosom to calm her startled heart. He already had removed his coat, vest, and cravat. The billowy white of his shirt hung open and untucked. Even his boots and stockings had been stripped.

"You frightened me nearly out of my skin, milord!" she said, breathless yet, both from his sudden entrance and his alluring appearance.

"For my own advantage, I would have done better to frighten you nearly out of that gossamer nightdress you wear," he said.

Coquette gasped, indignant practically to mortification at his inference.

He smiled and chuckled. "Come now, you merchant's daughter, you," he said. "We are alone, entirely isolated within my bedchamber. You need not act the offended innocent here. You seem to forget . . . you are my wife and have spent the night in my bed once before. Willingly enough, I may add."

Coquette felt her brow pucker, again frustrated with her lack of memory of her wedding night. "Did I not know the better of it for myself," he began, "by the expression on your pretty face, I would think you had forgotten completely the fact of it."

"I-I am simply unaccustomed to such light-hearted handling of . . . of such private matters," Coquette stammered. How she wished she could remember! But she did not. She remembered only her stunned astonishment at finding Valor to be her husband—the warm milk and nutmeg. Nothing else.

She watched him as he strode to the bed, lying down upon it and tucking his hands beneath his head for a moment as he seemed to consider the lion above. "Now then," he began, "would you prefer I play the attentive lover for a time? Or does your preference this evening run toward fulfilling your duty as quickly as possible?"

Coquette frowned, but not for the insensitive manner of his words—rather for the familiarity of them. She had heard these words before—on her first night in his chamber.

"I choose as I did before," she ventured. She was certain he had spoken these words to her on their first night. But what if she were mistaken? If she were mistaken, he would know at once her mind denied her memory.

"Ahh," he said then, smiling as he rose and strode to her. "You choose again the attentive lover, then."

"I do?" she breathed, completely unnerved as his strong, warm hands encircled her neck. Goose pimples broke over her entire body at his touch—a delightful shiver produced by the thrill fanning through her.

"Yes," he said, his eyes narrowing as he looked at her. "And it pleases me you should admit the preference."

"It does?" she asked, breathless as he bent, placing warm lips against her ear.

She startled as the standing clock struck. Almost instantly, there came a soft knock on the door.

"That would be Victoria with our drink," Valor said, releasing her.

Coquette swayed slightly, having been rendered rather giddy and light-headed by his attention.

Opening the door, Valor removed two silver chalices from the tray Victoria held.

"Thank you, Victoria," he said. "You may leave us."

Coquette fancied Victoria paused before leaving. Further she fancied the serving woman rather glared at her master with disapproval for a moment.

"Good night," Valor said, closing the door with his foot.

"There you are, milady," he said, offering one of the chalices to her.

Suddenly Coquette wondered if she should accept the drink. It occurred to her only then that the previous time she had taken warm milk with Valor, her memory had been denied her. Still, it had been Victoria who had prepared the milk. And how could milk and nutmeg deprive a person of their memories?

"It is good, this concoction Victoria blends," he said, drinking his milk as Coquette accepted the chalice from him.

The milk was good—warm with heat and spice—and Coquette could not help but empty the chalice.

"Come," Valor said, taking the chalice from Coquette's hands and setting both vessels on the mantel. "Now what were we about before Victoria intruded?"

"I believe you were endeavoring to seduce me, milord," Coquette answered, feeling suddenly less unsettled and more secure.

Valor's eyebrows rose in seeming wonder. "Was I, milady?" he asked, yet going to her and taking her face in his hands.

The very air of the room seemed to soften and warm, and Coquette was momentarily mesmerized by the beloved face of Valor Lionhardt before her. How his eyes burned with . . . was it desire? His hair so soft, so tempting she could not keep her fingers from reaching up to twist one velvet lock.

"Are you truly so much changed as you appear?" she asked.

"Much changed, yes," he told her, his eyes glowing amber. "I am everything your charming little suitor of the past was not," he said. He smiled at her then, the dazzling brilliance of it causing her to quietly gasp. "Dark, dominant, and demanding."

Her heart hammered brutally within her bosom. She fancied her toes tingled as she looked at him—watched as his dazzling smile softened to a mischievous grin, his eyes narrowing as he looked at her.

"For I am Lord of Roanan and will easily seduce innocence."

"Seduce innocence?" she said. "Do you mean such as the devil himself does?"

His smile broadened, and he chuckled. "So that is who you kin me with, is it? Still, seduce you I will—and yet, as I have said, the manner in which I do was this night, again, your choice."

Coquette's breath caught in her throat, her heart pounding in her as he leaned forward, letting his lips lightly brush her ear.

"Which manner of lover's lure do you wish me to use this night, my beauty? Do you wish for the gentle, careful lover's kiss?"

She was breathless, trembling as she felt his lips linger a moment at the nape of her neck.

"Should I linger?" His voice was deep, rich like sun-warmed honey. He kissed her neck once more, one hand resting lightly at her waist. "Should I breathe a kiss to you?" he asked, his hand at her waist pulling her body closer to his. He moved his attention from her neck, letting his mouth hover a breath from her own. "Do you prefer the soft, measured kiss of tender youth?" he asked, his breath warm on her slightly parted lips.

She was undone! Her mind fought with her

heart and body, reminding her this was not her beloved Valor before her but a cruel and heartless beast. This was not Valor's tempting whispered kiss but the breathed kiss of seduction. Yet everything in her, every shred of her soul, wanted him to gather her in his arms, press his lips to her own.

"P-please, milord," she said, feeling somewhat giddy and weak. He must not kiss her! He mustn't! She feared her longing to have her lost Valor, her heart's dream, would be her undoing.

"Soft," he said as his lips pressed to hers lightly. "Measured?" he asked, kissing her again.

Coquette inwardly scolded herself for not pushing at him—for not even attempting to evade him. Yet as his lips pressed to hers a third time, she was near gasping from restraining her desire to return the kiss.

"It is teasing in a manner," he said, his mouth still hovering a breath from her own. "I find it frustrating and juvenile."

His words saddened Coquette. For was this not the very kiss he'd so often stolen from her, gifted her so long ago when they were happy lovers? It angered and hurt her he would reprove it.

Suddenly he took her chin firmly in hand, his eyes smoldering with emotion as he looked at her. "Preferable to me, and methinks to you as well, is the aggressive advance of impatient, matured masculinity," he growled. "Simply take what I desire."

Coquette melted as his mouth took hers! Driven, moist, severe, this kiss was unlike any kiss her beloved Valor had administered. Heated with demanding desire, this kiss was passion-bred! And though she did not return it, Coquette was wholly overcome by it. Clenching her hands into fists at her sides, she endeavored to remain unwavering—resolute in not involving herself in the kiss, in not returning it, in not simply throwing her arms around his neck and drinking in such passion. She felt her knees weaken, her heart hammering in her bosom. The very hairs on her head tingled where they were attached. He must stop! If he did not, she would weaken—give in—and he would know. He would know the Valor Lionhardt he once was, even the Valor Lionhardt in whose arms she now trembled, owned her very soul!

"Thus," he whispered, breaking from her, "which choice is yours, milady?" He leaned forward, kissing her cheek softly. "Soft and measured?" his rich, deep voice asked. "The adolescent's kiss?" he asked, kissing her again. "Or ambitious with appetite?" he added a moment before his mouth captured her own in the moist, driven kiss of passion.

At once, Valor pulled Coquette into his arms and against the strength of his powerful body. Exhilaration and pleasure burst full in Coquette's stomach, fanning out to every limb and appendage of her body. As Valor's mouth endeavored, coaxing hers to join in the fevered exchange, Coquette's resolve to resist him began to vanish. She could no longer hold her hands in fists at her side or deny her mouth permission to accept his kiss, return its fervor.

Letting her hands travel the breadth and strength of his shoulders, she trembled at the joy of finally embracing him. This was Valor, after all—her heart's greatest desire! His kiss was ambrosia—moist, heated, tinged with the flavor of confection! Coquette reveled in the feel of his roughly shaven face against the tender flesh of her own. In those moments, she did not care what heartless beast he had become; in those moments, she knew only her fixed dream had come to fulfillment. She belonged to Valor!

The raging desire of passion within Valor threatened to consume his sanity. What a taste her kiss was! Warm and delicious nectar! And her touch—it was his undoing! How could he put her away from him when every thread of his being wanted only to hold her for eternity? His mind raced, visions of life in Bostchelan, visions of remembered hope and happiness, burning through it like a rogue fire.

Yet he was no longer simply Valor Lionhardt.

He was Lord of Roanan—the dark lord and beast who knew only hate and dominance. This he reminded himself even as he continued to quench his thirst for Coquette's kiss. What a thirst for her burned in him! And her acceptance of him, of his passion's kiss—the knowledge of her acceptance—was nigh to dropping him dead at her feet. More than acceptance was her involvement, her response, nay her returning the affection of his mouth with her own. This was a dangerous farce he played at, and he knew it. Yet was it farce? Was it folly?

Silently, he cursed Victoria. Hadn't she measured the tonic correctly? It seemed Coquette should be unconscious, not returning his kiss with such eager zeal. One more minute and he might lose himself in the feel of her in his arms, the warm flavor of her nutmegged kiss.

And then, a moment before the Lord of Roanan was nearly lost to a memory of a past character, he sensed Coquette's embrace weaken, her kiss lighten. Beyond regretful, he broke the seal of their lips, gazing into the ethereal beauty of her face. Her eyes narrowed, heavy with the fatigue brought on by the tonic. He watched their emerald fire soften as deep weakness began to overtake her.

"What then, wife?" he said. "What manner of seduction—"

"Any manner will find me helpless in your . . . in your arms, Valor," she mumbled.

He caught her unconscious body in his arms, lifting her and cradling her effortlessly.

He grimaced, suddenly stung by his own guilt in such deceitful trickery. What a coward he was. What hypocrisy had he allowed to own him! To threaten the girl's innocence and yet put her deep to sleep by use of Victoria's tonic instead of relishing that which by husbandly right was his—it was pure cowardice.

He called upon his anger, lest he be lost to the heart he owned in the past. He called upon his fury at seeing Antoine de Bellamont in his gardens at Roanan. Valor had been furious nearly to violence at seeing the man, the lowest of fathers, the shallowest of characters, who had stripped him of his happiness, the man who had denied him the only thing he had ever wanted—the merchant's daughter. Antoine de Bellamont was a pretender as well. Valor ground his teeth at the knowledge of how the man had embellished the story of their conference to Coquette. He wondered then if her father had even told her of losing his ships, of Valor's restoring his wealth. He thought not, for she seemed willing enough to accept the descriptions of her father's success, fleet, and wealth written in her sister's letter.

As he gently laid Coquette on his bed, he endeavored to rid himself of the passion she evoked in him—endeavored to remember she had chosen her spineless father over him—endeavored to conjure the memory of the pain of heartbreak. And it was not difficult to find.

Still, as he studied her peaceful, beautiful face, guilt and self-loathing bathed him. She was innocent. What good, caring daughter would deny her father's will, rebel against his protective authority?

Dropping to one knee beside the bed, Valor closed his eyes, raising one powerful fist to his forehead. Drawing from everything harsh within him, he remembered disappointment, anger, heartache, and loss. Endeavoring to rebuild his resolve, he clenched his jaw tightly, attempting to ignore the flavor of Coquette's kiss still lingering in his mouth, the blissful sensation of her body held in his arms.

Would that she could heal him; would that she could still want him. But as he studied the beauty lying on his bed—ebony hair softly strewn over his own pillow—he knew too much had changed in him. A beast he was—heartless, cold, and unfeeling. It is what he told himself as he gazed at her.

He mused then this beauty before him was not so innocent. Unwilling to defy her father and marry Valor Lionhardt, she had quite easily agreed to marry a stranger to save the cowardly father's life. He glared at her, appalled she would marry an unknown man without any pause when she had found it so easy to spurn him.

Standing, he reminded himself of his vow—his vow to never consummate his marriage to Coquette without her willing consent—without her desire to do so. Still, his anger at her father and his heartbreak and anger at her hand for choosing the will of such a weak-minded fool as Antoine de Bellamont over the love and happiness he would have gifted her—at last his anger returned his strength and resolve to him.

No. Husband or not, he would never force intimacy upon Coquette. Still, as rage and resentment pulled him from his knee at her bedside and to his feet, he thought, *Yet let your mind imagine what it will, Coquette, for I have no heart—no heart for compassion and no heart left for you to break again.*

Reaching for his boots, he stormed from his bedchamber. He did not trust himself to linger in the same room with such a passion burning within him. Further, he would seek out Victoria, determined the reprimand he delivered her would be harsh.

He found her sitting in the kitchen, a book of poetry in one hand, a pastry in the other.

"What are you about, Victoria?" he growled. "It was nearly . . . I was nearly undone, for it took the tonic some time to affect her."

"What do you mean, master?" Victoria asked,

an innocent perplexment in her expression. "What do you mean you were nearly undone?"

"Do not trifle with me, Victoria!" he growled, slamming one powerful fist on the table before her. He ran trembling fingers through his chestnut mane and said, "You nearly cost milady her incorruptibility this night!"

Victoria put down her book. She set the pastry on the table linen before her. Reaching out, she placed a comforting hand over Valor's fist. "She is your wife, milord," Victoria said softly. "Why do you deem it corruption to take her when you are—"

"You nearly cost her most dear this night, Victoria," he interrupted. Perspiration beaded at her master's brow. Rage, desire, and an obvious lingering minimum of self-restraint wracked his trembling body. *Why does he deny himself?* Victoria wondered.

"While I am her protector against all else, you are her protector against me," he whispered. "Do you understand me, Victoria? Do you understand you must protect milady from this beast I am? You serve me, and you must do what is best."

Victoria's eyes narrowed as she studied her master. Undone he was! Entirely! "I do understand, milord. I must've lightened the tonic quantity too much," she told him. "I will not fail you any longer."

She watched as her master swallowed hard, nodding he was pleased with her answer—though she knew how thoroughly he misunderstood it. She would not fail him any longer, it was true. No. She would not mix the tonic to put his lady abed. Next time, she would not simply lessen its strength: she would neglect it entirely. Whatever darkness kept him from the beauty within his reach, it was time he faced it. "I will not fail you, master," she said.

He straightened and wiped the perspiration from his forehead with one yet trembling hand. "Th-thank you, Victoria," he stammered. "You will look in on milady?"

"Yes, milord," she said.

"Then I will away to the stables. I must ride out this fever over me in the cool of the night," he mumbled.

"Yes, milord."

Antoine de Bellamont—coward! Selfish seller of daughters! Goliath's gallop was strong and swift. The night air did serve to somewhat cool Valor's fever brought on by his dalliance with Coquette. Yet it would take far more to keep him from her the length of the night.

Over and over he considered returning to his chamber, attempting to raise her from her tonic-induced slumber. Over and over he thought of taking her mouth with his own again—selfishly taking more than her kiss. But he would not!

Antoine de Bellamont—merchant, proud mongrel. The fault was none but his! The merchant had stripped Valor of his happiness, and Valor hated him for it. Hated him for his lies to Coquette. And yet what better liar was Valor? What less hurt and pain was he heaping on her now?

"On, Goliath!" he growled. "She chose her father," he mumbled. "She chose him over me, and she yet does! So be it. Let her think what she will of me. Let her wonder what happened between us this night!"

Yet guilt was his best companion as he rode on—rode on and on into the dark of night.

The sun broke the horizon as Valor quietly entered his bedchamber. He breathed a heavy sigh—a sigh of great fatigue, defeat, and near despair. He looked to the bed to see Coquette yet slept. He wondered how long she would remain in peaceful, innocent slumber. Removing his boots and shirt, he strode to the bed and carefully laid himself upon it—next to Coquette, yet with ample space between them.

Again, great fatigue caused him to sigh. He would not look at her. Surely it was not wisdom to gaze at her peaceful beauty when he had spent the entirety of the night trying to forget it. Instead, he stared for a time at the mural above— studied the lion so kingly on his throne of firm rock. What a strong beast this lion was—strong and dominant of all he surveyed.

Sleep quickly overtook Valor. The effort of restrained desire coupled with the long night of riding had weakened him, vanquished his vigor. Even as he slipped into deep slumber, he forced his thoughts to bitterness toward Coquette.

Let her think what she will, he thought. *Let her awaken to find me at her side. Let her mind burn with wonderment.* And yet as he slipped deeper into sleep, he thought he felt his own mouth whisper, "Forgive me, Kitty."

TO WEAVE SUCH A WEB

A low, breathy moan entered her mind, stirring her from the deepest of slumbers. Coquette opened her eyes to bright sunlight. Her eyes still heavy with awakening, Coquette rubbed them to encourage awareness.

Almost instantly, she was alert and remembering. Gazing blindly at the lion sitting protectively overhead, her hand went to her mouth as she remembered the kisses placed there by Valor the night before. Closing her eyes, she drew upon the delicious memory of being in his arms, his touch, his mouth heated and moist and melding with her own. Tears sprang to her eyes as she remembered nothing else! Again, her memories somehow had been bested, erased. She wondered if she had simply fainted from the euphoria induced upon her by his kiss. Or was there more to Victoria's nutmegged milk than simple warmth and spice?

Suddenly she remembered Valor's abrupt appearance the previous time she had awakened in his chamber. She moved to raise herself to sitting, but as she turned, she saw him, Valor, lying as a tangible dream on the bed next to her. She held her breath, afraid she had disturbed him and that he would suddenly open his "predator's" eyes and see her there beside him. He did not stir, and she paused in contemplation of the man next to her.

He wore nothing save his breeches. One strong arm lay across his stomach, the other outstretched at his side. His massive, muscular chest rose and fell with the slow ease of slumbered breathing. His eyes were closed, his face serene and free from anger and frowning. It gave him a look of peace Coquette had never before witnessed in his countenance. His hair, rather tousled, caused a smile to spread across Coquette's face. Boyish, it enhanced his peaceful appearance, and she desperately wanted to reach out and weave her fingers through its nut-brown softness.

She was possessed with the intense desire to take his face in her hands and kiss him exactly on the mouth! She wished he would awaken, see her gazing at him, and pull her into his strong embrace. She wished to see into his very soul, to see beyond the beast, to see if his core were really as black as it appeared. Such thoughts both delighted and frightened her. She carefully removed herself from the bed. Tiptoeing to the door, she lifted the latch, looking over her shoulder to ensure he still slept. He did.

Once outside his chamber, thankful that no one else lingered in the hall, she quickly made her way to her own room.

"Oh!" Victoria gasped as Coquette entered her bathing room. "You startled me, milady."

"I could not remain asleep," Coquette quickly explained. "I thought I might wander in the gardens awhile before breakfast."

"Certainly, milady," Victoria said. "Would you wish I should cease in preparing your bath then?"

"Um . . . no. No, I think you are right. I think a soothing morning bath would serve me well," Coquette replied.

"Good," Victoria said, smiling as she poured an amount of oil from a glass vial and into the waiting tub. "I do love this scent, milady— sweetened vanilla bean. So heavenly. How did you come by it?"

"My father is a merchant, you remember," Coquette answered. "I have loved it since first he brought it for my mother when I was a child."

"Lovely," Victoria said, corking the small glass vial of scented oil. She stirred the surface of the water in the tub with her fingers, patting them dry on her skirt. "And . . . and how do you find the master this morning, milady?"

Coquette swallowed. Did Victoria know? she wondered. Did Victoria somehow know the bride of Roanan could not remember the nights spent in his lordship's chamber? Suspicion rose in Coquette's mind once more, for it was Victoria who had again brought the nutmegged milk. Still, what reason would Valor's housemistress have for wanting her to forget her nights in Valor's chamber? And Valor certainly could not be responsible—he who wanted nothing from her save she should provide him with an heir. She would consider on it later, when she was again alone in her chamber with her thoughts.

"The master is yet asleep," Coquette answered, making her way to the waiting tub of warmed water and scented oil.

"Good," Victoria said. "Then he will have no need of either of us for a time. Here, let me help you to the bath."

"Oh," Coquette said, quite astonished Victoria should offer to assist her in bathing. "I am quite capable of—"

"Oh, yes, milady," Victoria said. "I only meant I might linger and talk with you awhile, if you wouldn't mind."

"Very well. I suppose." It seemed an odd ritual—speaking to the housemistress while bathing. Still, Coquette surmised it might be commonplace in titled households. In fact, she suddenly remembered her mother once telling her and her sisters of a favorite maid in her own father's house who, on occasion, sat and talked with her of careless things whilst she bathed.

Victoria turned and began to arrange a mound of towels set on a nearby table. Coquette, though still somewhat disconcerted, knew this was her prompt to enter the tub. Removing her nightdress

148

and underthings, Coquette swiftly slipped into the warm, fragrant water.

"Oh, it is a nice fragrance, is it not?" she sighed as the comfort of warmth and scent enveloped her.

"It is, milady," Victoria said. "I bathe often in the evening—when the house is all settled and the master quieted for the night. Godfrey . . . now there is a man who does not enjoy the comforts of life."

"How so?" Coquette asked, though she had often thought Godfrey a bit stiff and was not surprised at Victoria's opinion of him.

"He bathes in barely tepid water, or so the stablemen tell me," Victoria explained. "And he has nothing whatsoever to do with pastry. How can a person enjoy life without indulging in pastry? Even the master has his confections— peppermints and other candies he purchases from the shop in Roanan. It is ever I am finding half-eaten bits in the pockets of his breeches."

Coquette giggled and fancied it felt good to do so. "Yes," she said. "He bought several pieces from the shop yesterday. He has always been fond of confection and candy—ever since I can remember. Why, even when we were in Bostchelan," Coquette giggled again, thoroughly amused by the memory washing over her. "I remember once when Father brought me chocolate he'd purchased from a French chocolatier, I thought Valor would eat himself to sickness with it! He had not had it much, you see—for his father was ever so strict and . . ." Coquette gasped, realizing what she had revealed. She looked to Victoria to find her smiling, a triumphant expression on her face.

"There is more to this business with you and your father than his lordship has told us," Victoria said. "Godfrey and I knew as much . . . though we know not what it all means."

"He must not know I have said anything, Victoria! Please!" Coquette begged, tears brimming in her eyes. "I do not know why he keeps the past so carefully guarded in himself. I suppose hate and bitterness have forged such a pride he cannot tolerate it ever happened. Oh! I have said too much! I have said far too much!"

Panic began to overwhelm Coquette. If Valor were to discover she had revealed the secret of their past together, what anger would it evoke in him?

Instantly, Victoria was kneeling beside the tub. Taking one of Coquette's hands in her own, she said, "I would do nothing to cause you pain, milady. Nor would I harm milord. He has been ever good to me—to everyone in this house. I owe him loyalty beyond comprehension, but I am loath to see him so unhappy. And, milady . . . it is worse since first your father came and then you. Why? Why is it his bitterness is fed with you here?"

She was helpless—trapped! She could not very well leap from the tub of scented water and run naked across the room to gather herself a towel. She wondered for a moment if indeed Victoria had intentionally trapped her. She knew she had. She thought then of the nutmegged milk and how she could remember only brief moments after having drunk of it. Still, she sensed the woman's intentions were not malevolent.

Valor's unhappiness had increased since his reunion with her father. Victoria had only been worried for her master. Beast though he was, it was plain then to Coquette that Valor was good to his household. How else would he have earned such loyalty?

"You have tricked me into this, Victoria," Coquette said.

"I have, milady," Victoria admitted. "And you may dismiss me from my position at once. As Lady of Roanan you may, but I beg you, first enlighten me where his lordship is concerned. Help me to see why darkness resides in him where I know once there was light."

"How do you know there was light once?" Coquette asked. "Perhaps he has always been cruel, unfeeling, and hateful."

"There is a light in his eyes when he looks at you, milady. I have only seen it once before . . . when first he came here," Victoria explained. "Three years ago, when first he arrived to claim his uncle's title, his eyes burned with something residual, something other than hate and bitterness. I watched it slowly disappear, until I was certain it was gone forever. And it might have been but for the morning . . . your first morning at Roanan Manor—the morning you fainted in the stables. He thundered into the house with you in his arms, and the light was there—fiery, passionate, fearful—and I wondered how you could have lit his eyes so quickly with such emotion. I was . . . I was . . . Godfrey told me milord had known your father. I knew of his great hatred of him, of his desire for revenge. But revenge for what, I wondered. And now . . . now you talk of candy and chocolate, and you call him Valor in the same sentence. Send me away if you must, milady, but I beg you, reveal the reasons for milord's hatred of your father and the light in his eyes when he looks upon you."

Coquette sniffled and brushed the tears from her cheeks. She knew then Victoria loved Valor— loved him as any mother ever loved a son. She could only imagine the agony the woman experienced in watching Valor transform into the beast he had become.

"I will not send you away, Victoria," Coquette said, "for if Valor is capable of love . . . it would be to love you as his own mother."

Victoria brushed tears from her own cheeks.

"He was not always the heartless beast he appears to be now, was he, milady?"

"No. He was not," Coquette whispered through her tears. "I knew him long before he was Lord of Roanan . . . when he was Valor Lionhardt, only son of Lord Alfred Lionhardt of Bostchelan. Once he was as handsome of spirit as he is of face and body. Once he . . . once he loved me . . . enough to ask my father for my hand."

"What?" Victoria gasped. Her eyes widened with astonishment. "And . . . and your father refused," she breathed as realization washed over her. "Pray, tell me more. I beg of you."

Coquette paused, fearful of revealing the full length of the past to Victoria. Valor had kept his past a secret, unspoken, and she was certain it was not for her to reveal. Yet it was her past as well, and she was Lady of Roanan. Why should she keep silent of her own past if she wished to tell the tale? Still, she knew he would be enraged to find she had revealed such secrets.

"You may trust me to be your confidante, milady," Victoria assured her. "I would see no harm come to you by way of your own words."

Coquette turned to Victoria, smiling as she read the woman's earnest expression. Still, she paused a moment, somehow unwilling to relive the pain of memory herself.

"We were young lovers once," Coquette

whispered, "innocents, and Valor Lionhardt was everything to me."

"I bid you go on, milady," Victoria pleaded.

"He began to court me when I was sixteen," Coquette continued. She felt as if her very spirit were being freed from some sort of bondage. Before she could stop herself, reconsider what and how much she was telling Victoria, she had begun. "From the first moment I saw him, he was the only man I ever wanted to see again—the only man I ever wanted to belong to. Such the young gentleman—so attentive, thoughtful, filled with wit and humor. He was everything I had ever dreamed, and for two years he courted me patiently, proving himself to my father. Valor's father was a titled man in his own right, with enormous wealth and position. Yet Lord Lionhardt was the worst in moral character. It was said Valor's mother died of a broken heart—humiliated to literal death by her husband's blatant infidelity. But Valor was not his father. Valor had followed his mother's lead and was strong, faithful, pure of heart, and kind. Still, my own father judged the son by Lord Lionhardt's deeds, and when Valor came to him asking for my hand, my father emphatically refused. He accused Valor of being of the same fabric as Lord Lionhardt—said he was destined to be so. I stood at the door to my father's study, unable to comprehend why my father would refuse Valor.

He had courted me for two years, Victoria!"

Coquette took Victoria's hand in her own as all the pain of the incident flooded her body and mind once more. "Yet my father did refuse. I . . . I was astonished. I could not think my ears had heard what they had heard. Valor fairly flew at my father, shouting, accusing him of being low in character and unworthy to judge Valor or his own father. He left the room where my father had refused him, and I was there—in the entry of the house—I was there, astonished to silence, heartbroken, and confused. Valor came to me. He said, 'We will not listen to your father's will. We will away at once.' And I wanted to go with him. Oh, how desperately I wanted to go with him! Yet my father had refused, and I was undone. I could not think with clarity in those moments, and when I did not instantly speak, Valor left me. He stormed from the house. I was heartbroken."

"Oh, milady!" Victoria breathed. "Milady! What devastation this brought to you both. I see it now. You could not disobey—"

"But I did!" Coquette cried in a whisper. "Though Valor knew not of it—knows not of it even yet. Within the hour that same day, I arrived at Lord Lionhardt's door. I had taken the time to prepare a small valise, only a few possessions—my mother's likeness, a few personal necessities—and yet when I arrived at the manor house of his father, Valor was vanished! No one knew where he had gone. No one. I begged his father to tell me, yet he knew not. At least he knew not that day, and he was dead shortly thereafter—run through by his mistress's husband. And I knew not how to search for Valor. Undoubtedly my father would not have helped. Likewise, I was certain he would no longer want me. I was certain he thought I would never defy my father and thereby had given me up—and he had."

"Oh, milady," Victoria breathed, brushing tears from her cheeks. "What sad circumstance found milord here those three years ago. And none of us were the wiser. And you, milady, how did you endure?"

Coquette brushed the tears from her face and forced a smile. "I . . . I . . . I lived on. What more can one do when all is lost? Simply sit down and die? Though I admit the thought seemed preferable to the pain of losing Valor. Yet I had my family—my father, my sisters. And Valor's memory in my heart and mind." She smiled at Victoria, who sat clinging to the lip of the tub, weeping beside her. "So you see, Victoria," she began, "it is revenge that finds me here. Revenge and fate—Valor's revenge against my father and my fate for having paused that day without my father's study."

"Oh, milady," Victoria repeated. Her empathy was obvious in her tears and painstricken expression.

"You should have laid eyes on him then, Victoria," Coquette said. She smiled at her own memory. "Always smiling, ever the gentleman, kind to every worthy soul he met."

"None of the brute beast was in him then?" Victoria asked.

"Oh, he was brute enough when occasion demanded," Coquette admitted. "He had no patience for those who showed any disrespect to women, especially me." Coquette shook her head, smiling. "I remember the day he put a fist to Henry Weatherby's nose—broke it—simply because Henry had taken my arm without permission." She brushed more tears from her cheek with the back of her hand. "And he dealt with other miscreants harshly enough, I suppose. But the hate driving him now was absent. And I think . . . I endeavor to believe he loved me then."

"He loves you still, milady," Victoria told her. "If only you knew . . . knew his . . . knew his great respect for you, milady."

"Respect? When he barks at me at the slightest provocation? When his eyes burn ash into mine?" Coquette asked. She shook her head. "No. No. He owns no respect for me, and he can never love me. I . . . I broke his heart, and it hardened to stone. I know that now. The past cannot be mended, and I can only endeavor to give something back to him. I can only endeavor to bear an heir as he asked me to—

in gratitude for his not taking my father's life."

"Gratitude for not taking your father's life?" Victoria repeated. "What do you speak of, milady?"

"I speak of the rose my father stole from Valor's garden," Coquette said, lowering her voice. "Surely you know of it."

"I do. But an heir? In exchange for your father's life?" Victoria asked.

"I have said too much, Victoria," Coquette whispered. Already she had revealed Valor's deepest secrets to his housemistress. She could risk no more disloyalty to him. "Please do not press me further. I beg you."

"But, milady—" Victoria began.

"And I further beg you," Coquette interrupted, "please let me count you as my true friend, Victoria. Please do not trick and deceive me again as you did today. I . . . I cannot endure not having an ally."

Victoria let her head fall forward. Her guilt was heavy, even if it came at the master's bidding. Valor Lionhardt, beast he had become, owned ever her love. As her own son she loved him, and she would no longer stand in watching him suffer—no longer watch his lady suffer.

"The playwright said, 'It is a tangled web we weave, when we play at deception,' " she whispered. "And I will deceive you no longer where my part in milord's web is concerned."

"What do you mean?" Coquette asked.

But Victoria only smiled, placing one warm palm against Coquette's cheek.

"You need respite, milady," she said, rising to her feet. "I will leave you to your bath and your garden walk." She paused before leaving and added, "And do not worry, milady. What has passed between us will be held safely and silently in my heart."

"Thank you, Victoria," Coquette said.

"Milady," Victoria bid her and left.

Sitting back in the tub, Coquette closed her eyes and inhaled deeply the faint scent of sweetened vanilla. The warm water did seem to soothe her. Still, she wondered, was it the bath or the purging of her secrets to Victoria?

How comforted she was to know of Victoria's loyalty and love for Valor. How good was Victoria to see beyond the beast to Valor's soul—rather to the soul that had been his. She thought of Valor, of the peaceful countenance of his sleeping form as she had seen him only a short time before. Surely, as he slept so soundly, anyone might be able to imagine beyond the beast to his having as much beauty of spirit as he did of face and form.

She opened her eyes, thinking again on the nutmegged milk, pondering the feelings of her body and mind each time she had drunk of it. She thought of Victoria's promise to never deceive her in any way again—thought of the woman's references to Valor's weaving a tangle of web. Had Valor endeavored to weave such a web—demanded Victoria mix something other than nutmeg into her milk? Certainly, she knew physicians and apothecaries had such knowledge of herbs and remedies to make such a potion as to put a person deep into sleep. Her own mother had taken such a tonic on occasion just before her death, when the pain in her body had often kept her from a good night's rest.

Coquette frowned, certain then Valor had forced Victoria into tainting the warm milk with something other than mere nutmeg. Still, it made no sense. Why would he put her to sleep, render her unconscious, thereby utterly useless if his only desire in marrying her was vengeance on her father and producing his heir? Her head began to ache with thinking, and yet one thought more came to her. When next he offered her a chalice of Victoria's nutmegged milk, she would refuse it. What then she knew not. Still, come what circumstances may, she would not drink the tainted milk again.

"You've received another letter from Bostchelan," Valor said. They sat together, Valor and Coquette, in quiet finishing of the evening meal. He tossed a letter to the table before her. "It is from your dearest father, I think."

Coquette retrieved the letter from the table. Her father's hand was indeed on the front of it.

"Read it then," Valor demanded.

"Aloud?" Coquette asked, remembering the tantrum the last letter she had read to him caused.

"Yes, aloud," he said. "Let us hear what your dear father has to tell you of late."

With trembling fingers, Coquette broke the seal of the letter, unfolding the parchment.

"My dearest Coquette," she began.

"Well, you are his dearest," Valor mumbled. "We well know that."

Ignoring his sarcasm, Coquette continued, *"Inez is betrothed! This day! And to none other than Henry Weatherby. Though your sisters may already have written to you, I thought you would like to read it from my own hand. They are to be wed come October, and Inez has asked that you attend. How grand it would be to have the Lord and Lady of Roanan attend such an occasion in Bostchelan."* Coquette paused, frowning. The Lord of Roanan had threatened her father's very life, yet Inez requested his presence at her wedding?

"Apparently, he has forgotten that I wished to kill him," Valor said, his eyes narrowing as he looked at her.

"There is yet more," Coquette mumbled.

"Dominique has a suitor as well! A French merchant . . . a friend of my own. I have known him for years, and you must but guess at his specialty . . . tapestries! Will not Dominique be happy with such a man for a husband? Our newly increased wealth has presented many venues of success and happiness for your sisters. It is only I wish you were near to us to enjoy it. Yet you have wealth beyond imagine there in Roanan, so I am content to know you are cared for. We think of you often, dearest Coquette, and are happy in the knowledge you are living in great comfort and position. Lovingly, Father."

"I told him I would treat you badly," Valor said then. "I boldly told him I would . . . and yet he writes of his happiness in knowing you are comfortable."

"Will we attend my sister's wedding?" Coquette asked, horrified by his repeated revelation and yet determined not to confirm her feelings to him. In those moments she indeed remembered his telling her after Inez's letter—remembered his telling her of his promise to her father to treat her badly.

"Even still, you want to return to Bostchelan?" Valor asked. "They have all but forgotten your sacrifice on their behalf."

"But they are yet my family, and I love them," she said. "Perhaps this is how my father endures knowing that I came to you for the sake of his own life. Perhaps lightheartedness is his sanity." Yet even as the words passed through her lips, she did not believe them.

"I will never let you return to Bostchelan!" Valor shouted. "You belong here now. You belong to me! You must forget your asinine father and insipid sisters. You are Lady Lionhardt, and Roanan is your home."

His outrage did not startle or frighten her. It was expected because of his way of thinking. "May I . . . may I write in response to the letters from my father and sister?" Coquette asked, folding the letter and placing it in her lap.

"If you wish," Valor said, rubbing at his temples with one hand. Quickly looking at her, he added, "Though you will not tell your father or sisters you arrived at Roanan Manor to find *me*. That I will not allow."

"Why not?" she asked. "Revenge . . . is that not your purpose? Why not salt the wound then? The threat of death to my father, his sacrifice of a daughter . . . and in the end to the man he thought unworthy of her? It seems to me you would want him to know."

Valor shook his head, rubbing at his temples once more. "I am tired, milady," he said. "I cannot speak of it now."

"Milord," Godfrey said, entering the room. "This has just arrived." Godfrey held a silver tray toward Valor. On it lay a rolled parchment tied with black ribbon.

"Thank you, Godfrey," Valor said, taking the parchment. He loosed the ribbon and read the contents of the correspondence. "Answer at once that we accept, Godfrey. Though as tired as I am in mind and body this night, I wish avoidance were a choice."

"Yes, milord," Godfrey said. "Milady," he bid to Coquette before clicking his heels, turning, and leaving.

"We will attend Lord Dickerson's dinner in two weeks," Valor sighed. "It will be your first official appearance as Lady of Roanan."

"Lord Dickerson?" Coquette asked, though she remembered well enough the man who had witnessed her strange marriage.

"An old friend of my uncle's . . . now my friend as well. You know him," Valor answered. He suddenly looked overly fatigued as if he hadn't slept in days. Yet Coquette had slept but hard the night before and awakened to find him at her side. Why then did he appear so fatigued?

"Are you indeed well, milord?" Coquette asked. Her heart raced with sudden concern for his well-being.

"I-I am but distracted and fatigued," he said. "And please do not play at concern for my well-being. It will not save you from my advances this night."

"Save me from your advances?" she asked, vexed he should think her concern was pretense.

"Yes. No pretended concern will keep me from finding you in my chamber again if I demand it be so," he said.

"In the first, I do not make to pretend to be concerned," she told him. "You are weary—it is purely obvious. I only meant to—"

"I will expect you at eight," he said, rising from his chair. "Be prompt. I have no patience this evening."

"You have no patience any evening," Coquette mumbled under her breath.

He glared at her. "For that you will meet me within the hour, woman!" And he stormed out of the room.

"As you wish, beast of a man!" Coquette grumbled. Lowering her voice to a whisper, she mumbled, "But I will not drink the warm milk you offer if you offer it. Let us see what transpires then. Tonight I will see beyond the beast to the very core of your blackened soul—whatever it may cost me."

Coquette rose from her chair. Glancing at the letter in her hand, the letter from her father, she tossed it into the chair she had only just abandoned. Her response to her father would wait, for she meant to spend the night in Valor's company—spend it in full consciousness no matter the consequence.

TO SOOTHE THE BEAST

"Victoria!" Valor called, storming through the kitchen doors. "At once, Victoria! Brat of a girl," he grumbled as Victoria rose from her chair at the kitchen table.

"What is it, milord?" Victoria asked.

Valor looked from the startled face of one cook to the other. Such matters could not be discussed in their presence.

"I would have a word with you," he said.

"Of course," she obeyed.

Once they were alone in the small parlor adjoining the kitchen, Valor growled, "You will prepare your tonic once more for milady, Victoria. And this very night!"

"Only . . . only once more, milord?" Victoria asked.

Valor ran a hand through his hair—ground his teeth for a moment. He had sworn he would not give her the tonic again. After spending the night astride Goliath, Valor had sworn he would not use the tonic to further deceive Coquette. He had vowed to keep himself from her—forever if needs be. Still, the impertinent woman had vexed him, provoked him to threat, and he knew not what else to do. He had woven a thick web of deception in order that Coquette would believe their marriage was consummate while simultaneously preserving her virtuous innocence. Yet how she vexed him! How she provoked! How thoroughly her very presence tempted him! In that moment, he was bemused at what other path might appear. And so, in a fit of temper, in having to hear her defend her loathsome father yet again, he had threatened. And now, the only choice before him was Victoria's tonic.

"Only once more, Victoria," he confirmed. "It will not harm her to have it administered two evenings consecutive, correct?"

"Of course not, milord," Victoria said. "You have consumed double her amount before she arrived and after, when you worried for her. And you were not ill affected."

Valor felt a sickness rising in his stomach. He was loath to give her the tonic again. Yet what other choice lay before him? Truth? Certainly not. Still, Valor's self-loathing only increased, for he knew he had become the equivalent liar to her father. But he could not resist her otherwise. He was certain of it.

He considered other venues. He would go to her, begin an argument, leave his chambers in a fury. Still, it would not serve. He would not triumph in her eyes that way. He must allow Victoria to brew the tonic once more.

"Bring it to my chambers at the half an hour," he said. "No, wait." He must triumph. Coquette must understand she belonged to the dark Lord of Roanan, to Lionhardt the Heartless. "No, Victoria," he said. "You will not bring the milk to my chambers. But at half the hour, you will bring it to her own."

"Yes, milord," Victoria said. "I will bring the nutmegged milk to milady's chambers at half the hour. I will bring it to you, milord."

"Thank you, Victoria," Valor said. He would triumph. He would! One way or the other, Coquette would come to know she must forsake her lying father—forsake him in favor of her lying husband.

He grimaced, disgusted with himself for his treachery. And he tasted it bitterly, tasted it with intention. He was a beast, and a beast he would remain.

Coquette sat at her vanity before her looking glass, brushing her hair. Still she was vexed with Valor's behavior after dinner. Her anxiety in anticipating being in Valor's presence, in spending the night in his chamber, had begun to lessen. The beast roared of having his way with her yet put her to sleep in the next breath, and Coquette was determined something was amiss with him—something beyond the beast he had become—and she was curious as to exactly what was amiss.

"For that you will meet me within the

hour, woman!" she growled at her reflection, mimicking Valor's last threat. "Hmph!" she breathed. "Well, dark Lord of Roanan, tonight we will see, will we not? Tonight we will see—"

Coquette gasped, fairly leaping from her chair as the doors to her bedchamber suddenly burst open. Valor stepped through the entrance, swiftly closing the doors behind him.

"Ah," he said, as if he had simply happened into the room to find her there. "There you are." He strode into the room, looking this way and that as if he had never before seen the furnishings therein. "I favor red," he said. "It speaks so strongly of passion. Do you not think so?"

"I thought I was to meet you in your chambers, milord," Coquette said. At once, she was ill at ease over her attire. Certainly she had appeared before him twice previously—dressed in the nightdress of a recent bride. And though the soft white nightdress she wore this night was as modest as any other he had seen her wear, his being in her chamber rather than his unnerved her.

"But you were," he said. "Still, I cannot have you assuming you are safe from my attentions simply because you have your own chambers in which to retreat, now can I?"

"Am I to have no privacy then, sire?" she returned, attempting to convey more courage than she actually possessed.

"None," he said. He fumbled with the sapphire cravat at his throat, stripping it from his neck and tossing it into a nearby chair. "This is my house," he said as he removed his coat and vest. Coquette watched as they too found residence in the chair. "Everything in it belongs to me. Including you." He unbuttoned his shirt, and Coquette's eyes widened as he swiftly stripped it off over his head in one smooth motion. "What? No argument?" he asked, running a strong hand through his nut-brown mane.

"What argument could I offer, sire?" Coquette said. "I have joined the long list of your possessions, and I am well aware of it."

His eyes narrowed as he studied her with suspicion. "There is the softness of a woman in this room," he said as he looked at her.

Coquette swallowed the lump in her throat, for he did not take his eyes from her as he moved ever nearer.

"Cast-off stockings in the chair next to the bed . . . timid candles aflame on the mantel . . . the light fragrance of the vanilla bean." His voice had dropped to a low, alluring tone—a quality of voice to cause goose pimples to break over Coquette's arms. "Did I not know the better of it, I would think you endeavored to lure me here for your own purposes at seduction." He reached out, placing one strong hand around her neck.

Coquette's courage began to abandon her then, and she stepped back and out of his grasp. "It is . . . it is thus every evening, milord," she said.

"Then it is every evening you wish to lure me to your own purposes?" he asked, reaching for her again, this time with both hands encircling her neck.

"I assure you, I meant no lure," she said, suddenly breathless as she gazed into the warm amber of his eyes.

"Your existence in itself is a lure, milady," he said.

"You own me, milord," she said. She was both hurt and vexed he should toy with her. "As you have reminded me only a moment ago, there is no need for you to play the attentive lover."

His brow furrowed then into the deepest of frowns. "As you wish, milady," he growled. The next instant, she was in his arms. He held her body firm against the warm flesh of his bare chest with one hand, while his other, fingers woven through her hair, held her head to his as he kissed her.

At the first touch of his lips to hers, all vexation, all rational thought, fled Coquette's mind. A tonic in himself was he—savory, intoxicating—and she felt her knees weaken as he held her. No beast could kiss her thus, evoke such blissful feelings in her. Surely the adept mouth sealed to her own

171

was Valor's, not that of some brutal beast. In the flavor and feel of his moist kiss, she knew this to be true!

Breathless, ravenous in her desire for his affections, Coquette felt her own arms return his embrace, reveled at the warm, smooth feel of his skin beneath her palms. With no tainted spiced milk to dull her mind, Coquette drank deeply of the passion Valor drizzled over her, evoked within her. Yet even for her euphoria, her pure joy at being the object of his passionate attention, a painful pang of regret traveled the length of her body—regret in that she had not instantly defied her father three years previous— regret in not having spent each day since rapt in Valor's affections.

She was bewitching him! By matching his attentions, reciprocating his kiss, Coquette threatened to destroy Valor's oaken will! He drank deeply of the affections of her mouth, reveled in the feel of her body in his arms, her soft hair between his fingers. Where was Victoria? He would be undone in one minute more—undone and unable to keep himself from her!

He tried to call on his pain of three years previous—the excruciating pain left in him when she had chosen her father's will over his. He thought of the heart he once owned, the breaking of it at her hands. But it was of no consequence, for the beloved beauty in his arms threatened to soothe the beast.

Though she heard it, Coquette did not heed the knock on the door. She wanted nothing, save to stay thus with Valor forever. Yet he broke from her instantly, almost—she fancied—desperately.

"Victoria," he breathed as he rather stumbled toward the door. "She will have brought warm milk to us."

Coquette stood breathless, nearly panting as she watched Valor open the door. Victoria stood without the room, a silver chalice in each hand. She bore them on no silver tray as she had twice before, and Coquette felt her own brow lift with curiosity as Victoria handed one chalice to Valor, saying, "I have brought you the warm milk you requested, milord."

"Thank you, Victoria," Valor said. Coquette did not miss the breath of utter relief he released next.

"And for you, milady," Victoria said, offering the other chalice to her. Victoria looked quickly to Valor, whose attention was drawn to the chalice as he drank. Nodding with reassurance, Victoria winked at Coquette, bidding she accept the chalice.

Coquette understood at once. Victoria had promised only that very morning—promised she would never again deceive Coquette. However, she had made no promise concerning her master. Whatever had been added to Coquette's milk the two occasions previous now lingered in Valor's. She wondered for a moment, was it safe for him to consume? Yet Victoria's gentle nod as Coquette accepted her own chalice reassured her.

"Leave us then, Victoria," Valor said.

"Of course, milord," Victoria said, turning to walk away as Valor closed the door behind her.

Valor tossed his empty chalice to join his discarded clothing on the nearby chair.

"Drain your cup, milady," he demanded, "and with haste."

"But such a sweet drink, should it not be savored?" Coquette asked. She studied him as she sipped from her chalice. She fancied he was far more unsettled than he wished her to know.

"Passion is to be savored, Coquette!" he growled. "Not spiced milk." A delightful shiver passed over her at the sound of her name spoken from his lips. He had not referred to her by name since her coming to Roanan. She wondered then if the tainted milk were already affecting him.

"Very well, milord," she said, swallowing the last mouth of milk from her own chalice. Slowly, she set the chalice on the nearby vanity and waited. *What next then?* she wondered, trepidation and exhilaration battling within her.

He advanced upon her then, taking her arm and pulling her against him. She fancied he winced as

174

he looked at her, and there was regret, sadness, reflected in the lion-amber of his eyes.

Raising one hand to her face, slowly caressing her cheek with the back of his fingers, he mumbled, "You are yet more beautiful than even I remembered." Taking her chin softly between his thumb and forefinger, he kissed her tenderly once, then twice. Letting his mouth hover to hers, he whispered, "Once you cared for me, Coquette. Remember?" His speech was slower, and he closed his eyes for a moment.

Coquette knew whatever tainted the milk was fast overtaking him. Suddenly, she regretted it, She did not want him to fall into such a deep sleep as to render him unable to whisper to her, touch her, kiss her! Still, as the light in his eyes began to dull, she knew it was already too late.

"I remember it," he whispered against her mouth, kissing her lightly. "I remember the way your eyes flashed when—flashed like emeralds on fire—the way they flashed when I took you in my arms. I remember when you gave your mouth to me . . . kissed me freely . . . because you wanted to. Do you remember it, Kitty?" He grimaced, as if some pain had momentarily taken his breath from him.

She said nothing, only fought the tears suddenly springing to her eyes. The beast was soothed, and Valor spoke to her now. The tainted milk had turned his mind to the past, and her heart ached that he did not care for her now—broke in knowing he was hardened, vengeful, and did not love her. When fully conscious, he was a beast incapable of positive emotion. Wasn't he?

"Do you remember it, Kitty?" he asked, his body slightly swaying. "Do you remember when you . . . when you loved me?" he whispered as he kissed her.

He struggled in keeping his eyes open, and guilt washed over her. Certainly he deserved this—the same treatment she had suffered at his hand. Certainly he deserved it. But she had loved him once—loved him so desperately she had often thought she might die from it. And she loved him still—the Valor he had once been. And though the inward admitting frightened her, she loved the beast he was!

"Yes," she whispered. "I do remember."

He closed his eyes for a moment, a sad smile curving his lips. Coquette gasped, guilt-ridden and anguished, tears flooding her cheeks as she saw a single tear escape his eye, slowly trickling over his cheek.

"That is good," he whispered, releasing her and stumbling toward her bed. He attempted to steady himself, gripping one bedpost weakly for a moment. Putting a hand to his forehead, he mumbled, "I-I know what you have done, Kitty."

Coquette wept as he collapsed onto her bed, struggling to turn onto his back. Frantic, she went to him, worried for his well-being.

"I am sorry, milord," she whispered, placing a hand to his forehead to ensure he did not suddenly burn with fever. "Only . . . you did no less to me."

"It is the beast residing in us all that finds us weaving such webs. And ever we find ourselves caught up in them."

"I am sorry," Coquette said, brushing tears from her cheeks.

"I know what you have done, my beauty," he repeated. "And . . . and I want you to understand . . . I want you to know . . ." he stammered, his speech ever more slurred. "I want you to know that I do not think ill of you for killing me, Kitty. For I more than deserve it."

"Killing you?" Coquette gasped. "How have I killed you?" she asked. Had Victoria misjudged her concoction? Panic overtook her then. "Valor! You are well! Tell me you are well!"

"I can feel it," he whispered. "Whatever tonic you put in my drink . . . it is killing me now. I can hardly keep unconsciousness at bay."

"No, no, no," Coquette said. "The chalices were only exchanged, Valor! You will be well come morning. As I ever was."

"Hush, Kitty," he mumbled, another smile spreading across his handsome face. "All is well. You killed me before . . . and this time it is less painful somehow. I-I thank you for it."

177

"No, no, Valor," she said. Her panic intensified. He was thinking she had meant to murder him! "No! It is only the tainted milk you have given to me each time before you . . . before you . . ."

"I have never taken you, Coquette," he said, reaching up to cup her cheek with one warm hand. "Surely you know it. Surely if your body did not speak it to you . . . your mind or heart did."

His touch sent pleasure racing through her body. Goose pimples broke over every inch of her flesh! She wanted his touch—his arms around her once more. She desperately desired the feel of his lips pressed to hers, his whisper in her mouth, the taste of his kiss. She had known it! Deep in her soul she had ever known he had never forced intimacy upon her. Why then did he pretend? Yet it was proof enough to her—proof the beast in him could be soothed. Valor, the soothed beast, lay before her in a strange stupor, and she was desperate he not lose consciousness while yet he thought she meant to kill him.

"Valor," she began, taking his face between her hands and patting his cheeks until his eyes opened once more. "Valor. It is only the spiced milk you have given to me twice before. I would never . . . I would never harm you, Valor!"

"It is all right, Kitty," he mumbled, smiling at her through narrowed eyes. "I-I no less than fully deserve it."

"No, Valor. Please," she pleaded. "All will be well come sunrise. All will be well. I would never harm you."

"Hush, Kitty. Hush and kiss me," he mumbled. "Let my last taste of life be your sweet mouth. Let it be your mouth—sweet and, best of all, willing. I beg you, Kitty," he said. "Do not let me die without one last breath and taste of you."

"But you are not dying, Valor," she told him.

"You deny me?" he asked, a frown puckering his brow, another tear escaping his eye. "That is as it should be."

"Valor," she whispered as she watched his weary eyes struggle to remain open.

Valor Lionhardt, Lord of Roanan—the hand-somest man the world had ever seen. Had Coquette never loved him, still it would be true. And as she gazed at him, peaceful in his belief she had murdered him, warmth and moisture flooded her mouth. She wanted his kiss, wanted to feel the sensation of his lips to hers again, taste the heated flavor of his mouth. He desired the same. He desired it else he would not have asked it of her. She would not let him lie before her, believing she had murdered him, and yet deny his last request—her own greatest desire.

"There was a time . . . a time your kiss was all I could ever think of, dream of, and wait for," she told him.

He tried to smile and whispered, "It is good

to know it, Kitty. Were that it were still as true."

"But it is," she whispered so softly she knew he could not hear. And then, ever so slowly she bent to him.

Her fingers left his cheek, their sensitive tips traveling caressively over his lips. Moisture flooded her mouth, her heart hammering with anticipation and desire. She could not draw breath, and she cared not for it. Gently, tentatively, she kissed his parted lips. As ever, her body began to tremble as she increased the pressure of her lips against his. Gently, he returned her kiss. Disappointment, sadness, flooded her as she realized his inability to take her in his arms and compel her to submit to a more forceful exchange.

"Kitty," he breathed as she drew away for a moment, thrilled as she watched him moisten his lips and open his mouth further, an invitation to a deeper exchange—an invitation she accepted vigorously in the next moment. Mouths melding, he kissed her and she him. The milk had dulled his reflexes, subdued his ability to kiss her with vigorous passion, yet his kiss was as emotionally powerful as ever it had been, past or present.

Coquette then let the tears flow freely over her cheeks as she kissed Valor. As his mouth worked a bewitching spell over her—an enchantment of pain mingled with desire, joy mingled with sadness—she cried for the knowledge she did not carry his child, never would carry his child. For in those moments, she wanted nothing more than to own a part of him once more.

His hand at her cheek, his warm mouth separating from hers, caused her to sob as he closed his eyes and said, "Thank you, my beauty . . . my Kitty. Thank you. And do not feel any bad thing for your having killed me. I died long ago . . . and I have proved myself worthy of nothing better since. You are free of me . . . at last."

He slipped then into unconsciousness—a deep, peaceful unconsciousness—and she wondered whether he, like her, would remember nothing when he awoke. Would he awaken confused, anxious, and wondering what had taken place? Or would he awaken angry, hateful, and mean-spirited—the beast she had come to know?

She studied him as he slept, his strong square jaw, the slight cleft in his chin, the dark chestnut of his whiskers, the perfect angle of his nose, and the artistic line of his lips. Oh, how she had loved him! Oh, how desperately she still did love him.

"I would have married you," she whispered, caressing his face with the back of her hand. "I would have married you, and you would have been my happiness. I would have been yours." Coquette brushed the tears from her cheeks. Reaching down, she took one of his heavy hands in her own. Raising it to her lips, she kissed the back of it, pressing her cheek to it as she cried.

"I would have gladly been the vessel to give you . . . to give us both sons and daughters. Sons with your strong chin and dark eyes, daughters with your nut-brown hair."

Carefully, though she knew he would not stir, she lay down beside him, let her body stretch the length of his, nestling against him. Wrapping her slender arms around one of his strong ones, she pressed her face to his shoulder and inhaled the scent of him. The sensation was overwhelming! The familiarity of his scent—cedar and leather— it sent new tears streaming over her cheeks.

"I would have belonged to you," she whispered. "I *should* have belonged to you!"

It returned then—the resentment, the pain, the bitterness she had tasted the day her father forbade her to accept Valor's proposal. She hated her father in those moments. In those moments, she was glad he was in Bostchelan and she was in Valor's manor house. She would stay with Valor through the night—sleep next to him. *I belong here,* she thought.

Certainly, she would have to wake before the cock crowed. Valor could never know she had stayed the night with him, clung to him as desperately as ivy clung to stone. Still, raising her head, she maneuvered his arm to cradle her against his strong body. She let her hand rest on his chest as it rose slowly up and down with his peaceful breathing. His skin was warm beneath her palm, his breathing rhythmic as some restful, hypnotic ocean wave.

Coquette was where she had so long dreamt of being, and she slept sound and comforted until the cock crowed and Valor finally stirred.

THE TURN OF
THE CHALICE

Valor slowly opened one eye, then the other. It was unfamiliar to him—to awaken to full-risen sunlight pouring into a room. He felt somewhat stiff, as if he hadn't turned the length of the night—also weakened and bemused. Had he dreamt he had heard a door open and then close? Had he dreamt the sound of soft fabric moving across the room? And was it his imagination toying with his senses—sending him certain he smelled Coquette's familiar scent? Or did the faint fragrance of sweetened vanilla truly linger on the bed beneath him?

Awkwardly, for the weakness he felt was unfamiliar to him, he turned on his side, pressing his nose against the mattress on which he lay. He inhaled deeply the faint scent of vanilla. He was suddenly quite aware—quite aware he was not in his own chambers, but rather in Coquette's.

How came I to awaken here? he wondered. Glancing about the room, he was rather unsettled, anxious somehow that Coquette might suddenly appear and find him so disorientated and disheveled. But then, as his mind began to rise completely from the fog of sleep, he frowned. He yet wore his breeches and boots—no shirt and certainly no nightshirt. He bent and inhaled the fading fragrance of vanilla still clinging to the linens beneath him. What had transpired?

At first, he had no memory of how he had come to be in Coquette's bed still wearing his boots and breeches. He closed his eyes, trying to recall the events of the night before. Coquette had received a letter from her father. Yes. He remembered it well—remembered telling her to retire to his chambers. He remembered his conversation with Victoria—instructing her to mix the sleeping tonic for Coquette. He remembered entering Coquette's room, taking her in his arms, tasting of her lips. Victoria had come, bringing the nutmegged milk, and he had watched Coquette drink it—had drained his own chalice.

Panic seized him then, for he knew! Coquette had not been the one to consume the tonic; he had! He remembered then the feeling of freedom, of fatigue, as it gradually had overtaken him. And he remembered Coquette—at least he remembered the taste of her mouth. He felt his stomach tighten, as did both fists, as he realized he had been rendered unconscious in her presence. In his relaxed state, under the influence of the preparation, had he faltered—spoken words so long cached in silence in his dark heart? Had cruel things slipped from his lips? Yet perhaps worse, had he verbalized the barely restrained truth? Had he, in weakness, spoken words of lost love and admiration to Coquette? Instantly he called up his best companions—resentment, bitterness, hate. What had passed between them? What words had he spoken? What action had he taken?

Remembering the passion and desire blazing in him as he held and kissed Coquette in those moments before Victoria arrived, he could only hope he had quick expired to sleep. Yet what if he had not? His mind ached with fear and worry over what his lips might have whispered to her when his strength and resolve had been compromised.

Burning with self-revulsion, panicked to near frenzy, Valor rose from Coquette's bed, fairly running from the room. Pausing not a moment, not even long enough to close her chamber doors behind him, Valor stormed across the hall to his own rooms. His hands, arms, legs—his entire body—shook with consternation and self-loathing. On the two previous nights spent in Coquette's company, he had played at being a beast. Yet with the turn of the chalice, had the beast been too soothed? Were all his brutal plans of victorious vengeance vanquished? Thwarted or not, he was undone. Entirely undone!

Carefully, slowly, Coquette entered her bed-chamber from her sitting room. The first moment Valor stirred, Coquette had awakened, quickly and carefully moving from her bed and into her sitting room. It was mere moments later, while peeking through the barely ajar door adjoining the rooms, she had seen him bolt upright in bed. He was entirely overcome with confusion. She watched as he ran his fingers through his tousled hair and seemed to sit in miserable lack of memory for a moment.

At first, she enjoyed feelings of triumph. *Let him know what it is to lose an entire night of memory,* she thought. In the very next instant, she was awash with guilt and regret. As unsettled and as frustrated as she had been with her two nights lost, she knew such a man as Valor would be entirely undone by it. It had been cruel to allow him to drink the tonic. Though guilt washed over her, regret was easy to fend off, for she had seen glimpses of her beloved in those blessed moments before Valor fell unconscious. In those moments, she had seen Valor, touched him, tasted of his kiss, and that she did not regret.

She dressed quickly, determined to arrive downstairs and to her breakfast before he had a chance to gather his wits. Some tiny hope had begun to flicker within her. With the turn of the chalice the night before, Coquette had found evidence of Valor still lingering in the beast. Soothe the beast, and Valor would be there. She knew it now. Perhaps her Valor was not lost to her forever after all—and little hope was still better than none.

"Good morning, sire," Victoria greeted as Valor stormed into the breakfast room. The morning sun streamed in through the open windows, and Coquette sat calmly eating a morning cake.

"Good morning, milord," Coquette greeted.

"What is this?" Valor asked.

"Breakfast, of course, milord," Victoria answered, a puzzled frown puckering her brow.

"And what are you doing here?" he growled at Coquette.

"Eating, milord," she answered. "Do you wish me to leave? After all, you did instruct that I begin each day by eating a hearty breakfast."

"How is it I came to awaken in milady's bed, Victoria?" Valor growled. As he had washed and dressed, he had begun to suspect it was Victoria's intention he consume the tonic. Had she not handed him the chalice with her own hand, rather than serving the drink from a tray and indicating with a nod which he should choose as she had done previously?

Eyebrows raised in astonishment, Victoria whispered, "Milord!"

Valor felt his cheeks heat, almost a blush at his realization of the inappropriate nature of his question to his housemistress. He studied her for a moment. Surely Victoria would not intentionally administer the tonic to him instead of Coquette. He scolded himself for suspecting she had.

"You were somewhat overcome with great fatigue last evening," Coquette said. "You came to my chamber to speak with me and were overcome. It was very strange. Frightening in truth. I did not sleep one peaceful moment for worry over your well-being."

He did not miss the blush that rose to her cheeks, the tremble of her pretty hand as she held her fork poised above her morning cake. "That is all?" he asked. She did not seem any more unsettled than usual. Certainly, if he had spoken anything that he might regret, it would play out on her face before him now. "Nothing more passed between us?"

Victoria nervously cleared her throat. He was suddenly irritated by her presence. Could he not have one conversation alone with his wife? Still, it was not Victoria's fault he had no memory of the night before, for even if she had by accident given the tonic to him instead of to Coquette, it was he who had ordered it brewed. No. No one but he alone could be held accountable.

Coquette sat nervous, anxious he would press her further about what had transpired. Surely he had surmised the chalices had been turned, having twice before witnessed her reaction to the tainted milk. Yet what kept him from erupting into fury? It

189

entered her mind then he was unsettled not merely at his lack of memory but by his lack of knowing what, if anything, had transpired between them. It saddened Coquette to know he did not remember being her Valor for a time, did not remember their shared kisses.

"I will have my breakfast in the east gardens, Victoria. Will you see to it at once?" Valor asked.

"Yes, sire," Victoria said with a nod. She turned and left. Valor advanced toward Coquette.

Coquette gasped as Valor suddenly reached out, taking her chin in hand and forcing her to look up at him.

"There is nothing else? Nothing else of the night I spent in your chamber?" he demanded.

Coquette swallowed, hoping her eyes did not reveal too much to him—hoping they hid her desire for his touch, his attention. "Surely, if there were something else, your mind and body would speak it to you," she said. He frowned, and she knew her words rung familiar and he could not fathom why.

One day passed and then another. Valor grew silent, pensive, and Coquette began to worry for him. In the privacy of her own thoughts, she mused she missed the beast, for if she could not have Valor, then at least the beast conversed or rode out on Goliath for hours on end. Yet with the beast seemingly soothed, Valor had withdrawn over the days since partaking of the tonic, and it worried her.

It was nearly every day for a week when out for her own meander through the gardens, Coquette would come upon Valor sitting on the bench at the pond. Ever she did not disturb him, did not let him know she had seen him—seen him rubbing at his temples as if they pained him or raking one hand through his hair as if tormented.

"He is deep in contemplation," Victoria told Coquette upon her return from her garden walk one afternoon. "He wonders what was spoken or not spoken between you that night. No doubt he is guilt-ridden as well, for his own deception of you. It is good to see him thus, milady," she said. "It is man battling with beast."

Coquette was worried still, even for Victoria's reassurances. Perhaps both would be lost to her—Valor and the beast.

And then a letter. As Coquette sat in silent dining with Valor one early autumn evening, Godfrey entered with a tray bearing a letter.

"This has arrived for you, milady," he said, extending the silver tray to her.

"Thank you, Godfrey," Coquette said, resting her fork on her plate and taking the letter.

"What joy," Valor grumbled. "Which member of your beloved family has chosen to taint our meal this night?"

Angry and irritated as she should be, Coquette found she was somewhat relieved at the sound of his sarcasm. Perhaps the beast in him lurked nearby this night. "It . . . it looks to be in Elise's hand," Coquette answered.

"Then open it and let us see what news of Bostchelan," he grumbled.

Coquette paused, studying him with sudden curiosity. She wondered at his wanting to hear the letters from her family read aloud when they so entirely vexed him.

"Very well, milord," she said. Breaking the seal, she unfolded the letter and began to read. *"Dearest, oh dearest Coquette, Father says you are not to come to Inez's wedding! He says he has received a letter from you—which I might tell you he refused to read to us—and in it you said you would not be able to travel to Bostchelan for the wedding! I am heartbroken! I so long to see you, Coquette . . . to know you are well. Naturally, Inez was furious when Father told her you would not come. She was in hopes to be telling people the great Lord of Roanan would be traveling to Bostchelan to attend her wedding. Dominique, however, has explained that with Father's wealth and our new accommodations, we need no great lord to impress the populace of Bostchelan."*

Coquette paused, daring to glance at Valor. It was as she thought; the angry amber of his eyes was perfectly affixed to her. He wore a rather self-satisfied expression as well—as if to say, *You can fool me not longer, for I see you are beginning to acknowledge the shallow nature of your family.*

"Read on, milady, do," he said. "These letters always interest me."

Coquette sighed and continued, her own annoyance at her family's shallow nature thick in her veins.

"*I speak now of something that has been pressing quite heavy on my mind since first you left, Coquette.*" Coquette paused, surprised by the sudden change of the letter's tone. "*I do not feel at ease as Father, Dominique, and Inez do . . . about your leaving to marry the Lord of Roanan. In truth, I believe them to be so entirely consumed by wealth and in seeking after their own possessions and pleasure that I consider them to have utterly forgotten your sacrifice. Without your willingness to go to Roanan, thereby saving Father from literal murder, we girls would be penniless, helpless, and alone. How can they go on and on about money, possessions, and position when you have away to marry a complete stranger? Though I imagine and tell myself this stranger treats you better than he did Father, that your beauty alone would keep him in constant awe of you . . . I worry. Are you truly well, Coquette? In your letter to me you wrote of—*" Coquette ceased in her reading, not wishing to read aloud to Valor what was next in the letter.

"Go on," Valor said. "Read on. What did you speak of in your letter to your sister?"

"Nothing of consequence," Coquette said. She blushed then, knowing full well he would mock her if she read on.

He held out his hand to her, however, and demanded, "Give it to me. I will finish it for myself . . . and for you."

What choice had she? Either read the contents herself and be humiliated or allow Valor to read them and be humiliated. She chose the latter, for it was somehow easier. Slowly, she handed the letter to him. As he took it, his fingers brushed against her own. Unexpectedly, her flesh broke into goose pimples. She had the sudden urge to leap from her chair and throw herself into his arms. It was entirely disconcerting that one slight and unintended touch should so affect her.

Valor cleared his throat, obviously unaware of Coquette's senses suddenly coming alive, and began to read. *"In your letter to me you wrote of this Lord of Roanan . . . of this man who threatened to kill our father. You wrote he is the handsomest of men . . . even as handsome as your Valor was, though I am difficult in imaging any man being more comely than Valor."* Valor paused in his reading. "Perhaps I may come to like Elise again after all," he said, an amused grin spreading across his face.

"Give it over to me," Coquette said, suddenly overly humiliated at his reading the letter. She reached for the letter. He simply pushed his chair backward so she could not lay a hand on it.

"Nay. I must continue," Valor said, still smiling. *"You write he is good to his townspeople and those of his household and that he has not harmed you in any way. You write of being anxious to produce an heir that he may be glad of having you, Coquette. And yet he threatened to kill Father, and I am led to wonder . . . how can you so willingly succumb to this man's beauty and position? For you are not like Dominique, Inez, and I. Ever you have longed for Valor and Valor alone, and I cannot fathom that you—"*

"This was meant for me! Not you!" Coquette cried, bolting from her chair and snatching the letter from his hands. He frowned at her but remained sitting as she folded the letter, tucking it into the bodice of her gown.

"Do you really suppose that if I wanted the damnable letter, I would be too timid to take it back from you simply for where you have cached it, milady?" he asked.

"Why shouldn't I lie to them?" Coquette asked, ignoring his inference. She was hurt he would mock her attempt to champion him in the eyes of her worried sister. "Why shouldn't they live in peace . . . thinking I am happy and hopeful?"

"Because they do not deserve it!" Valor said, rising to his feet. "This good sister, perhaps," he said. "But the others, no. And especially your father. Has the man no conscience? You do not own pure knowledge of what passed between him and me. I assured him of your misery and unhappiness at my hand. And still he sent you to me." He paused, his eyes narrowing as he added, "As I knew he would."

"You would have killed him!" Coquette argued. "Stand before me now and tell me you would give your own life for the sake of protecting your daughter's happiness."

"I would give my own life for it," he growled. "I would easily have taken a villain's sword to my guts rather than see a daughter sent to such as your father understood you were to endure!"

"And what great horror have I endured, milord?" Coquette asked. "Fear? Anxiety? Perhaps. But what other than that? What other? For even I know, for all your threats and implications . . . even I know it is impossible that I carry your heir."

"What?" Valor breathed, his face draining of color.

"I have learned well of deceit at your hand, milord," Coquette said. "The turn of the chalice has proven to me you are not but threats and deceit."

196

"You know nothing of what has passed between us!" he roared. "Simply for the sake of my drinking from the wrong chalice—and, yes, I admit to asking Victoria to brew it for you. I cannot fathom how it came to me instead of you. Yet you have no knowledge of what passed between us or what did not!"

"But I do, milord," she said, "for you told me yourself. You spoke the truth from your own lips the night the chalices were turned."

Valor commanded his expression to remain unchanged, though despair and defeat inwardly consumed him. He had spoken to her after drinking the tonic. He had, and as he had feared, he had confessed the truth to her—that he had not endeavored to have her as he implied. *Vengeance attend me now,* he thought.

"And so I spoke the truth of it to you, did I?" he growled. "I spoke to you that you could not possibly now carry my heir. And did I tell you why? Did I tell you why I have not touched you, even though the law would find me just in doing so?"

He watched as the triumphant determination on her face vanished, confusion in its wake. He knew in that moment he had withheld some knowledge from her at least.

"No, milord," she admitted.

He was somewhat surprised she had admitted

it. The beast roared within him then, the vengeful, hateful, heartless beast. "What reason do you give then?" he asked her. "What reason would I have for keeping from you these past weeks when an heir is the only possession I desire that I do not already possess?"

"I know not, milord," she said. He watched the hurt brim in her eyes, even as her self-worth and confidence diminished. She was thinking he did not find her pleasing, that she did not evoke masculine desire in him. He winced, knowing the pain such thoughts would induce, for he had felt similarly when she had chosen her father's will over his love so long ago. Beast he was, yes—but he would not have her think she was not beautiful or was unwanted by him.

"I own hatred for your father, this you know," he told her. His mind fought frantically for something, something to assure her of his desire for her without revealing the true reason for his keeping from her. It came to him then, and he said, "As much hatred as I own for him, I own far more wanton lust for you. But to satisfy my desire for you would find your father victor over me."

"What?" she exclaimed.

He felt relieved somewhat at her blush, for it told him she believed he found her beauty desirable.

"You speak in riddles," she said.

"What vengeance would I gain by having you?" he asked. "Even I, beast that I am in your eyes, even I who have stripped you from your beloved father, from your cherished sisters . . . yet even I would not use intimacy as a means to revenge."

Coquette felt her brow pucker into a frown. She did not understand him. He spoke in riddles, roaring broad threats that remained only threats, never seeing fruition.

"But you told me . . . you told me you wanted nothing from me save the birthing of your heir," she said. "And yet you keep from me. How does it keep your vengeance strong . . . your keeping from me?"

"I told your father I would have an heir by means of you," Valor said. "After you arrived here, I came to find he kept this from you. I told your father, and this I have said before to you, though in not the same words as I used with him . . . I told him I would have my heir of you no matter what manner of treatment it may cost you. I . . . I told him once my heir was born, I would put you off as I would an old dog. Did he tell you these words I told him, milady? No. When he told you that you must away to marry a stranger to save his life . . . did he repeat the heartless words I spoke to him?"

Suddenly Coquette felt dizzy. "No," she whispered. "In truth, he did not even tell me you wanted a wife simply for want of an heir. Only you told me that the first night I came to Roanan." Her father had misled her. She thought she understood why—to ease the task she faced, marrying a stranger to save his life. Still, he had misled her.

"Denying myself you keeps my vengeance strong," he told her then. "Strong and steadfast. At least for the time being, for I did not deceive you when I told you I will have my heir, milady. It is only I must wait until my vengeance finds conclusion."

"Yet what conclusion can this vengeance find?" she asked.

Valor's heart began to hammer as he saw the tears in her eyes, tears of pain. He winced, knowing the pain was borne not only his own deceit of her but of her father's as well. Long he had wanted her to know what a coward, what a selfish coward, her father was. Yet now, as the pain of the knowledge glistened in the moisture of her emerald eyes, he regretted it.

"What conclusion can this vengeance find, milord," she repeated, "when my father is not aware of it?"

"What?" Valor asked.

"He writes of joy, happiness, wealth, and satisfaction. What vengeance will come to you when he does not even seem to consider that giving me to you was any loss at all? Further, I have assured my family of my well-being. Therefore, what vengeance have you had?"

A tear traveled over her lovely cheek, and he felt he might drop to his knees and beg her forgiveness.

"Who then do you seek to harm with this vengeance you speak of, sire?" she asked him. "Is it the merchant Antoine de Bellamont, who wounded your pride three years previous by refusing you my hand? I do not think so. Rather . . . rather I think your vengeance is looking to me."

Valor wanted to shout, *No! No! It is your father I hate! He merely provided the means that I might own you. To at last own you: that was my true undertaking.*

Still, the wounded, hateful beast in him could not speak the words. Instead he said, "You are wrong, milady. You are wrong. And in that you may be assured it is your father I loathe. I will . . . I will allow that he should know you are miserable. For in your infinite misunderstanding of me, yet your point in that is clear. Therefore, I will review every letter you send in response to those of father and sisters. You will no longer be allowed to lie to them about your happiness . . . rather, your lack of it."

"And what then, sire?" she asked, another tear traveling over her beautiful cheek. "After you have made my father as miserable as any man can be, what then of me?"

Too wise she was. She knew his riddles were woven to distract her. He could no longer attempt to weave a web of confusing words—offer no further feeble reasons for keeping from her. He had loved her once and as such respected her, yet he could not confess this as his reason for protecting her innocence. Twisted as it was, she could not know he yet longed to be her champion in some small regard.

"Then there will be no more turning of chalices, milady," he told her, "for I am desirous of an heir—an heir to be born of you. When I am well certain of your father's destruction, Victoria's blessed tonic will not save you by any means."

She was glad of his words, hopeful in his threat, for there was something unspoken in the sound of his voice. He meant her to know he desired her and that his vengeance was not to her.

Suddenly, Valor reached out, pulling her into his arms and kissing her with such a ravenous nature of passion to all but consume her. Confused and in the deepest pain of mind, still Coquette melted to him. She could not fathom Valor's reasoning in his deep hatred for her father, yet he had assured her of his desire for her, of his vengeance aimed at her father and not herself. This knowledge, coupled with the realization her father had sent her to a stranger while possessing a threat she would be maltreated, stripped her of any rational thought, and she wanted only Valor.

Driven, moist, and warm, Valor's kiss threatened to force consciousness from her with its passionate demand. Yet it seemed to Coquette she could not quench her thirst for his kiss, the feel of being held in his arms. Perhaps he felt no residual memory of love for her, but in those moments she cared little for it, for she loved him. Even for his hatred of her father, for she understood it somehow; even for his harsh words, for she remembered the softness, the tenderness, of his words the night the chalices had been turned. In those moments, she thought, *Better to be in the arms of a tormented beast than in longing for Valor and living in Bostchelan with another who deceives.*

Suddenly Valor released her. "Write to your sister and answer how you will, excluding any high praise of me or my character. Then write to your father and tell him of how badly I treat you. Tell him I beat you with some regularity, and we will see what comes to pass . . . the fruition of my full vengeance or your full enlightenment." He turned then, storming out of the room and leaving Coquette's mind and body reeling with conflicting thoughts and sensations.

Coquette's thoughts were then made clear. She would write to Elise. She would write to her father as well—she would bait him and see what his reaction would be to a knowledge she was being ill-treated. Yet even as she planned to test her father, to dangerously involve herself in Valor's vengeance, she knew—she knew she preferred life with the beast who was once Valor to life without him. In those moments, the entirety of Coquette's soul became his—though he may never know it.

"Is there anything you require, milord?" Godfrey said upon entering the great hall to see the Lord of Roanan sitting in shadow.

"I require respite, Godfrey," his lordship responded. "And I fear you cannot gift me that."

"Perhaps you might find respite in milady, milord," Godfrey ventured, "if his lordship would but allow it."

"Respite?" Valor roared. "Respite? At her hand? Why, Godfrey," he chuckled, "have you lost your wits? Milady gives me nothing, save anxiety and frustration."

"But I believe that is your choice, milord. Not hers," Godfrey said. He was on tender ground, he knew. Godfrey had stood silent, watching the young Lord of Roanan endure the conflict raging within him.

Godfrey had friends—many secret friends—and through one of these secretive friends, he had recently learned the truth—the origin of his master's grief. With a knowledge of Valor's pain of the past, Godfrey far better understood the beast in him—though he would not reveal his knowledge, nor understanding, to his young master. Further, he understood the conflict rampant in his mind and body—to own the one woman he had ever loved, yet love her too perfectly to wholly own her, to loathe her father with such pure loathing and yet struggle in allowing the girl to believe her father was yet honorable.

"My choice, is it?" Valor asked, the fight and strength suddenly gone from him. "What would you have me do, Godfrey? I know you well enough," he said then, his eyes narrowing with suspicion. "I am certain that by some means you have come to a full knowledge of the past—that you know I was once in love with Coquette de Bellamont, that her father refused me her hand."

"I may know something of it," Godfrey admitted. Godfrey had learned long ago it did not bode well to play at pretense in Valor Lionhardt's presence.

"Then you know she chose her father over me. I loved her once, and she chose that fool over me. What fool would I then be to allow myself . . . to allow myself to have her in any regard, to allow any emotion to drift toward her?"

"Pardon, milord," Godfrey said, "but only a fool would not have milady."

"She yet chooses to believe his lies, Godfrey," Valor sighed.

"And you do not tell her the whole truth of it," Godfrey said.

"And crush her spirit more than I have already?" Valor mumbled.

"Perhaps it is in your power to restore her spirit, milord," Godfrey said. "Forgive me, but it seems her spirit was crushed some years ago."

"Unlike the beast here before you, she appears well enough in spite of it," Valor said.

"She chose a different path, milord," Godfrey said. He was angry himself then. The utter stupidity of it all was too much. "Take her, milord!" he growled, slamming his fists on the table before Valor. "Enough of Victoria's tonic and your misguided honor! Reach out and take her for your own, milord. Beat down the walls between you! She only keeps herself guarded because she believes it is what you want!"

"You would have me choose villainy over honor? That is the choice I own, Godfrey—honor or villainy. Which would you have me choose where milady is concerned?" Valor growled in return.

"Have you not chosen both in a manner?" Godfrey asked. "Your honor is somewhat misguided, for you refuse to make her truly your wife out of respect for her innocence while you simultaneously withhold the truth from her concerning your dealings with her father and your own feelings!"

"I have no feelings!" Valor shouted, slamming his own fists on the table. "No feelings save hatred and loathing toward the man who stole my life from me three years past."

"Then that is your choice, milord," Godfrey said, straightening his posture. "But I tell you only this—perhaps this merchant stole your life from you, as you put it, three years past. Yet it is you who chooses not to reclaim it now."

With a click of his heels, Godfrey turned and walked away. Yet he was not wholly despairing, for never before had the Lord of Roanan allowed any person to address him in such a manner. Anticipation rose in him, for he felt Valor Lionhardt weakening, and he knew—the beauty of, and in, Coquette de Bellamont Lionhardt was profound. His hope was renewed that beauty would vanquish the beast.

TRUE INTENT

Coquette indeed did as Valor instructed: she wrote to her sister as well as her father. To Elise she wrote of the beauty of the gardens and of her hopes in seeing her again one day. She did not overly praise her husband as she had done before, yet she did not speak too harshly of him, for she had no desire to upset Elise. Still, in writing to her father she professed unhappiness, wove false tales of abuse at her husband's hand, and pleaded for his compassion and help. Valor, of course, insisted upon reviewing the letters.

"Your letter to you sister is as it should be—trivial," he told her. "And the one to your father . . . you have told him I am a beast of a husband—cruel, unfeeling, violent."

"It is what you wanted me to tell him," Coquette reminded.

"Yes. And it will at last prove to you the shallow nature of your father's character, for I would wager all I own that he will give little thought or concern to what you have written to him."

"You're wrong, sire," she said. Still, she wondered. Was Valor about to be proven exact in his thinking?

Coquette posted the letters to Elise and her

father and then waited—waited for response. Yet in the course of ten days, none came, and she began to further wonder if Valor were correct in his entire assumption of her father's character. Though she was loath to believe her father would be indifferent to her unhappy situation, she could not discount the fact he had sent her to wed a stranger in the first of it.

Valor had all but curtly ignored Coquette in the days since their quarrel the night Elise's last letter had arrived. Light conversation at dinner was nearly the only attention she received from him, and she found herself nearly mad with wanting more—more conversation with him, more of his attention! An argument, a ride out to Roanan, or especially a night spent near him with one or the other of them falling prey to Victoria's tonic was far preferable to his nearly ignoring her. She found she was agitated, unhappy—far more than she had been since her arrival—and she knew not how to proceed.

She would write again to her father, beg for his support. It was the only venue left to her—provoke Valor in order to receive his attentions. Thus she found herself in Valor's study one afternoon in search of parchment and ink.

Finding the inkwell on Valor's desk empty, she went to a small adjoining room meant for the storage of parchments, inks, and other correspondence necessities. While she was in the storage room, she heard the hum of voices. One was Godfrey's, the other Valor's, and they were near upon the study. Suddenly she was unsettled, nervous about being found in Valor's study. Perhaps it was sheer excitement at the sound of his voice; perhaps it was fear of vexing him by entering his study without his knowledge. Whatever the reason, Coquette found herself pulling the storage room door nearly fully closed behind her as Valor and Godfrey entered the room.

Struggling to keep her breathing steady, her body motionless, lest she be discovered, Coquette waited, hoping they would fulfill whatever their purpose was and promptly leave.

"Oh, Dickerson is a good man, Godfrey," Valor said. "Still, I loathe his dinner parties, and I am unsettled in subjecting Coquette to such gossip."

"I understand, milord," Godfrey said. "But as you say, Lord Dickerson is a good man."

"And what *is* being said, Godfrey? What talk?" Valor asked then.

Coquette's hands trembled, apprehension rinsing over her. If he found her there, if he became aware of her presence, her eaves-dropping—still she could not reveal herself now. She was trapped—trapped with her curiosity at its peak.

"It is said you do not deserve her, milord," Godfrey answered.

Coquette startled as Valor's laughter filled the room then.

"That I do not deserve her?" Valor repeated. "Is this the talk you speak of? What news is this, Godfrey? 'Tis nothing more than veritable truth." He laughed again, saying, "I do *not* deserve her. For once the gossip is more than gossip. For once there is legitimacy to the talk of Roanan."

Coquette smiled in the darkness of her hiding place. To hear Valor refer to himself as unworthy of her—it was proof he admired her in some regard. Was it not?

"You *are* a good man, sire," Godfrey said.

"Am I?" Valor said.

The defeat, the doubt in his voice, caused Coquette to desire to see the expression of his face. Carefully she peeked through the small crack of the slightly open door, watching as he ran his hand through his soft brown mane. Would that her fingers could feel of its softness. Her heart fluttered at the thought.

"Yes, sire," Godfrey confirmed.

"If it were true, and it is not," Valor began, "then it would take a greater man than I, even it would take an extraordinary man, to deserve her . . . even for all her misplaced loyalty. And I, being only a *good* man, am truly undeserving." He inhaled deeply and straightened to his full height once more. "What more talk is there?" he asked. "I want to hear it, Godfrey. Tell me

211

of the scandalous gossip of the Lord of Roanan. Scandalous fabrication is far more interesting than truth, as you well know."

"Very well, sire," Godfrey continued. "They say you kept her sequestered a week upon your marriage, milord."

"A week," Valor said, nodding. His eyebrows raised in approval. "Then I *am* a good man. What then? How many children born this month with mothers claiming I am the father?"

"Only one, sire," Godfrey answered.

"Only one?" Valor asked. "Hmm . . . what was it last month . . . three? I shall have to play the better virile villain when next I am in town."

"It appears so, milord," Godfrey said.

Coquette frowned. Could it be as it appeared? Was Valor indeed the target for such malicious slander as this? He had told her of such gossip the day they had ridden out together for Roanan. Yet she had been disbelieving, for everyone seemed so gracious. Yet for Godfrey to remain so calm in appearance when discussing such matters—certainly, Godfrey was ever stoic, yet this instance was different—and for Godfrey to discuss such matters so unaffected, it was if the subject of gossip, the full measure of its falsehood, were commonplace between them.

"Is there anything else?" Valor asked. "Anything more I should know before the loathsome gathering at Dickerson's two nights hence?"

Godfrey put a fisted hand to his mouth, clearing his throat. "You will put milady aside in favor of a mistress in no less than one month."

Coquette's eyes widened. How could he endure such gossip? And then the thought struck her— how could she? Further, her fear and anxiety entered into it all. What if he did put her off in favor of a mistress? What if he already had? Perhaps it was the reason for his nearly ignoring her of late. Tears sprung to her eyes, her stomach tightening into knots. Yet she clung to her knowledge, her familiarity with the depths of his soul. He was not like unto his father; Valor was honorable. She knew it.

"One month, is it?" he asked. "What little faith these people put in me."

Coquette was somewhat relieved, but somehow only mildly.

"It is their way, sire. It is what entertains them—speculation concerning the lives of titled men and noble women," Godfrey explained. "It is as I always tell you, sire . . . do not dwell on such idle and malevolent gossip. It does you no good service."

Valor nodded, running his hand through his hair with frustration once more. "And yet, pray tell me, Godfrey . . . what is said of Coquette? What is said of milady?" he asked.

Coquette's heart began to hammer with rising angst. She had to concentrate to steady her breathing. In all the horrid things she'd heard Godfrey reveal to Valor, she'd feared most the gossips' assault of her.

"As I said before, you are not deserving of her," Godfrey answered.

"But this I already know," Valor told him.

"She is proclaimed a great beauty, milord—your match in favor of feature and face. She is hailed as kind and gentle . . . in these your opposite," Godfrey began.

"And there is the truth again," Valor said.

Coquette's heart fluttered once more at his veiled compliment.

"Odd, is it not? The manner in which they all judge her so perfectly when she has been to Roanan but once. Go on."

"Among the men, she is admired. And by one or two . . . well, sire . . . it is said you should be at the ready to defend her honor."

"Who?" Valor exclaimed. It seemed he erupted to fury in the instant. "Who would dare to imply . . . to threaten her in such a manner? Who would dare to cross me thus?"

"This I do not know, sire. Only that it has been said," Godfrey explained.

Coquette felt a chill as icy fingers seemed to travel up her spine. To this line of conversation, she suddenly did not wish to be privy.

"Our gender does us no good credit at times," Valor grumbled. "So driven by desire, so ignorant and weak of mind." He slammed one powerful fist onto the top of the desk near which he stood. "Let me hear one word of who would dare to speak such things of her, and I will slit his throat without pause or remorse!"

"Yes, milord," Godfrey said.

"Enough gossip, Godfrey," Valor said then. "You warn against its ill effect on me. I am always regretful at not heeding your advice."

Through the slight crack in the door, Coquette could see Valor rummaging through a stack of parchments on his desk.

"Here, Godfrey," he said, handing a parchment to Godfrey. "These then. Send these to his miserable self, and let us be done with him."

They left the room then, and Coquette paused before leaving the small storage room. She was thankful it had not been a full inkwell they had come in search of, as she had.

Mistresses? Talk of Valor having to defend her honor? Coquette was not pleased by the subjects of conversation between Godfrey and Valor. Still, some things did cause a tiny flicker of gladness to burn in her bosom—Valor's talk of his being unworthy of her, of his not deserving her, and confirming her beauty. Perhaps he did not despise her as thoroughly as he wanted her to believe.

The tiny flicker in her heart began to burn brighter. She would champion him. Yes! She would! As they attended Lord Dickerson's dinner, she would prove to the gossips of Roanan that Lord Lionhardt had no need of a mistress and that no man would dare to impose upon Lady Lionhardt in any regard.

Cautiously, she left Valor's study, determined to capture his attention at Lord Dickerson's dinner, if only for a few short hours. She smiled, thinking of the stunning emerald gown Valor had acquired for her to wear to the affair. She would find a way to be beautiful. She would! For him. No one in attendance at Lord Dickerson's dinner would have cause to believe malicious gossip. And though Coquette yet felt anxious at Valor's seeming lack of interest in her, she was determined he would not be able to ignore her at Lord Dickerson's.

Drawing upon all the memories of her sisters' vanity, Coquette endeavored to believe she could be beautiful—beautiful enough to capture the attention of the Lord of Roanan and thereby anyone else at Lord Dickerson's table.

"For milady, sire," Godfrey said, entering the dining room bearing a small silver tray.

Coquette's heart leapt at the sight of two letters lying on the silver tray. Surely they would be from her father or Elise—both perhaps.

Exhaling deeply, Valor nodded, indicating Godfrey should give the letters to Coquette. He frowned at Coquette as he watched her retrieve the letters Godfrey offered.

"Well?" he nearly growled. "What news of Bostchelan to spoil our dinner this evening?"

Coquette looked at him. She could feel her eyes burning with triumph. Now he would see. He would see how much her father cared for her, for she recognized her father's hand on the first letter. Now Valor would admit her father cared more for her than he gave due. Still, something in her heart trembled. Somehow she still feared Valor was correct in his estimation of her father's character.

"I have no wish to spoil your dinner, sire," she told him. "I will read the letters when we have finished and you have retired."

"You will read them now," Valor said, setting aside his fork.

"As you wish, milord," Coquette said. "Of the two, there is one in Elise's hand and one in Father's. Which do you wish me to read first?"

"Begin with your sister's," he said. "I suspect hers to give you false hope."

"And you wish to see my hope in my family crushed," she said.

He did not respond, yet his eyes narrowed, his frown deepening.

An odd sensation of foreboding rose within him, and Valor frowned. He was certain Coquette's father would further abandon her, and he was suddenly loath to see her hopes vanquished. For a moment he considered snatching the letters from her, thereby sparing her further hurt and disappointment. Yet she must know. Coquette must know the true nature of her father. Perhaps then such a beast as sat sharing an evening meal with her would not seem so vile.

Still, as he watched her break the seal of the first letter, such thick anxiety rose in him as to cause him to feel somewhat feverish. He reached up, loosening his silk cravat, attempting to appear unaffected.

"*My darling Coquette,* Elise begins," Coquette began. "*Such goings on! You would not believe the excitement over Inez and Henry's impending marriage. The entire household is in utter chaos! The dressmaker is frantic over the need for more fittings for Inez's wedding gown, as well as the gowns for Dominique and I. Father's tailor is quite excitable as well, not to mention the cooks! Oh, and you should hear of the plans for the flowers, Coquette. How I wish you could attend to see us in all our finery! How I long to see your face again, to see your smile and know you are happy. Perhaps if you may not come to us, I may come to you one day. Do you think your Lord of Roanan would allow me a visit to see you? Perhaps after the occasion of Inez's wedding I may visit. Still, it looks to me as if Dominique will shortly follow in Inez's footsteps soon. Her old French merchant is quite entirely taken with her, and Father expects a request for Dominique's hand any day. Oh, but he is terribly old, Coquette. Nearly as old as Father! Can you imagine? For my sake, I hope to be married to a dashing young man the likes of your Lord of Roanan . . . not to some moth-ridden friend of Father's."*

Coquette paused when she heard Valor chuckle. She looked up from the letter to see him grinning, obviously amused. "I remember Elise was always rather amusing in her honesty," he said.

"Yes," Coquette agreed. "She does not choose her words all too carefully." He nodded, and Coquette smiled, pleased at Elise's letter having brought him some trifle of happiness.

"Father's ships have set out once more," Coquette continued, *"though I cannot fathom how Father came by such large and magnificent ships, and he did not ever tell us what became of the others. We have not seen them since his return. Perhaps the old ships were sold as payment for the new ones. Still, the ships will no doubt return heaping with treasure. It should please Inez and Dominique. Still, for me, I am beginning to wonder which part of me will win over in the end . . . for there are two parts of me, battling so fiercely within my bosom I can hardly endure. One part, I call it my head, tells me to*

enjoy Father's wealth, to bask in the glory of things and vanity. Yet my other part—and it is my heart, I think—my other part longs for simplicity of a kind, love, and, in truth, escape. Often I think of you there with your handsome Lord of Roanan and wish I too could leave Bostchelan. In truth, I envy you . . . as I envy John Billings for quitting Father for his own endeavors. He has quickly become quite the admired stable owner. However he came by the means to—"

Coquette stopped, gasped, and looked up to Valor. He only glanced away from her and to the unfinished meal before him. Billings! She had forgotten all about the purse Godfrey had given Billings the day he had driven her from Bostchelan to Roanan. Yet now, sitting near to Valor, she remembered it. Likewise she remembered Valor having told her years before of his admiration for Billings, of his wish for Billings to be able to make his own way. Valor had provided the means of Billings's escape—his escape from servitude to independence. Something in her heart leapt with joy, for was it not a sort of proving, an evidence that Valor still lingered within the beast?

"Read on, then," he said, "for we have yet your father's letter to hear."

"You had Godfrey give him a purse," Coquette said. "The day I arrived . . . Godfrey handed Billings a purse and said he should use the contents for his own good pursuits—his own stables."

"Yes, yes, yes," Valor said, sighing heavily and rubbing at his temples with one hand. "What of it? Read on."

Another memory, another realization washed over her then. "It was why Billings was encouraged in leaving me. He knew . . . he knew it was you who would have me. He seemed so relieved all at once. I thought it odd in that moment, but I had not thought on it again. Too much else—"

"John Billings was a good man . . . once a good friend to me," Valor said. "He deserves his own way. Now read on, for I grow tired and must away to bed soon."

The warmth glowing in Coquette's bosom was delicious! Yet she knew Valor would speak no more of his giving Billings his way. She decided to be joyous in the knowledge; spoken or unspoken, the kindness and concern toward Billings came from Valor's warm heart, not the beast's cold one.

"Very well," she agreed. Still, she smiled as she continued reading Elise's letter, for she sensed what it would reveal next, and somehow it pleased her to have Valor hear of it. "Here . . . I begin once more. *He has quickly become quite the admired stable owner. However he came by the means to quit us and begin, I do not know . . . yet I am glad for him. I have ever thought him handsome and able and deserving of his own success. It is the part of me that longs for escape, the part of me that has ever admired John Billings from a distance, that wishes Father were not so determined to marry us girls to men who value only money and position . . . for I have ever wished John Billings would take notice of me. Remember the trips I would invent, begging Father for the use of his coach, simply so I might see John, speak to him even a little? Yet I am certain Father will have none of it, and it disheartens me more than you know. There now, I have talked myself into despair, Coquette. I must end this before I am reduced to tears and further confessions. Know that I love you and miss you desperately. Your Sister, Elise."*

"She proves herself wiser than she may appear," Valor said, "for John Billings is the best of men."

"She would be humiliated to know I had read such personal musings to you," Coquette said.

"Well, she will never know of it," he said. "Further, if she did know of it, I would commend her on her choice and encourage her to follow the part of herself who admires him." He looked to her then, and she knew she wore a puzzled frown. "What then?" he asked.

"How . . . how can you hand Billings a purse—a sum enough to enable him to quit my father and begin his own stables—and yet threaten murder beforehand?" she asked. She could not stop the question from escaping her lips, for the man, the beast before her, was nothing if not a conflict in himself.

"The other letter," he said, looking again to the service on the table before him. "Read it now."

He would not answer her question. She knew it. And so, with sudden and great trepidation, she broke the seal on her father's letter and began to read. *"Dearest Coquette,"* she began, *"I was, for a moment, disheartened at receiving your letter and reading of its contents; however . . ."* Instantly, anxiety and an odd sort of apprehension washed over Coquette. In one sentence she knew—she knew Valor had been right. With the reading of one sentence, her father's character was further in question.

A sort of panic flamed within Valor at the first line of the letter. He did not wish Coquette to continue to read it, for he knew it held only disappointment and heartache. Certainly he had wished, wished for years, for Coquette to know the true nature of her father's character—to know the true nature of the man she pledged loyalty to over him. Yet now, with the sure proof of it written in her father's own hand before her, Valor did not wish her to have confirmation.

"I grow weary of the evening and letter

reading," he said. "Leave the letter here. We . . . we will continue another time."

"No," Coquette said.

She looked to him, and he felt the sharp pinch of painful regret pricking at his cold heart.

"This is what you wanted. You wish for me to have a better knowledge of my father's low character. I think . . . I think this letter will—"

"I am greatly fatigued, Coquette," he interrupted, angry suddenly, but not at her—not even at her father. Rather at himself. "Leave the letter."

Coquette drew in a quick, startled breath. He had addressed her by name. Other than the night he had been overcome by the tonic, he had not addressed her by name since her coming. It warmed her, his addressing her so familiarly. Even for the anxiety growing within her in anticipation at the contents of her father's letter, Valor's allowing her name to fall from his lips warmed her.

"I will read it in silence if you prefer, milord," Coquette said. "You do not need to linger and—"

"If you are to read it at all, then read it aloud," Valor growled. She fancied he did not seem happy, did not enjoy his triumph as she thought he would, and she wondered why.

"Very well," she said. "I'll continue." Clearing her throat, she began again. *"I was, for a moment, disheartened at receiving your letter and reading of its contents; however, I write with my own assurance that all will be well. The bruising left of a beating does heal, my darling, and if you keep to the manor house until healing has been completed, then the population of the township will be none the wiser. Further, men are fierce and brutal creatures, Coquette . . . and violence is the companion to brutality. Still, with age, the majority of men do settle and calm. Take comfort in the knowledge your husband will not always be so brutal and that happiness will come to you as you learn to accept life as the Lady of Roanan. You asked that I come to you, help you in some regard, my darling . . . but I say to you that you belong to your husband now and thus must cling only to him. He is now your counterpart and will care for you in whatever manner he sees fit. It is what comes of growing up, Coquette . . . of marrying such a man of wealth and position. Therefore, I say to you, take heart! For your beauty will win such a beast in time. It is inevitable. And now, let us speak of your sisters and their happiness. You will find yours, and they, each in turn, seem to be finding theirs. Inez's wedding gown promises to be the most dramatic and beautiful ever before seen in Bostchelan! Henry is overjoyed at having won her . . . though I think any of you girls would have done for him. It seems he desires to be known for his relation to me."*

"Enough!" Valor growled, pushing his chair back from the table and rising to his feet. He trembled with fury and hatred of a man who would write such a letter to a daughter. Antoine de Bellamont deserved nothing! Certainly he did not deserve to own daughters. "Give the letter to me," he growled, holding a hand out to Coquette. He felt moisture in his eyes as he looked upon her, the sweet pink having drained from her pretty face, her shoulders drooping with disappointment and despair.

"B-but I have not finished."

Furious, Valor reached out, snatching the letter from her hand and ripping it into shreds.

"There is no need to finish," he said.

"You're right, of course," she said, casting her gaze to her lap, where her hands brutally twisted the cloth of her gown. "Your point has been proven, and there is no need to . . ."

Valor put a tight fist to his mouth. His rage was barely controlled, his desire to reach out and gather his beauty into his arms, to comfort her with the strength he possessed that her father did not, barely restrained. He saw the tears on her cheeks and knew—knew they were caused by pain borne of his endeavors more than the words her father had written. He had demanded she bait the maggot! He knew her father would fail her, and still he had demanded she pen such lies to him as to give venue for him to prove himself an unfeeling coward. It was his fault she sat destroyed, hurt, in pain—none but his.

"This letter is of no consequence," he said. "He . . . he knew he had been baited. I am sure of it."

He watched as Coquette rose from her chair, brushing tears from her cheeks. He watched, his heart throbbing with pain as she walked to him. She stopped just before him and raised her face to his. He thought he might surely collapse to his knees—beg her forgiveness for the pain he had caused her. He wanted only to reach out and gather her into his arms, kiss her, confess she was everything to him and that she need not worry, for he would find a way to make her happiness. Yet he paused—for it was a thick, black web of lies and deceit he had woven and a thick, black bog of fear yet enveloping his heart.

"You must tell me, sire," she whispered, tears streaming down her face. "You have been proven correct in your assumption of my father's shallow nature. Yet he loves me, I am certain. You must tell me, for I am certain he did not lie to me concerning every circumstance finding me here. You must tell me the truth now. Did you . . . did you truly threaten to take my father's life if he did not send me here?"

Valor swallowed, choking back the emotions of love, desire, and honesty threatening to overwhelm him. Coquette's father had proven himself selfish enough and thereby had broken her heart. Yet to tell her the truth of it, to validate Antoine de Bellamont had lied further, proved himself even more selfish. It might break her entirely.

And so Valor lied too. For the sake of Coquette's need to believe her father valued her in some regard, he joined her father in his society of low and lying men.

"I did," he answered. "I told him I would kill him, run him through with the very sword hanging at my hip now. I told him if he did not sacrifice you to me . . . I told him I would kill him, leaving his daughters without any means of support or protection."

Deep in his chest Valor felt the black pain of bitterness, the ache of a desire to win Coquette somehow. But such boyish musings were worthless now, for he had confirmed himself to be the worst of the two men she had once loved— her father and Valor Lionhardt.

Coquette gazed into the lion-amber of Valor's eyes. Her heart broken from accepting her father's true character, she stared at Valor, and she knew: he was lying to her. By the warm-amber, pain-filled expression of his eyes, she knew he had not threatened to kill her father. What he had done to convince her father to send her to him, she did not know, but she did know Valor had not meant to kill her father. Yet why did he lie to her?

There could be only one answer—he wanted her to loathe him. Valor did not want her love. Valor wanted an heir to his wealth and title. How much more complicated would life be for him were he expected to deal with an insipid, silly, love-stricken wife? Valor wanted her to loathe him. It was the only answer she could fathom.

Still, why had he endeavored to lessen the effect of her father's written word?

This letter is of no consequence, he had said. *He . . . he knew he had been baited. I am sure of it.* His words echoed in her mind, confusing her, leading her away from any rational explanation of his behavior and lying.

"Then I suppose we are both triumphant this night. Are we not?" she whispered.

He frowned, obviously confused. "What do you mean? What triumph is there for me in your father's failing of you? What triumph is there for you in it?" he asked.

"Your triumph is that now you may endeavor to have your heir, for you told me that once your vengeance on my father was complete, producing an heir was my next purpose," she said.

"Yes. That is true," he said, and Coquette noted the pain in his amber eyes increased. "Yet where is your triumph?"

"My triumph is over you," she said, "for you did not wreak vengeance on my father as you said you would. His letter only just proved to us both

. . . he feels no loss. You knew he would not. All along you knew it. And that is my one triumph—proof that your true intent of vengeance . . . was to me—not my father. My triumph is in having drawn out your true purpose in your vengeance."

In those moments, in Coquette's brief claim of victory, Valor knew—she had triumphed. As the web of lies he'd woven hung thick and viscid in his mind, as the pain in his heart threatened to crush the breath from him, his conscience affirmed what he had fought to accept: his vengeance had been to Coquette! All of the memories, thoughts, and emotions of the day Antoine had been found in his gardens—all of them returned to him in that one moment. He hated Antoine de Bellamont, it was true. Yet it had been the pain in his very soul, the flaming desire to own Coquette against her father's will, against her own will, that had spurred him on.

She had once chosen her father over him, and it had nearly killed him. It had succeeded in killing his goodness, his spirit. With Antoine's thievery, Valor had seen the venue to revenge—revenge and the fulfillment of his wonton desire for Coquette.

Sudden realization overwhelmed him, a realization that all the hateful things he had spoken to Coquette concerning her father, he had spoken for a dual purpose—to break her love for her father and to try and force her into finally choosing him over her father. Both had failed, for he could see that for all her father's treachery and lying, she yet loved him. Further, she had not chosen him over her father, never would. She had been forced to belong to him, but it was far different than choosing to belong to him.

Confess! his mind silently shouted. *Reach out and take her for your own! Mind, body, heart, and soul!* But he could not. He had proven himself the villain to her and in doing so had proven it to himself. Valor knew then, in those moments, he had doomed himself to finally being the beast he had set his feet on the path to becoming.

Coquette watched as the soft amber of Valor's eyes began to change, freezing to a cold tawny hue. There before her, whether for her father's true character being proven to them both or for impertinent irritation at her having guessed at his true course of vengeance, Valor's heart was hardening. Coquette's mind raced with memories of his veiled compliments of her to Godfrey as she stood cached in secret in the study eavesdropping—thoughts of his kindness toward John Billings, of his trying to ease her pain by commenting her father had been baited into such a heartless responding letter. He was two people inside himself, just as Elise had said she was. In Elise there dwelt the shallow, vain woman raised to be so, as well as the tenderhearted, humble lover of John Billings. In Valor, there dwelt the beast—hateful, vengeful, hardhearted—but there also lingered the heroic champion, the passionate lover, the kind governor. Yet how to vanquish the beast and release the champion Coquette did not know, especially now that she was assured of his bitterness toward her.

"We will leave promptly at six tomorrow evening, milady," Valor said. "I will not have us arrive late to Dickerson's dinner."

Lord Dickerson's dinner—Coquette had completely forgotten it. As Valor angrily strode from the dining hall, Coquette remembered her determination to prove herself worthy of Valor to all who would attend Lord Dickerson's dinner. She thought of her grand plans to appear as beautiful as possible to the attendees, to make certain the Lady of Roanan was a thing the Lord of Roanan would be proud to own.

She thought again of Valor's benevolence to Billings, his kindness to those under his employ, his quiet compliments of her to Godfrey. Surely if the beast could be soothed, it could as well be beaten.

Hopeless yet hopeful, Coquette returned to her chamber. Her father was a coward, careless of his youngest daughter's safety and happiness. Coquette was surprised at how easily her mind and soul accepted this fact. Yet had she not always suspected it? From the moment her father had told her of stealing the rose from Roanan Manor, had she not always doubted him? Doubted his good character the way she now doubted Valor's villainous character?

In the quiet of the night, in the loneliness of her chamber, as she found herself longing to be in Valor's company, in his arms, Coquette let go of her need to believe her father was of finer quality. In those moments she released all else but her desire to unearth her lover. A sudden sense of freedom, of purpose, rose in her then. Her father had proven himself unworthy of her worry, while Valor seemed more unsettled and bewildered than ever before.

Coquette closed her eyes, letting her mind linger on the night Valor had drunk of the tonic, of the warmth of his kisses, the tenderness of his touch and words. Moisture flooded her mouth at his remembered kiss.

"I am Coquette Lionhardt," she whispered to herself. "It is all I ever wanted. It is all I yet want . . . to belong to Valor and for Valor to belong to me."

Valor was there, across the hall, brooding and miserable. Coquette would find him—force him to forgive her for her pause three years before, force him to accept she still loved him. Somehow Coquette would force the beast to give Valor up to her, and then perhaps he might find he could still love her after all.

BUT AN UNWANTED ADMIRER

"Pardon me, sire," Godfrey began as he studied his master, "but you do not seem the least enthused at the prospect of Lord Dickerson's dinner this evening."

Lord Lionhardt sat with something akin to an air of defeat about him. Certainly he looked the perfect part of lord and master in his black coat, white shirt, and red silk cravat. However, his demeanor was far less than confident.

"That is because I am *not* in the least enthused, Godfrey. Another able observation on your part," Valor said.

"Yet no doubt milady will be the belle of the ball, so to speak," Godfrey said. "With such a beauty on your arm, it seems—"

"I do not wish to speak of milady, if you please, Godfrey," Valor grumbled.

Godfrey did not miss the way his master's hand fairly trembled a moment before he fisted, firmly pressing it to his forehead—another gesture of his being troubled. "She . . . she unsettles you this evening?" Godfrey asked, knowing full well the answer.

"She unsettles me every evening, Godfrey, you idiot!" Valor nearly shouted. "Every minute!"

"You possess far more self-discipline than any other man, milord, and I both praise and pity you for it," Godfrey said.

"Do not concern yourself with praise nor pity, Godfrey," Valor grumbled. "I am pitiful enough without your adding to it, and I deserve no praise for the treatment I have subjected her to."

"Then subject her to a different treatment, milord," Godfrey said, holding Valor's sheathed sword out to him.

"She would have no different treatment from me," Valor said, taking the sheathed sword and belting it to hang at his hip.

"Are you certain?" Godfrey asked, trying not to smile, hiding his satisfaction at Valor's discomfort. Milady had managed to slip deeply under Lord Lionhardt's skin. Godfrey was confident she would eventually win him, thereby vanquishing the cold stone encasing his heart.

"Quite certain."

"Then you are wrong, milord," Godfrey said. "Drop to your knees before her, confess your sins, confess your heart, and she will have you." Godfrey felt his teeth clench tightly as Valor unexpectedly chuckled.

"What?" Valor asked through his amused disbelief. "Confess my sins? Confess my heart? I have no heart, Godfrey! And well you know I have far too many sins where Coquette is concerned to merit time enough in all the world to confess them. You are ridiculous in your suggestion. That I would ever think to—"

"I daresay you think on it every moment, milord," Godfrey interrupted.

"Do you know what misdeeds I have heaped upon her, Godfrey? What pain?" Valor growled.

Godfrey was witness to the deep hurting already in his master's eyes, yet he said, "Yes. Years passed. You abandoned her without giving her a moment to consider on a harsh decision. Of recent you lie to her, endeavored to cause her to abhor her beloved family, put her off at every turn as easily as you would a happy puppy . . . to name a few misdeeds, milord."

"Indeed you spare no mercy for my already thick and sickened guilt," Valor mumbled.

"And yet she loves you, milord. All you need do is reach out, take her in your—"

"Godfrey," Valor began through clenched teeth. "I am Lord of Roanan—cruel, harsh, hardhearted. It is who I am—who I have become. She will never—"

"She will prove herself to you, milord," Godfrey said. "One day, milady will display her true feelings for you. It may be subtle, for she has little reason to hope you will accept her, but one day she will prove unguarded, weaken, and if your eyes are wide instead of blinded as they are now, you will see her heart belongs to you . . . as ever it has. Then, with the opportunity of redemption before you—then you must find the courage to take her heart into yours once more."

Valor frowned as he looked at Godfrey. Valor could not believe such heartfelt advice was falling from his first-man's lips—such a weathered, beaten, stiff soldier was he. Could he be in earnest? Could Godfrey be correct in his assumptions, his predictions? Surely not! Valor knew the devil he had become. Unworthy of Coquette and her heart, he would not waste his time and effort in hoping Godfrey possessed some great insight he did not.

Yet he could not deny the small glimmer of hope, desire, and wishes flickering in his chest. The mere thought of Coquette set his mouth watering, his knees weakening, and his hands tightening into fists. He must deter his thoughts, concentrate on facing Dickerson's dreaded dinner party and the social pressure to be endured. He could not think of Coquette. To think of her any longer would surely be his undoing.

"Inform milady of our need to leave now that we may be prompt in our arrival, Godfrey," Valor said. "At once."

Godfrey nodded and offered a slight bow. "As you wish, milord," he said as he turned to go. "She will show her hand one day, sire. Do not be foolish enough to fail to notice it and to act when she does," he said as he left the room.

Valor watched Godfrey leave, making certain he was gone before dropping to his knees. One powerful hand pressed his thigh for support; the other clutched his chest. He struggled to steady his breathing, struggled to find the strength to stand once more. She would kill him, he was certain of it. The battle within him—desire to release his heart from its stone encasement fighting with fear and the need to further harden it—had begun to take a very physical toll. His hands were numb while yet his arms ached with the pain of wanting to hold Coquette. His throat felt dry with resisting her, while his mouth constantly watered for want of her kiss. Her smile! It's what he most wanted to see before him—to let his last vision each evening be that of her beautiful smile. He wondered if he could indeed endure a life of torture—a life that thrust his greatest desire before him at every turn, yet denied him even the simplest touch or the happy beauty of her smile.

Tightly closing his eyes, Valor endeavored to calm his breathing, to remember the pain he'd known the day Antoine de Bellamont had denied him Coquette's hand—the same day his most beloved had chosen her cowardly father over him. He must draw upon the darkness that had saved him from utter failure and despair.

Yet his hands continued to tremble, his heart endeavoring to convince his mind of Godfrey's wisdom. Still, his own lies chewed at his thoughts and conscience, the knowledge of his own wicked deception reminding him of the loathsome beast he had become—a beast unworthy of beauty, of love, of the simplest kind of good.

Eventually, Valor found his physical strength—enough to rise to his feet and breathe more calmly. His determination and power returned none too soon as, in the next moment, Coquette entered.

However, Valor feared he might collapse to his knees once more as his eyes lingered on her beauty, beauty of body and of spirit—the brilliant green of her eyes so complemented by the emerald gown she wore, the cherry of her lips, the soft, ebony locks cascading over the smoothness of her shoulder. He swallowed the excess moisture flooding his mouth as he gazed upon her.

"We must away to Dickerson's," was all he could say.

"Yes, milord," Coquette said, and he feared the sweet sound of her voice might be his undoing.

Yet as he strode to meet her, he caught a glimpse of his loathsome self in a nearby hanging mirror. At his own reflection his determination was fortified, for it seemed all his lies, all the black bitterness in his heart, shone plain upon him. What beauty such as she could care for a beast like him?

• • •

Coquette swallowed the excess moisture filling her mouth as she watched Valor stride toward her. Dressed in the finery of a great lord, sword hanging at his hip, eyes aglow with strength and power, she thought she might lose herself, fling her arms about his neck. Ever she'd felt drawn to Valor—from the first moment she had seen him so many years before. She wanted to throw herself against him, beg for his kiss, plead with him to love her—but she must be patient. The beast was wary, and so must she be if she were to one day find Valor again. To confess her feelings and thoughts to him now—well, surely it would mean only disaster and further pain.

She must wait, be patient until the beast could be soothed, lulled to sleep, and Valor lured away. Still, she must touch him. She must!

"Forgive me, milord," she began as he stood before her, "but there is something . . . just there . . . on your cheek." Carefully she reached up, running one finger across his left cheek. There was nothing there, of course, but the feel of his flesh was purely invigorating. "There. Now you are presentable," she said.

"Thank you," he mumbled, glaring at her. He seemed quite unaffected by her touch, yet Coquette experienced such exhilaration as to send goose pimples breaking over her arms.

"You are chilled," Valor said.

Coquette was mortified at his having noticed the effect his presence had on her. "Yes. A little," she said.

"Autumn is full upon us," he said. "I will have Victoria gather a wrap for you as we leave."

"Thank you," Coquette said.

"Come then," Valor said, holding a hand toward her. "We must go. I do not wish to be late."

"Yes, milord," Coquette whispered, awed by the blissful sensation washing over her as she placed her hand in his. Again she swallowed the excess moisture flooding her mouth. Oh, how she wished he would pull her into his arms, devour her with ravenous kisses.

Valor stumbled, and she glanced at him, surprised by the uncharacteristic clumsiness. He seemed impassive, however, and she wondered if perhaps she had missed a step and not he.

An unexpected excitement rose in her bosom—pride in knowing all those in attendance at Lord Dickerson's would know Valor belonged to her. *He is magnificent,* she thought, daring to glance at him. She hoped he found her appearance acceptable—hoped she was a Lady of Roanan he would be proud to sit next to at a dinner party. He was magnificent!

Valor exhaled heavily, relieved to have reached Dickerson's estate at last. The ride in the coach with Coquette had been nearly unendurable. The only thoughts in his mind the entire length of the trip were those of restraint, battling to keep himself from ravaging Coquette. Wiping the perspiration from his forehead, Valor nodded to the coachman as he took Coquette's arm and led her into Dickerson's manor home. He sighed, relieved to know distraction waited within. Distraction would be his rescuer.

"Milady Lionhardt," Lord Dickerson greeted, taking Coquette's gloved hand, stooping to kiss the back of it. "You are more dazzling in your beauty than even I remember."

Coquette smiled at the kind, roundish man. "You are too kind, milord," she told him. "And I thank you for your invitation. It was very thoughtful."

"Thoughtful?" Lord Dickerson chuckled. He winked a friendly wink at Valor and said, "Thoughtful to wish to have the loveliest lady in Roanan at my dinner table? P'shaw! You do me honor, milady. Both you and your gallant husband. Good evening, Lionhardt," he greeted Valor.

"Dickerson," Valor said, nodding in greeting. "We do thank you for the invitation."

Lord Dickerson chuckled again. "Thank you? No doubt your lovely lady pulled you from your saddle or soft chair and dragged you here by that handsome mane of yours. I know how you feel about social events. It's why I'm all the more flattered to see you."

"Lord Lionhardt!"

Coquette turned to see a young woman of perhaps her own age approaching with the grace of an ascending dove. Auburn-haired, rosy-cheeked, and dressed in a lovely cream gown, the young woman's hands alighted on Valor's free arm as she raised herself on tiptoe and kissed him sweetly on one cheek.

"Lady Dickerson," Valor greeted as Coquette attempted to squelch the hot sting of jealousy rising in her bosom.

The young woman then gasped as she looked to Coquette. "Oh! Is this she? The new Lady of Roanan? Is this your bride, Lord Lionhardt?" she asked.

"Indeed, Lady Dickerson. This is Coquette—Lady of Roanan," Valor said.

"Oh, you are exquisite!" Lady Dickerson said, her lovely hands alighting on Coquette's arm. "When Dickie told me Lionhardt had wed, I at first could not believe it! But now I see how the Lord of Roanan was finally ensnared—by beauty herself."

"I am Coquette," Coquette offered, uncertain as to what else to offer in greeting. She was not at all convinced she liked a young woman who would so easily kiss Valor's cheek when his new wife was present. Yet she seemed a sort of innocent—happy in simply existing.

"And I am Juliann! Dickie says we are meant to be great friends, you and I. Isn't that right, Dickie?" the young woman asked her decades-older husband.

"It is undeniable," Lord Dickerson said. "Is it not obvious, Lionhardt? Our wives are destined to be the dearest of friends."

"Undeniable," Valor said, smiling at Coquette.

Coquette smiled too, delighted by the amusement she saw dancing in Valor's warm-amber eyes.

"We'll mingle just a bit before dinner, darlings," Juliann said. "Everyone is simply blissful to know you two are attending, so please do talk to a few guests, Lionhardt. I know how you like to try and hide in a corner. But not tonight! Not with your lovely bride on your arm."

"As you wish, milady," Valor said, leading Coquette away from the merry couple and toward a room full of waiting guests.

"We must brunch soon, milady," Juliann called as her husband greeted another guest.

Coquette smiled and nodded. Looking up to Valor, she could not help but whisper, "Dickie?" She heard the low chuckle in Valor's throat accompanying his amused grin.

"They have been married for near to five years, and she seems little changed from the first day

I met her," Valor said. "She is purely bliss for him, and I am glad. He is a good man—though I often live in fear she will invent some tender endearment for me and take to greeting me aloud with it."

"She seems very kind. Very affectionate as well—and very fond of you," Coquette said.

"It is hard for you to believe then? That someone could be very fond of me?" Valor asked.

"Th-that isn't what I meant," Coquette faltered. Yet she was not willing to admit her jealousy over Juliann's affectionate greeting.

"Ah," Valor said then. "There are Lord and Lady Winston. They hail from Brookstone. We should offer greetings."

Valor wondered, *Could it be Coquette is slightly vexed, somewhat jealous of Juliann's greeting kiss?* He thought not. More likely she was stunned in witnessing anyone finding Valor Lionhardt the least bit likeable. The evening promised to be long and taxing, yet he was somewhat intrigued by her notice of Juliann's affections.

An odd heat warmed his stomach momentarily, yet the warmth within and his advance on Lord and Lady Winston were halted as Lord Springhill stepped in his way.

"Lionhardt," Springhill greeted.

Valor forced a friendly grin. He did not care for Lord Noah Springhill. He found him irritating and held him in great suspicion. His black hair and hulking stature seemed to somehow deny his age, for there was nothing graying or weathered about him. Ten years Valor's senior, Springhill did not appear the elder of the two. It seemed a devil's trick in Valor's mind—something to be distrusted.

"Springhill," Valor said.

"Fancy meeting you at one of Dickerson's events," Lord Springhill said.

Valor noted the manner in which the man spoke to him, his eyes to lingering on Coquette, however. "Fancy it indeed," Valor said.

Valor was startled at Coquette's abrupt closeness. He glanced down at her, his body tensing as she suddenly began to cling to his arm with an odd sort of desperation. Something was amiss. He could sense it instantly—sensed the immediate fear and trepidation in her. Not but fear and trepidation would find her body pressed against his side, her slender arms clinging to his arm so frantically.

He looked again to Lord Springhill—witnessed him assessing Coquette with a lustful glint in his eyes, a barely masked wanton expression on his face. Coquette must've sensed the man's licentious thoughts, and realization filled Valor's mind: she clung to him for protection. Lord Springhill disturbed her. Yet no doubt Coquette had suffered such appraisal before. Her beauty would certainly attract the attention of gentlemen as well as filth.

"And has it been, I'd say, near to one year since last our paths crossed, Milady Lionhardt?" Springhill asked Coquette.

Valor felt her arms further tighten about his own, her hands clutching the fabric of his coat sleeve. And what was Springhill saying—that he'd met Coquette before?

"Yes, milord. I-I believe so," Coquette managed to answer politely.

Inwardly Valor was infuriated. Something in him suddenly desired to reach out and encircle the man's throat in the power of his hands—squeeze the breath from him. Instead he simply placed a reassuring hand over one of Coquette's clinging to his arm, slightly angling his body, a shoulder toward Springhill, placing more of his own mass between the man and Coquette.

"How is it you know milady?" Valor asked.

Springhill smiled, continuing to openly admire Coquette as he answered, "I have business with her father now and again. The merchant de Bellamont has provided me with several fascinating antiquities. He well has an eye for value in rare artifacts. I am a collector, you understand. A collector of beautiful things."

One of Coquette's arms released its bind on Valor's. Yet while the other remained, Valor drew in a deep breath at the startling and wonderful sensation of her free arm sliding across his back to awkwardly embrace him at his waist. He sensed she was terrified and wondered, did she know something of Springhill he did not or did she simply sense his vile nature?

Calmly, Valor removed his arm from her remaining grasp, placing it about her shoulders and pulling her snuggly against him. He trembled slightly as her now freed hand suddenly clutched the front of his shirt at his stomach. He felt her small, trembling fist tightly bunching the fabric there and covered it with his hand in order to both reassure her and to hide her frantic discomfort from the predator before them.

"Ah," Valor said then in response. "A collector of antiquities, is it? I then see how de Bellamont has proven of worth to you. Has he procured anything of value for you of late?"

"Ah, yes!" Springhill affirmed. "A Roman vase that would amaze you with its fine condition. But then the treasure you acquired from de Bellamont, though the method of acquisition is a mystery to us all, is far more beautiful than anything I have ever before laid eyes, or hands, upon, for that matter."

At this utterance, Valor felt Coquette's body go even more rigid against his own. She was terrified, and he knew he must end the conversation with Springhill—whisk her away from his loathsome presence.

"Well, then," Valor said, "we leave you to enjoy Dickerson's refreshments and others of his guests, Springhill." He nodded a dismissal to the man rather than offering him a hand, for both his hands were otherwise engaged in reassuring Coquette. He would champion her; he would not offer his own hand to a man whose mere presence caused her to feel so deeply assaulted.

"Good evening then, Lionhardt . . . milady," Springhill said with a smile and nod in Coquette's direction.

"Good evening, Springhill," Valor said, turning himself and Coquette away from the vile man. Never releasing the frightened young woman at his side, Valor directed her toward the nearby open doors leading to the veranda, fresh air, and, he hoped, some idea of privacy.

The night air was cool but did nothing to lessen the fires burning in him—fires of anger, rage, and barely controlled violence toward Springhill, fires of excitement, some odd sort of joy, and the flame of desire Coquette's clinging to him had sparked.

"It seems you have an admirer," he said.

"An unwanted admirer, milord," she said, her voice weak and quivering.

"What behavior has he displayed toward you in the past that you would shrink from him so entirely?" Valor asked once he was assured they were alone on the veranda. Still, she did not attempt to disengage herself from him, and he could yet feel the trembling in her.

"It is his expression . . . his very countenance. His thoughts toward women are not . . . not honorable," she said, and suddenly she was in his arms, pressed tightly against him, her own arms wrapped around his waist, her hands fisting the fabric at the back of his coat.

He could not help himself then and embraced her fully, holding her hard against his body, letting one hand rest at the back of her head as he pressed her face to his chest.

"Most thoughts of men in regard to a woman of your beauty are not honorable," he said, attempting to both teach and soothe her at once, but she did not sigh with relief or lessen her hold on him.

"He has always frightened me, Valor," she said, turning her lovely face up to gaze at him.

He thrilled at the sound of his true name falling from her lips and could not muster the resilience to correct her this time. In fact, he was certain she was unaware she had addressed him thus.

"He means nothing respectable toward me, I am sure."

"I am sure you are right," he said, his eyes narrowing as he looked into her wide, frightened ones. "Still, he shall not discomfort you any further this evening. I will not leave you to endure his wanton inspections at any turn."

Still, she clung to him, and he wished for her to do so forever. Yet his passion for her was rising at an increasing and powerful rate, and he must distract her from her present endeavors at seeking protection, lest he lose himself and take her mouth to his there on Dickerson's veranda.

"He knows well not to vex me," he added. "I would as soon slit his throat as look at him." Still she did not release him, only clung to him, the sweet scent of her hair filling his nostrils, the warm softness of her body against his threatening to destroy his resolve. He was the dark Lord of Roanan! Lionhardt the Heartless! And it was she, the very woman in his arms, who had turned his heart to stone. He could not weaken now.

Yet his mouth watered for want of hers, his powerful arms weakening as they held her. It wholly unnerved him. Another moment and he would be undone.

Coquette held back her tears, tried not to panic as Valor took hold of her arms, pushing her from his embrace, looking down into her face as if trying to help a frightened child to bravery.

"You are well enough then in the knowledge I will not tolerate his further discomforting you?" he asked.

The softer intonation of his voice was gone now, in its place the firm, angry voice she had come to recognize as the voice of the Lord of Roanan's. He had endured her fear, her physical assault on him, well enough and was now weary of it.

How ridiculous she had been! Clinging to him like a frightened child—weak and fearful in his presence—in the presence of he who feared nothing and no one!

"Forgive me, sire," she said, looking from his handsome, angry face. "I am sorry to act so—"

"Do you wish that we should take our leave? That I make an excuse?" he asked.

Coquette shook her head. "No. No, milord. I would not have Lord and Lady Dickerson, your friends, offended because I have had a moment of cowardice."

"It is not cowardice to read ill-intent and avoid it," Valor said.

Coquette forced a smile and looked up into his frowning face. "I am well, milord. It was . . . it was only he startled me . . . to see him here. It . . . it was so unexpected."

She would reveal nothing more to him. She would not tell him of her past experience with the vile Lord Noah Springhill—the occasion one year previous when the monster had attempted to force his intentions upon her during a visit to her father. Valor so rarely socialized, and she could see he harbored a liking to Lord and Lady Dickerson. She would not give him reason to run from those who might help her in her quest to peel away the beastly cocoon and free Valor. Lord Springhill had failed in his attempts to seduce her before, in his attempts to force himself upon her, and with Valor as her husband, he would dare not attempt any inappropriate behavior. She would endure his presence at the dinner party—for Valor's sake.

"You are certain?" Valor asked.

She read concern in his eyes, and it warmed her. "I am," she told him. "What ill-intent can he have toward me now . . . with you here?"

He slowly inhaled, a deep frown furrowing his brow as he studied her for a moment. "We will go at once," he said then. "I will make my excuse to Dickerson and Juliann. I will tell them I am suddenly overcome with . . . with an aching in my head."

"The Lord of Roanan is never overcome with anything, milord," Coquette said.

He was championing her! It thrilled her nearly beyond her ability to keep from taking flight. Yet perhaps he only did so out of duty. She was his wife, after all. Perhaps he only felt obliged somehow. No matter the reason. Valor was willing to leave Lord Dickerson's affair for her sake. It was enough—for the moment.

"No. I am recovered from seeing Lord Spring-hill here. I will not see your friends' evening tainted."

• • •

A deep sense of foreboding was slowly seeping into Valor's flesh. Coquette seemed recovered, yes. Still, her initial reaction to seeing Springhill had been quite dramatic, severe. It concerned Valor, for he felt there was more she was not telling him. A woman's intuition was sensitive and struck true nearly always. Yet Coquette's reaction to seeing Springhill seemed beyond mere intuition. His heart told him to take hold of her, drag her from the place if needs be. But Valor knew his heart was cold, void of wisdom. He could not trust it. Suspicion had settled in his mind, a permanent fixture, and it was surely what attempted to drive him now. Springhill was a reptile, it was certain, but the description fit many men of Valor's acquaintance. He did not want to disappoint Dickerson and Juliann. Further, he did not want to disappoint Coquette. She appeared so delighted to be out, to have met Dickerson's wife. What harm could be in staying through the dinner, especially if he made certain Springhill had no further contact with Coquette?

"Very well," he agreed at last. "Then we should return. Juliann will want to seat us to dinner soon."

Coquette could not help but smile at Valor. She could see the conflict in his eyes, suspicion battling with a want to please. But please whom? Dickerson and Juliann—or herself? Valor offered his arm, and she accepted it, thrilled to be touching him again.

Hope had been rising in Coquette. Every moment since the Lord of Roanan had been revealed to be Valor, hope had been rising. Certainly Coquette had experienced the depths of despair as well, yet always hope managed to find renewal in her and never so strong as it was in those moments. As Valor escorted her into the dining room, she nearly began to tremble with the renewed realization she walked with Valor. As if her father's letter of the day before had freed her somehow, as if confirmation of Valor's having been correct in his estimation of her father had released her from some sort of prison, she felt liberated, free to be Lady Lionhardt, free to fight the beast for Valor.

And certainly her feelings of freedom and joy only increased as Valor did not leave her side for any moment or reason as the evening progressed. Ever he remained at her side, no matter to whom he was speaking. Coquette was warmed by his attention, his attempts to guard her from any further discomfort at Lord Springhill's hand.

Even as they dined, he sat closer than was expected, his strong arm brushing her shoulder now and then, giving her further reassurance, however unintentional.

"Tell us then, my darling Lionhardt," Juliann began as the third course commenced, "why have we not seen more of your lovely bride? It comes to my ears you have visited Roanan only once since being wed."

A sense of panic began to rise in Coquette. For all Valor's heroism of the evening, would he yet reveal their marriage was a farce? She was certain he would not. Yet what answer could he give that would continue the appearance of all being well between them?

"I . . . I pause to answer, milady," Valor said. "Yet I will tell you my reasons are wholly selfish. I have not been willing to share the Lady Lionhardt with anyone. In truth, I am brutally jealous of even having to share her with you and your guests." He looked at Coquette, smiling his dazzling smile, and she blushed under his gaze. "For I am selfish with her attention, wanting everything about her for my own. She has my heart in its entirety, and I cannot be parted from her even for a moment without anxiety washing over me as a cold spring rain."

Coquette's blush deepened as she heard several of the women seated at the table giggle with delight.

Even Juliann clapped her hands together, exclaiming, "I love it! I love it! It was doubtful, I was, Milady Lionhardt . . . doubtful that any woman would ever capture the heart of the Lord of Roanan. But you have done it. It is full obvious!"

"Yet I say the brute endeavors to flatter you, Lady Dickerson," Lord Springhill said.

At the sound of his voice, every hair on Coquette's head prickled with apprehension. She could not keep from leaning closer to Valor and was somewhat comforted when she felt his hand cover her own where it lay at her knee.

"What do you mean, Lord Springhill?" Lord Dickerson asked.

Coquette risked a glance to Juliann, who only rolled her eyes with obvious irritation at Lord Springhill's remark.

"We, all of us, have known Lionhardt these past three years, and what one of us has ever seen any woman capture his attention for any amount of time? Yet Coquette de Bellamont arrives, and he is smitten? I call you out, Lionhardt the Heartless!" Lord Springhill chuckled and drew his chalice to his lips as he looked at Coquette. "I say your heart has not been won yet, for you are as arrogant, as proper, and as hardhearted as ever you were."

"Careful, Springhill," Lord Dickerson warned. "You endeavor to criticize my good friend."

Lord Springhill chuckled again. "There, there, Dickerson. Surely you know I only endeavor to jest with our newly wedded Lord of Roanan."

"What proof would you have me offer, Springhill?" Valor said, his hand tightening around Coquette's.

"You need offer no proof, my dearest Lionhardt," Juliann said, "for I see it in your eyes. Your eyes are fairly ablaze with admiration for your lady."

"A woman's answer," Lord Springhill mumbled. "But until a man is willing to display his defeat, until a woman can prove she holds the heart and mind of a man in the palm of her hand . . . I do not believe the man is conquered."

"Conquered?" Dickerson asked.

"By love, of course," Springhill said. "For example, you, Dickerson, and your lovely lady—you, my friend, are conquered by love, for you fear no public display of affection, are not humiliated by tender endearments. Love has conquered you, Dickerson . . . conquered and in return heaped happiness upon you both. However, Lionhardt . . . well, he hardly seems conquered."

"You seek evidence I am conquered? Is that it, Springhill?" Valor asked. "Then who am I to deny it to you?"

"He only teases to try and taunt you, Lionhardt," Juliann said. "Lord Springhill is renowned for his lack of manners."

"Still, it vexes me he should doubt the con-quering power of milady," Valor said, and before Coquette could think what to do, Valor had pushed his chair from the table. Rising to his feet, she was certain he meant to do battle with Springhill. She gasped, however, when he instead took hold of the back of her chair, pulling it away from the table as well.

"Oh, do not be so vexed as to leave us, our darling Lionhardt!" Juliann exclaimed, fairly leaping to her feet.

"I am not so vexed as to leave you," Valor said. "Only I feel the hero . . . that I must champion my lady before the breath of hell's doubt."

Every woman at the table gasped then sighed as Valor dropped to one knee before Coquette then.

"How can any man doubt her power over me . . . over my heart?" he said, reaching down and taking her foot in one hand.

"What are you about, Valor?" Coquette scolded in a whisper.

"If she but asked it of me, I would ever be her footstool," he said, running one hand caressively over the top of her foot where her slipper did not cover it. "I would chain my wrists to this slight ankle, adhere my lips to this sweet knee with permanence if she asked it of me," he added as his hand encircled her ankle, his head descending to place a lingering kiss on the fabric of her dress covering her knee.

Coquette could hardly breathe! Valor knelt before her, spouting the words of a poet. She glanced to Juliann to find the lady smiling and biting her lip with pure enjoyment. Several other women smiled, hands at their bosoms as they watched. Save Springhill, the men all boasted approving smiles. Coquette wanted only to dash toward the nearest door and escape. What was Valor thinking? His actions were entirely scandalous!

"Enough, Lionhardt," Lord Springhill grumbled. "You've made your point of it."

"There is no point to be made," Valor said, rising to his feet then, taking Coquette's hands and pulling her to her feet as well. "Simply a public admission of being conquered by love . . . owned by the only woman to walk the earth who could own me."

Coquette drew in a quick breath, her eyes widening as she realized his intent then. He meant to kiss her! There! Before a room filled with titled men and noble women!

"Valor?" she whispered as his head descended.

"She merely whispers my name and I am undone," Valor said, gathering Coquette into his arms as his mouth crushed against her own. The fire that instantly ignited in Coquette at the feel of his mouth to hers drove away all awareness of others being in the room. Warm and sweet, hot and spiced, his kiss led her heart to such swelling, her limbs to such weakness, she thought she might expire. In an instant she was returning his kiss, her hands lost in the soft mane of his hair.

He only means to silence Springhill, she thought. Yet she cared not, for to be thus held by him, to receive his kiss, so moist, so passionate and driven, it was worth any price—even the price of deception.

It was the applause that seemed to draw Valor's attention from the kiss. Yet as he broke the seal of their lips, his gaze lingered on Coquette, the fire-amber in his eyes blazing triumphant.

"Well done, my darling Lionhardt!" Juliann exclaimed as her small hands clapped approvingly. "Well done!"

"Well done, indeed!" Dickerson chuckled.

Valor released Coquette from his embrace, yet keeping hold of her arm as he assisted her to sit in her chair once more.

"You, my Lord Springhill, have just been bested," Juliann said, sighing as she returned to her meal.

"In more ways than you know, Milady Dickerson," Springhill said, raising his chalice to Valor a moment before drinking from it.

Coquette sat trembling, trying to return the delighted smiles and approving nods of each woman in turn at the table. It was well she knew every woman seated in the room envied her, for no man had ever broken so completely with propriety in displaying his affections for his wife. Valor had far more than bested Lord Springhill: he'd bested every man in attendance. Still, no man, save Springhill, seemed irritated at the fact, and by comparison, the women were utterly enchanted. She looked to Valor, fancying he had just acted as only Valor would have. No beast would bury his pride to heighten a woman's worth.

"You are not one to ever suffer defeat," Coquette ventured. She sat in the coach, across from Valor, studying him as he gazed out the coach window into the night.

"No. I am not," he said.

"I am in utter astonishment at the lengths you will go to ensure you do not—" she began.

"You must tell me if Springhill ever endeavors to speak to you again," Valor interrupted. "He is not an honorable man, and I did not like the manner in which he watched you this evening. Like a wolf watching prey, it was."

"He does not frighten me now," Coquette said, unable to stop the smile spreading across her face. "He dare not meddle with you. And he thinks he would be meddling with you if he were ever to attempt to threaten me as he did in Bostchelan last autumn."

"What do you mean?" Valor nearly growled.

"I mean, surely he knows . . . or at least he thinks you would never tolerate his attention to me—"

"No! What do you mean he threatened you in Bostchelan last autumn?" he demanded.

How she wished it were Valor her lover sitting

262

with her in the coach and not the beast Lord of Roanan! Ever she must be wary of what she said to the beast.

"I-I . . ." she stammered.

"Tell me! At once!" he demanded, reaching forth and taking her shoulders between his hands. "And do not try to diminish any part of it . . . for I will know if you are hiding something from me."

"It is of no consequence now . . . nor then," she said.

"Tell me!" he growled.

"He came to see Father," she began. "At least I assume he came to see Father. I was in the south garden. Mother's irises needed separating, and . . . and I did not trust them to anyone else. Lord Springhill came upon me then. He . . . he did not even pause to appear casual—simply took hold of me and . . . and forced a kiss and—"

"Stop the coach! Stop!" Valor shouted, banging on the roof of the coach. Already his hand grasped the hilt of his sword, and as the coach lurched to a halt, he had already opened the door.

"Milord!" Coquette cried, taking hold of his arm.

"He'll see his throat slit of it," Valor growled.

"No, no, no!" Coquette begged. "It was nothing! It was so long ago, and . . . and Billings happened upon us in the garden and—"

"Tell me he did no more," Valor growled, taking her chin in one hand, glaring down into her face. "Though it is enough reason to kill him!"

"Tell me you will have William make for Roanan Manor House, and . . . and I will tell you the length of it," she said. Valor was fierce! She could see the fury in him. In those moments, he meant to cross swords with Lord Springhill, and she would not see his life in danger for any reason, especially for her part.

"I will slit his throat!" Valor said, his eyebrows raised in warning.

"You will take us home," Coquette said, pushing against his broad shoulders with her small hands. "I will tell you of it then—once we are on our way once more."

"Milord?" William called from the coachman's seat outside the conveyance. "Is all well?"

"All is well, William," Coquette called as she reached over and closed the coach door once more. "I thought I had neglected something, but I have it here. Please make for home. With haste."

"Yes, milady," William said.

Valor was infuriated! Yet he remained seated, glaring at her in silence.

"That is my mouth he endeavored to taste!" Valor growled. "You belong to me! All of you!"

"It was not your mouth then," she reminded him. "You did not want it then, and that is beside the point."

"Your mouth has always belonged to me," he growled, reaching out and taking her chin in hand once more. "And it is ever I have wanted it!"

Coquette scarcely had time to gasp before his mouth was sealed to hers, moist, heated, and ravenous. Yet there was something more—an unfamiliar trembling in him. What it was she could not fathom, though it felt akin to fear.

"Tell me!" he demanded, breaking their kiss. "For I am mad with the fear of knowing all of it."

"He . . . he simply came upon me in the garden," she began, for she felt desperate to ease the fear in his eyes. "He said only, 'My mind is obsessed of you,' and then he . . . he took hold of me and forced his vile kiss on me. I struggled, tried to free myself, but he was so strong. Billings came into the gardens then, and Lord Springhill released me. He left, and I have not seen him since."

"That is all. Do you swear it to me?" Valor asked.

"He ever made utterly lewd implications before that day . . . yet I have not seen him since, and it was . . . it was the only time he ever attempted to . . ." she hesitated.

Coquette noted the beads of perspiration on Valor's forehead, the trembling of his hands. Fury still threatened to overtake him, but he sat back in the coach seat and said, "You will tell me if ever you lay eyes on him again. I feel in the deepest regions of my soul that I should confront him now. But you do not wish it. Either that or you do not think I may truly best him."

"You would easily best him, milord," Coquette said, for she did not doubt it. "But he is not worth your attention." She looked away from him, a heated blush crimson on her cheeks as she said, "And he cannot have mistaken your display at dinner. He must think you would champion me . . . that you would kill him for ever trying such a thing again."

"I would kill him," Valor said.

"It is, all of it, in the past," Coquette said. "I do not wish to discuss it further, if you please, milord."

"As you wish, milady," Valor grumbled, returning his attention to the darkness without the coach.

Coquette breathed a heavy sigh. Fear still caused her innards to tremble—fear that Valor would confront Springhill and be injured somehow. Yet his fury over Springhill's assault buoyed her hope as well. She sensed it was more than merely Springhill's having touched her, Valor's possession, that drove him to such fury. And as she remembered his display at dinner, whether for the benefit of the witnesses or not, it gave her flesh cause to erupt into goose pimples. The beast Lord of Roanan was in danger of being vanquished at Valor's hand, she was certain—as much in danger as Lord Springhill would have been had Coquette allowed the coach to return to Lord Dickerson's.

THE WHISPERED KISS

"Victoria!" Valor called as he entered the kitchens. Victoria was where she usually was in the late hours—in the kitchen enjoying a book of poetry and a pastry.

"Milord?" she asked as he entered.

"We have arrived home," Valor said.

"I see that, milord. Was it a nice dinner party?" she asked.

"I am very fatigued, Victoria," came his answer. "Would you be so kind as to bring me some of your warm spiced milk when you come to tend to milady?"

"Milord?" Victoria asked.

He could see the worry and trepidation on her face. "Not to worry, Victoria," he said. "I'm simply tired. Just milk and nutmeg warmed, if you please. No additional ingredients, you understand."

"Yes, sire," she breathed with relief.

"But please do tend to milady," he added as he turned to go. "The evening was wrought with discomfort for her, I believe."

As Valor entered his chambers, stripping the cravat from his throat, he thought on the events of the evening. Springhill! He should have returned to Dickerson's and called the villain out. His mind burned with fury at the thought of Springhill's having even looked at Coquette in the past, but to know he had laid hands on her, pressed his foul mouth to hers—his mind and body could barely endure the knowledge.

Furthermore Godfrey's words, spoken prior to Dickerson's party, echoed through his mind repeatedly. *She will prove herself to you, milord,* Godfrey had said. *One day, milady will display her true feelings for you. It may be subtle, for she has little reason to hope you will accept her, but one day she will prove unguarded, weaken, and if your eyes are wide instead of blinded as they are now, you will see her heart belongs to you . . . as ever it has. Then, with the opportunity of redemption before you—then you must find the courage to take her heart into yours once more.* Over and over again these words echoed through his consciousness, and he could not send them to silence.

As he removed his shirt, as his mind recalled certain measures of the experience at Dickerson's—Coquette's perceptible jealousy of Juliann's displayed affection to Valor, her clinging to him for security and protection when Springville had appeared, her willing acceptance and return of his kiss in front of the dinner party. It was scandalous, what he had done at dinner to convince Springhill of his passion for Coquette.

And yet scandalous or not, she had involved herself in it. Something in him, something weak and hurt, something once damaged, whispered Godfrey's words to his mind over and over, and he began to wonder—was Godfrey correct? Had Coquette indeed, as Godfrey foretold, proven herself to yet harbor strong feelings for him? A throbbing ache began to take root in his stomach and chest as if something were trapped in him and battling to get out.

He needed sleep. He was tired—too tired to think with any amount of rationality. He would drink Victoria's warm nutmegged milk, void of tonic, and sleep hard. Perhaps in the morning all would be clear. For the moment, however, there was only the sickening ache in his body, the painful fatigue in his mind, the sweet taste of Coquette's kiss on his tongue.

There came a knock on his door, and relief washed over him.

"Come in," he called.

Victoria entered carrying a silver tray and chalice. "This should soothe you, milord," she said as she offered the chalice to him. "And Godfrey asked me to bring this to your attention as well," she added, handing him a letter that lay on the tray.

Valor accepted the chalice. "No tonic?" he asked, accepting the letter as well.

"Just milk and spice, sire," Victoria said. She

frowned as she looked at him. "You look overly fatigued, milord. Though these dinner parties of Lord Dickerson's do seem to wear on you."

"It was a night not to be taken lightly," Valor said as he sipped the warm milk and frowned as he studied the seal on the letter.

"I leave you then, milord—to your rest," Victoria said.

"Thank you, Victoria," Valor said. "Please be certain milady is well looked after."

"Yes, sire," and she was gone.

Again the pain in his gut ached, and he fancied he labored to draw breath. His limbs also felt weak. For all appearances and sensations, he wondered he had not been fighting some great battle.

Once more his thoughts lingered on Coquette, her clinging to him, her willingness to toss propriety to the wind and receive his kiss at the dinner party.

She will prove herself to you, milord, Godfrey's voice echoed in his mind. *With the opportunity of redemption before you—then you must find the courage to take her heart into yours once more.*

"What heart do you speak of, Godfrey?" Valor asked the air as he drank for the chalice. "For mine is cold as stone and—"

He was interrupted by a sharp twinge in his chest, in the vicinity of his heart. Uncomfortable it was, and he wondered if Lady Dickerson's menu had not agreed with him.

Sitting down on the side of his bed, he drank from the chalice once more. The warm milk soothed the pain in his chest a bit. He liked Victoria's concoction, even without the tonic. Setting the chalice aside for a moment, he broke the seal on the letter and began to read.

"And how was the dinner party, milady?" Victoria asked as she carefully placed Coquette's emerald slippers in the nearby wardrobe.

"Fine," Coquette answered.

Yet Victoria was suspicious. Had something unusual taken place at the dinner party? With milord looking so fatigued and milady so rosy-cheeked, she could but wonder.

Victoria's mischievous nature took hold then, and she said, "I have just come from the master's chamber."

"Oh?" Coquette inquired.

Victoria smiled, for curiosity was bright on the young woman's face.

"Yes," Victoria said. "He asked me to bring him the nutmegged milk."

"He did?" Coquette exclaimed with a gasp.

"Indeed," Victoria answered, however not offering any further information. She knew milady assumed the milk was laced with the tonic. It was what she wanted her to assume.

"But why?" Coquette asked. "Why did he ask for the milk?"

Victoria shrugged, feigning ignorance. "I suppose he was overly tired and wanted the soothing drink to help him sleep. Oh, and there *was* the letter Godfrey delivered."

"A letter? From whom?"

"I'm not certain, milady. Although, I could swear I've seen the manner of writing on it before. Definitely a woman's hand . . . but I can't recall why it seemed so familiar."

"Excuse me, Victoria," Coquette mumbled, hastening toward the door. "I . . . I must see milord before he . . . before he falls asleep. There is . . . there is something I've forgotten to ask."

"Then you best hurry, milady," Victoria said. "For he did indeed look greatly fatigued. I'm sure sleep will find him quickly."

Rushing across the hallway, Coquette was heedless to all else except speaking with Valor before the medicine of the nutmegged milk overtook him. She cared not for the fact she had neglected any slippers, had not even properly refastened the bows at the back of her ball gown. What woman had sent him a letter? She must know!

Without even knocking, she burst into his chambers to find him sitting upright on his bed reading the letter.

His eyebrows raised, his eyes widening as he

saw her. Next to him, on a tiny table, sat a silver chalice.

"Milord," was all she could say. It was only then she realized she had no excuse to offer—no excuse as to her sudden and rather rude appearance in his chamber.

"Yes?" he asked. He did appear overly fatigued, nearly weak somehow. His eyelids looked heavy, his hair tousled.

"I-I neglected to . . . to . . ."

"Neglected to what?" he prodded, laying the letter on the small table and taking hold of the chalice.

"I neglected to thank you for your display at the dinner table this evening," she managed at last. "I know it was for Lord Springhill's sake."

"It was for the sake of all," he said, still holding the chalice. "Actually, I'm not certain I'm in earnest in saying that."

"What?" Coquette asked. Surely he meant to let Lord Springhill know there was no doubt of his loyalty to Coquette.

"I think I did it for my own selfish reasons," he said, sipping from the chalice.

"No!" Coquette said, dashing toward him and attempting to take the chalice from his hand. "That is to say . . . I'm sure you did it for no other reason than to—"

"I did it for reasons I reason to be good reasons," he said.

Coquette released a heavy sigh. She was too late. He had partaken of the nutmegged milk and would soon be lost to deep slumber.

"Very well, milord," she mumbled. "I will leave you to your respite. Good night, sire."

"But wait," he said, and Coquette paused in leaving him. He tipped his head toward the small table on which the letter now lay. "Your sister Elise—Elise has written to me in her own hand," he told her. "She's written pleading with me to allow you to attend Inez's wedding five days hence," he said.

Coquette drew in a quick breath as she watched him raise the chalice to his perfect lips, draining it of its contents. No! She did not wish for him to be unconscious! She wanted to be with him—in his presence and he fully aware.

"I have little wish to go, milord," she told him. For it was true. She had no desire to leave him, even for a short time.

"You do wish it. Furthermore, I am inclined to allow it," he rather mumbled as he stood and rather unsteadily walked to the fire. "You . . . you are Lady of Roanan. Not a prisoner of it."

"And what of you, milord?" she ventured. "Do I travel alone to Bostchelan?" Oh, how desperately she hoped he would accompany her! How victorious it would be to see the expression on her father's face when he realized Valor was the Lord of Roanan. How glorious it would be simply to travel with him!

"I will remain here. I have no wish to return to Bostchelan. Godfrey will see you safely there," he said.

Coquette's heart landed solidly in the pit of her stomach. She had little wish to go to Inez's wedding and even less wish to go without Valor.

Valor frowned as he gazed into the fire. Elise had written directly to him, and how could he refuse such a heartfelt plea? Furthermore, his heart was beginning to speak to his head, and it told him he should allow Coquette to return to her family. She'd been miserable in his company, and although her family was the worst of shallow-minded fools, he knew she loved them, even her cowardly father. For a moment, he wondered if Victoria had indeed included the tonic in his milk, for his thoughts were most unselfish. Still, he was no less aware than he had been before he had drained the chalice. He would send word by carrier—affirmation he would allow Coquette to attend the wedding.

"I see you've consumed Victoria's nutmegged milk," Coquette said.

"Yes," Valor admitted. "I knew sleep would elude me tonight." He exhaled slowly as he sensed her moving closer to him, as the mischief in his mind won over his good sense. Coquette knew the milk had been tainted before. Why should she believe otherwise now? An opportunity had presented itself. Valor realized in feigning the symptoms induced by the tonic, he might indeed be privy to conversation and events he might not otherwise be.

"Then . . . then you are . . . you are overly relaxed, I assume," she said.

Valor was puzzled, curious. Coquette's easy approach, her reference to the nutmegged milk, it intrigued him. Never had he known exactly what had passed between them on the occasion of the turn of the chalice—the night he had consumed the tonic meant for Coquette. He had revealed to Coquette the fact of their marriage having never been consummated. Beyond that, he remembered nothing of what had transpired, and now his mind was alive with more than mischief: it was alive with deception. Deception—it had become a part of him and yet lingered, and he would make pretense of having consumed the tonic. In that moment, Valor was determined to witness similar to what had transpired the night the chalice had been turned.

"Yes," Valor said. "I grow more weary with each passing moment."

"Do you, milord?" Coquette asked. In the next moment, he felt her close behind him, felt her hand alight on his shoulder. "Then perhaps you should sit—make yourself more comfortable."

Yes! Much would be revealed this night. Valor sensed it with every inch of his flesh, every measure of his mind and soul.

"Perhaps," Valor said, turning from the fire and to Coquette. Upon seeing her again, he wondered, doubted he could continue the farce. Donning the emerald dress she'd worn to Dickerson's, her eyes flashed with mischief. She was entirely enticing, completely alluring. Simply by standing in the room she weakened his resolve to resist her, and yet . . . the mischief in her eyes was too tempting. He would play out the game.

Cautiously and feigning fatigue, he allowed her to lead him to the chaise lounge near the fire. He watched the mischief flicker in her eyes as she knelt beside him, never taking her gaze from his.

Coquette was delighted. The tonic Victoria's delicious, wonderful tonic! It would melt away Valor's resolve, vanquish the beast. Oh, how she cherished the memories of the night Valor had consumed the tonic instead of she—how she yet reveled in the remembered feel of his affections. Silently she prayed the tonic would not lead him to deep slumber too quickly, while simultaneously she hoped it would defeat his defenses as it had before.

"You seem sleepy," she said as she studied his handsome, beloved face. "Do you wish me to leave so you may rest?"

"No," came his reply and with it the most dazzling smile. "I wish you to stay here . . . near to me, thus, so that I might . . . that I might . . ."

"So that you might, what, milord?" Coquette asked, her heart hammering madly within her bosom. He would kiss her again this night! She was determined he would. He would kiss her and not for the sake of impressing dinner party guests.

The fire smoldering through Valor's veins was like none he had felt in seemingly so long—like none he had felt until Coquette had come to Roanan, that is. Under the guise of being influenced of Victoria's tonic, Valor knew a freedom he had not known in years—a freedom to play at being Valor Lionhardt, the lover of Coquette de Bellamont— Valor Lionhardt who desired only to please her and possess her heart.

Tentatively, for he yet feared she would recoil, he raised one hand to her face, cupping her cheek. Amazed when she did not flinch at his touch, he fancied her eyes fairly twinkled pure pleasure, her smile revealing delight. He again began to consider on whether Godfrey had been right. Did he merely have to reach out and gather her to him to win her? Did Coquette still care for him, want him? Even did she love him still?

"You are fortunate you arrived after I drank,"

he mumbled, feigning the tonic intoxication. He would venture further. "For I would aggress toward you were I able."

"I fear I might allow you to aggress were you able, milord," she whispered.

Valor felt his heart struggling against the cold stone encasing it, and it pained him excruciatingly. His own flesh tingled as her hands grasped his forearm, as she pressed her cheek more firmly against the palm of his hand.

Surely this could not be! Surely he was dreaming! He fancied that there had truly been tonic in the milk Victoria had given him and that he was hallucinating, imagining the flirtatious words passing between them. Yet he persevered. He would see the farce through, whatever it brought—whether joy or pain, he must know what would transpire.

Valor chuckled low in his throat. "Such lies do not diminish your beauty in the least," he said, reaching up and trailing limp fingers over her neck. "Nay, such lies only complement it." He let his hand loosely encircle her neck, his thumb resting in the tender hollow of her throat. "Further, it is dangerous to tease a beast of any breed, Coquette. Even one so fatigued, so weak as the one before you now."

"I am in no danger," she said, blissful at his touch. This was her Valor! This was her lover,

279

her friend, her heart's desire! "For when you are thus fatigued, you are Valor Lionhardt, he who was once my lover and protector, and I am secure that neither I nor my virtue linger in impending danger."

"Still," he said, dropping his hand from her and closing his eyes for a moment, " 'tis dangerous to tease a beast—no matter your confidence in the man you once knew."

"I still know him," she whispered, her fingers weaving through his soft hair. "He has never left my heart. He is yet companion to my soul, though I miss him with every breath of my life."

It was too much! Valor felt moisture in his eyes, felt the ice around his heart threatening to thin. Yet he knew he could not reveal himself as being fully aware. He closed his eyes, resigned to feign unconsciousness. Better to pretend sleep than to falter or reveal too much of himself, of the struggle within him.

"Valor?" she said, and he did not miss the disappointment in her voice. "No, Valor! Do not sleep yet." Still, he feigned. Every muscle in his body wanted to reach for her, pull her into his arms, but he resisted, trying to concentrate on the darkness within him, the bitterness of his soul.

In the next moment, however, his senses were more alive than ever before as he felt her lips press softly to his.

"Valor?" she whispered. "Do you indeed sleep? Are you lost to me so soon?"

"No," he breathed, barely able to keep himself from gathering her into his arms and crushing his mouth to hers.

"Do you remember, Valor," she began in a whisper, "when you used to kiss me? Do you remember when you would whisper into my mouth?"

Instantly, waves of familiar, long-restrained emotion washed through him. He felt hot and cold, weak and powerful in the same moment. Of course he remembered! Did she think him an imbecile? Yet he knew she did—at least she thought it of the fully conscious beast he had become. Still, how could even a beast forget it! Visions of the past flashed through his mind, of his manner of weakening Coquette's resolve to resist him. The trifle act of affection had never failed to find her trusting, willing in his arms— never had it failed to win her to him. It pained his very soul to remember it, to linger on wondering if the simple gesture would still win her to him.

"I do," he mumbled.

Coquette's heart leapt, wild where it already pounded madly within her bosom. She closed her eyes for a moment, remembering, nay reliving just such an instance from the past. She saw it clearly in those moments, her timidity, her awkwardness at holding the attention of the most

281

beautiful man imaginable. She could nearly smell the scent of lilacs, feel the warm sun on her face as Valor Lionhardt had kissed her tender lips—a light, careful kiss at first.

She remembered the expression on his most handsome of handsome faces, the spark of desire in his eyes as he held her face between his hands, so powerful even then. She had been frightened—frightened of releasing her tightly guarded manners, fearful of revealing the full depth of her feelings for him, terrified in knowing he may break her heart as easily as a footstep snapped a tender twig. And it had been in those moments—as he kissed her again, his lips pressing more firmly against her, understandingly patient, yet coaxing her own lips to part in further acceptance of his kiss—it was in those blissful moments Valor had first broken some invisible seal of fear and released her passion.

"Do not be frightened, Coquette," he had said in a voice so deep and resonate as to melt a woman's very bones. He had kissed her again, coaxing her lips to part, and as they did, he paused in the kiss, at the same time lingering, his lips still touching hers. It was then he had whispered, "I love you. I love you, Coquette de Bellamont."

Instantly the memory of his warm breath entering her mouth, the moisture of his tongue's soft touch to her lips as he had whispered the words, caused the flesh of her body to break involuntarily into goose pimples, just as it had done so many years before. She shivered, delighted by the thrill the memory drizzled over her—the memory she had kept beloved within her heart for so long.

It had been her undoing, the whispered kiss, his whisper of love carried from his mouth into hers! Instantly she had melted against him, passion exploding between them as his tender kiss ignited to a frenzy, his mouth crushed against her own. The very memory of it caused excess moisture to flood her mouth, and she smiled, remembering how Valor had not forgotten the effect and used it often to deem her weak and helpless in his arms. Never had he misused his power over her. Never had he pressed her beyond impassioned kissing. And Coquette was thankful to him for it, for she was even yet uncertain she could have ever denied him anything once he had whispered into her mouth.

"Lean close to me, Coquette," Valor whispered. The sound of his voice wrenched Coquette from her reminiscence.

"Pardon?" she asked. His eyes were yet closed, and she knew he was close to losing consciousness.

"Lean close," he repeated.

Her heart pounding like a hammer against an anvil, she did lean to him—close then closer until her face was only a breath from his.

His eyes opening into narrow slits, he said, "I am a wanton man now, Kitty," he said. "But I am weak in my fatigue. You are safe to place one tender kiss . . . one kiss the like of the past. Place one kiss to my lips, Kitty, and I will whisper to your mouth . . . though it may not please you as much as it once did, for circumstances are vast in their change."

Coquette's heart beat so brutally the sound of it was nearly deafening in her own ears. He was tempting her! Tempting her as the devil himself tempted the innocent. Yet how could she refuse? Her mouth watered at the thought of his whisper in her mouth, craved it as one craves a sweet, sun-ripened peach on a summer's day. She would have his whispered kiss once more. She would! And if his whispered words were of a nature only driven by physical desire, yet she knew they would linger on her tongue like confection.

She was breathless, unable to inhale as she leaned forward and pressed her lips tenderly to his. She let her lips linger against his, overcome by the pleasure of his lingering against her own. And then, as her heart nearly stopped from such wild beating, Valor began to whisper.

"He who you loved is altered, beauty," he whispered, his warm breath filling her mouth with a sweet ambrosia, the light touch of his tongue as he whispered causing her to tremble. He paused, kissing her more firmly, and then another whisper, "You belong to the beast who once knew him." Again he paused to kiss her, and Coquette's arms gave way, her torso relaxing fully against his own. "And the beast will have his heir—the beast will one day have you, beauty," he continued, and she was herself intoxicated by his charm. "But never against your will." She felt his weak arms band around her, as tightly as powerful arms weakened by a mischievous tonic could band around her. "This is my promise to you," he whispered, and she was undone.

Taking his face between her hands, Coquette freed the withheld passion, so long pent up within her. This was her Valor—the love of her heart, soul, body, and mind! In those moments, no matter what his whisper warned, it was Valor's voice promising safety. The beast would have her, and silently she hoped the beast's wanton desire for her grew from the love her lost Valor had once owned for her. The beast would have her, have his heir, yes—but Valor would protect her will.

His arms tightened about her, his mouth matching hers in its delicious, abandoned vigor. This was Valor! This was her knight, her prince, her heart's desire, her soul's mate! This tasted of Valor, felt of Valor, and it was Valor whispering into her mouth each time the seal of their lips broke for breath.

"Does my kiss please you?" he whispered.

"Yes," she whispered in return.

"Greatly?" he asked, still in a whisper.

"You can never know the bliss of it," she whispered.

"Then show me," he asked, his voice deep, rich, and enticing.

Coquette was undone! Frantically, she took his face in her hands, pressing her mouth to his in her own demanding, passion-fed frenzy, and he did not draw away. Instead Valor's mouth endeavored to match the fervor of her own, even for his weakened state. In mere moments, he had both surrendered and returned to dominance within the exchange, and she feared she might swoon in the bliss of the knowledge he possessed her.

Suddenly, however, and yet somehow expectedly, his kisses began to weaken. Coquette knew the tonic was winning him over, and she cursed its power. But how could she curse the power that had twice freed Valor of the beast? And so, as his kiss weakened, his eyes never opening again, she let him go—placed her soft fingertips to his lips as he drifted into unconsciousness.

It was then, when she was certain he slept and would not remember, it was then she spoke to him, confessed what she had wanted to confess for so very long.

"Valor?" she whispered. "You are asleep, and I am a coward. I am a coward, for I could never confess a thing such as this to you were you conscious."

• • •

Valor tried to appear unconscious, tried to breathe slowly and with regularity—a nearly impossible feat considering the passion blazing in him. What would she reveal? Within his still body, Valor's heart and mind battled. One part, his stone-covered heart, shouted she loved him still and would accept him—love him if he could but find the courage to release himself. The other part, his mind, shouted he was a fool—a fool to believe she could forgive him his horrid deceit and bitterness. Yet as the battle within him raged in silence, he strained to hear her whispered confession. What could one such as she possibly have need to confess?

"I abandoned my father that day in Bostchelan, Valor," she whispered. "After Father refused your proposal, I went upstairs. I cried as I packed a small valise, and . . . and I walked to Lionhardt Manor. Cecilie answered the door. She said you had gone and that you had left no word as to your destination. I could not believe I had paused—paused long enough to lose you. I inquired of your father, but even he did not know where you had gone. I inquired of everyone . . . everyone I knew, but you had gone. I know it does not matter now. The past is passed, and you cannot care to know this. Yet something in me wishes you to know it! I want you to know that I did not choose my father over you. I was only astonished at his refusal, confused, and frightened."

Valor struggled as he had never struggled to maintain the appearance of unconsciousness while his mind called out in misery and regret, shouted remembrances of his own stupidity and impatience.

"I loved you, Valor! I only wanted you! I only ever have wanted Valor," she whispered. "I'm sorry for my ignorance and weakness. I should not have paused. I knew it the moment my mind was clear, and I realized I had done it. Please forgive me. And know this: hell has me in its clutches," she whispered. "For it is I would rather burn with this beast forever in the hell he knows than to ever keep from you again, Valor."

He felt her soft lips linger against his once more, heard the swish of her ball gown and the latch of his chamber door. Opening his eyes, he drew labored breath, coughed, thought he might lose the contents of his stomach. Sitting up, he shook his head, spit out the lump in his throat, heard it sizzle in the fire. Perspiration began to trickle over his forehead, and he struggled to stand, even falling to his knees once with the weakness heaped upon him by what Coquette had revealed to him.

She had abandoned her father after all! Left to seek her lover out—her lover, he who was too impatient to wait even an hour to see if a mighty change would come about. In his pain, in his certainty to endure deeper hurt and pain, he had fled Lionhardt Manor and Bostchelan, leaving his broken heart and she who had broken it in his furious wake. One hour! Had he waited but one hour, she would have been at his side! The knowledge sickened him, and he again feared he might heave the contents of his stomach to the floor.

His body trembled, his chest burning with pain and anguish. His legs and arms felt weak and numb, and he was certain he would lose consciousness at any moment. He must ride! Ride out the passion in him begging fulfillment, ride out the disgust he felt for himself and his actions, ride out the sickness of his mind and body.

Awkwardly he pulled on his boots, shirt, and coat. His body wracked with pain and agony like he had never before experienced, he made his way to the stables, the fresh air of autumn night buoying his strength and resolve to ride. Saddling his mount, he took his greatcoat from the hook in Goliath's stall, for the night would be cold in the depths of the dark.

"Goliath!" he growled. "Ride this fever from my brain, this pain and weakness from my body! On, Goliath!"

The sound of leather and horse's hooves beating the ground further strengthened him. He would ride—ride to his death if he must. And if he did— well, what more did such a beast as he deserve?

• • •

Coquette lay in her bed gazing at the dying embers of the fire in the hearth. On her lips the sense of Valor's kiss lingered. She imagined she could yet feel his arms around her, his breath on her cheek, the solid muscles of his chest against her own soft form.

She thought of his display at dinner and could not help but smile. If Valor thought the gossips of Roanan had fodder before, then he had fed them well this night. She only wished she did not have Victoria's tonic to thank for his most recent attention to her. If only he could shower such affections on her without the aid of it. Yet it was something—all of it. His championing her at the dinner party, his unguarded, tonic-driven affection—all of it was proof Valor yet battled to win over the beast. And he would—he must! Coquette grimaced as her heart experienced a stab of pain at the thought of the beast somehow vanquishing Valor. It could not be. She would not let it be.

"He is there," she whispered to herself. She fancied she heard the heavy beat of horse hooves outside the manor. "Valor is there, and one day, my beast will be vanquished by him."

Her eyelids heavy, her body relaxed, Coquette drifted to sleep bathed in bliss-filled memories of Valor's whispered kiss.

THE WOUNDED BEAST

Valor heard the thunder of fast-approaching riders. He wondered who else would be riding so near Roanan Manor at such an early hour. Spent with fatigue from a long night of riding, he did not feel up to a social instance, no matter how trivial. Reigning Goliath to a halt, he turned, intent on bidding the other riders a good morning with a mere nod. Instantly, a frown puckered his brow. His muscles tightened as he saw three riders approaching. They were dressed in capes and masks common to highwaymen. It was certain these devils meant no good intention toward anyone.

He paused for a moment, just long enough to remind himself he dared not face three at once as he might have weeks earlier—before Coquette had come to Roanan. Something in Valor was changing. He did not view the approaching highwaymen as a challenge the way he might have in the days before Coquette was again near to him. Now they were a threat—a danger. He would turn his back and ride away rather than risk injury.

"On, Goliath!" he shouted. Still, he drew his sword as he turned the horse and urged the beast to a gallop. He knew he had paused too long in considering what course to take. In mere moments, they were upon him. Valor shouted as one of the villains plunged a sword into Goliath's hindquarters. The horse stumbled and fell, throwing its master to the ground.

Valor was on his feet at once, sword at the ready, as the three highwaymen dismounted and encircled him.

"You chose the wrong man to rob this day, cowards," Valor growled. Still, his great fatigue and instability of mind worried him. His strength was not what it would be had he received a proper night's sleep.

"Rob?" one of the men said. "Why, Milord Lionhardt—we do not intend to rob you."

"Of your valuables, at least," another one chuckled.

"Rather, it is your life we will rob you of this day," the third said.

A long-absent form of fear welled within Valor. All he could think of was Coquette—his need to see her face, his obsession with owning her. He would not die and lose the sight of her smile. Even at that moment, even when faced with such a threat as being murdered, his mouth watered at the thought of her—the thick stone and ice around his heart thinning further.

"Then you have certainly chosen the wrong man to murder," Valor growled a moment before he lunged at the first cloaked villain. Steel clashed, and disarming his first opponent, he spun to avoid the attack from behind. Stepping aside, he took hold of one man's wrist as he lunged at Valor and missed.

"I have no wish to drain you of your blood," Valor said. He pulled hard on the villain's wrist, causing him to lose his footing and fall to the ground.

"But we wish to drain you of yours!" the first man shouted, wielding his sword over his head as he approached.

"Then you will die!" Valor warned, raising his sword in defense.

Swordplay between the first man and Valor continued. The clash of steel to steel echoed in the quiet autumn morning.

An arm encircled his throat from behind. He kicked his facing opponent in the midsection, causing him to stumble. Flipping the hilt of his sword in his palm, he spun the weapon to face away from his frontal opponent and toward the attacker behind him. Valor clenched his teeth and plunged his blade into the man at his back. The arm around his neck slackened and then fell away. But there was no moment to reflect, for the two remaining men were upon him.

Valor shouted. He grimaced as he felt the hot sting of a blade deep in his left shoulder. Still, he fought, matching sword stroke for sword stroke with each man.

"Cowards!" he shouted as they fought. "Idiots! To assume three of you would be enough to . . ." He plunged his sword straight into the midsection of one of the men, adding, "To vanquish me!" as he watched the man crumple to the ground. Inhaling deeply, he wiped the blood from his sword on his left thigh and raised the blade toward the last man standing.

"You and I," Valor said, "we will go 'round a bit, but you will fall in the end."

The man paused, looking from one fallen comrade to the other. Valor could see his opponent's hand tremble as he wielded his weapon.

"I may let you live," Valor said, "but only if you confess your reasons for this ambush!"

The man continued to look at the fallen men on either side of him.

He tightened his grip on his sword. "Do you really think you can best me?" Valor asked. "You do realize that I am the Lord of Roanan, do you not? You do realize I have never been bested in swordplay, whether for recreation or in earnest."

"Y-you will let me live?" the man sputtered.

"If you confess to me why this was attempted, then I will consider it," Valor said.

The man swallowed hard. Valor could see he was fearful, terrified, and well Valor knew he should be.

"Lord Springhill," the man finally replied.

"He hired we three to . . . to vanquish you, Lord of Roanan. I do not know his reasoning."

"Springhill?" Valor roared. "Springhill paid you for this? Why?" he asked, lunging toward the man and holding the tip of his sword at his throat.

"I do not know, milord!" the man pleaded. "I do not know! I swear it!"

"Unmask yourself, that I may know you!" Valor shouted.

"B-but, milord—" the man protested.

"Reveal!" Valor demanded.

He watched as the man slowly reached up and pulled the mask from his face. He did not recognize the man and was glad of it. He had feared someone in Roanan had been willing to murder him.

"Pl-please, milord," the man began, "I beg of you . . . do not kill me."

"I should run you through here and now," Valor growled. "But I want to know why Springhill would see me dead."

The man shook his head and winced as Valor's sword cut into the flesh at his throat. "I swear, I do not know, sire! I know only that you have wronged him somehow . . . taken . . . taken possession of something promised to him. A merchant's promise of a thing of rare beauty, he said."

Valor frowned and whispered, "A merchant's

295

promise? A thing of rare beauty?" In the next moment, his mind was cleared, and he breathed, "Coquette!" Holding the man at bay by his sword, he growled, "I have let you live. Therefore, you will honor me by riding to Roanan and sending the constable to Roanan Manor House. Do you swear you will do this? Swear it! For if you do not swear it, I will run you through! If you do not do as I demand, I will find you and run you through! Swear it!"

"I swear it! I swear it!" the man gasped.

"Then go! For I must make for Roanan Manor," Valor said. Sheathing his bloody sword, he went to Goliath. The horse's wound was deep. Valor feared riding him, and yet—Coquette!

Quickly, he gathered the reins to a horse belonging to one of the dead men. Mounting, he shouted, "Make for home, Goliath," and rode off at a gallop, his greatcoat flapping in the misty autumn breeze.

"His lordship rode out quite early this morning, milady," Victoria said.

Coquette enjoyed another bite of one of cook's breakfast cake. Though she'd had the cake before, it tasted better to her for some reason. The morning sun seemed brighter; the autumn leaves dancing on the breeze appeared more brilliant in their hues of crimson, gold, and orange. To Coquette, everything was improved upon, enhanced, and she knew it was for the fact her heart was full of hope and joy.

The evening before, spent before the fire and in Valor's arms, tasting of his kiss—it had inspired her to hopefulness. The beast would lose its battle to retain Valor—Coquette would win. She was certain of it.

"I can see why he enjoys these morning rides," Coquette said with a contented sigh. "And morning rides in autumn must be best of all." Finishing the last bite of cake on the plate before her, Coquette rose from her chair and retrieved her wrap from across its back. "This morning is too lovely to ignore, Victoria," Coquette said, tightening the wrap about her shoulders. "I think I cannot neglect a walk in the gardens any less than milord can neglect a ride."

"Certainly not, milady," Victoria agreed. "Autumn is the most glorious of seasons, and the Roanan gardens proclaim it with perfect vibrancy."

"You will call for me if his lordship returns and is in need of my company for any reason. Won't you?" Coquette ventured.

Victoria smiled, quite delighted in the bright color on her mistress's face—quite proud of herself for risking the Lord of Roanan's wrath and leading milady to believe he had drunk of the tonic the night before. No wrath had yet appeared, and though she did not know what, if anything, had transpired between milord and milady, by Valor's urgent need to ride out in the late hours of night and Coquette's nearly constant expression of secret delight, she knew something had happened. An impassioned kiss, perhaps? She could only hope it was so.

"I will be sure Godfrey informs you when milord has returned," Victoria answered.

"Thank you," Coquette said. Then she took her leave.

Victoria's smile broadened. Poor, poor Valor. He could not resist her much longer. Coquette would melt the cold ice and stone surrounding his heart. Victoria knew it was true—to the very tips of her toes, she knew it.

The gardens of Roanan Manor were indeed glorious! Tender rosehips lined the paths, rich with deep maroons and pleasant golds. The leaves in the maples wove a canopy of crimson and green as the cool breeze breathed a delightful chill on Coquette's soft cheeks.

The frost had gone. Though Coquette had admired its artist's-fancy on her windowpane upon rising from her bed, she wished now it had lingered longer so she may admire the weave of its crystal lace on the leaves and rocks.

"Good morning, Lady Lionhardt."

Gasping, startled from her tender reveries,

Coquette spun around to find Lord Springhill standing not far behind her.

"Lord Springhill!" she exclaimed. She was instantly frightened, terrified! The man's very presence had always frightened her, but his unexpected appearance in Valor's gardens—surely he had not been invited to visit, especially so early in the morning and with Valor away.

"Yes," Lord Springhill said. "I thought I might join you on your morning walk."

"I was only about to return to the house," she said, stepping onto a nearby path that would lead around him and yet back to the house.

"But you have only just begun," Lord Springhill said, stepping onto the same path and in her way.

"Milord will want to know you're here," she said. "Surely he will want to join us."

"Your lord will not be joining us, milady," Lord Springhill said. "Is he not out for a morning ride on that great black beast of his?"

"Surely he has returned by now," Coquette said, every inch of her flesh alive with apprehension and panic. "He will be along shortly, for it is our habit to walk the gardens in the morning," she lied.

"How came you to be wed to the Lord of Roanan?" Lord Springhill asked. "How came you to be wed to such a beast, when it was only three months past your father promised your hand to me?"

"What?" Coquette breathed. "What . . . what are you referring to? My father would never . . ." Coquette's own words caught in her throat. Had not her father sent her to wed a supposed stranger? Still, surely Lord Springhill spoke in lies. Surely.

"Wouldn't he now?" Lord Springhill said. "Wouldn't Antoine de Bellamont promise the hand of his youngest and, I must say, most beautiful daughter to a wealthy and titled lord? Especially if there were something to be gained for himself in it?"

"I do not know what you're talking about," Coquette said, making to move past him. What did he speak of? She knew nothing of such an agreement between her father and any man. Furthermore, certainly her father would not enter into negotiations concerning her hand with such a vile creature as Lord Noah Springhill. Yet again she was reminded—he had sent her to wed the Lord of Roanan, had he not?

Lord Springhill's hand took hold of her arm, staying her.

"Release me," Coquette demanded, her heart hammering with fear. "The Lord of Roanan will—"

"The Lord of Roanan will do nothing, pretty Coquette," Springhill said, pulling Coquette against him.

Coquette struggled, kicking his shin with her

small foot. "Let me go! Let me go! You disgust me!" she cried, pushing herself away from him. Yet before she could fathom it, he had drawn his sword, holding its tip at her stomach.

"I disgust you?" Lord Springhill growled. "You will pay for that remark."

Coquette gasped then screamed as she felt the hot sting of steel at her side. Looking down, she was horrified to see her own blood soaking the fabric of her morning dress. The wound was painful indeed, but her fear dominated her sense of the pain.

She was in danger, in danger of being brutalized or even killed! The knowledge washed over her suddenly and with great force until her soul cried out by venue of her voice.

"Valor!" she cried. "Valor! Help me!"

"Valor?" Lord Springhill chuckled. "Valor will not be coming to your aid, Coquette. And it is sad to see one widowed so young. Yet your first betrothed, the man you were meant to marry—I will see you are taken care of."

"Do not speak to me!" Coquette cried, covering her ears with her hands. "Valor! Come to me, Valor!"

"You will die for this, Springhill!"

Coquette allowed the tears to spill from her eyes, dropping to her knees in grateful thanks at the sound of his voice. "Valor!" she whispered. "Oh, my Valor!"

Looking up, she thought her heart might burst with joyous relief at the sight of him. There he stood, Valor, the damp locks of his chestnut mane falling around his face and neck. He looked tired, winded, as if he'd been battling hard and long. Further there was blood soaking his clothes at his left shoulder. He had been wounded!

"Lionhardt?" Lord Springhill growled.

"Oh, yes," Valor said, drawing his sword as he approached. "Your foolish henchmen could no more vanquish me than they could a wounded pheasant."

"Foolish, indeed," Springhill said, drawing his own sword. "Still, I see the wounded beast before me . . . but wound you was not what their appointed task was, and they will pay with their lives when I have taken yours!"

"They have already paid, Springhill," Valor growled. "And now . . . you will join them!"

Steel met steel as Valor advanced, engaging Springhill. Springhill's counter was brutal and strong, yet Valor's parry was swift and effective. Valor was already winded, fatigued, and Coquette's heart beat madly with fear for his life. Springhill would kill him if he could—she knew it!

Sobbing, she turned and fled for the house, calling for Godfrey as she went. Frightened she was to leave Valor, yet wounded and so obviously spent; she must summon help to him at once! She could hear the blades meeting with brutal force as she ran, but she must find Godfrey, for her heart knew he would be the best to aid.

She reached the back steps of Roanan Manor House, and as she began to climb, Godfrey himself appeared by way of a side door.

"Milady? Did I hear you call?" he asked, frowning as he looked at her.

"Come quickly, Godfrey!" she panted. "Yet arm yourself, for milord is being attacked in the south gardens! Lord Springhill means to . . . he means to—"

"Milady!" Godfrey shouted, his attention suddenly captured by the blood at her side.

"I am well, Godfrey! Please! Valor is tired, wounded, and Springhill is fresh!" she cried.

Drawing a dagger from a sheath in his boot, Godfrey raced down the path from which Coquette had only just come. Turning, she followed him, though his speed far out measured her own. Her side stung with pain, and she could feel the warm blood soaking her dress. Yet Valor was in danger!

Rounding a corner and only a short distance behind Godfrey, she could see Valor battling Springhill in the distance.

"Hurry, Godfrey!" she called through her tears and breathlessness.

Suddenly, Godfrey stopped. Instantly he was still, and Coquette could not fathom it.

"Godfrey!" she cried as she reached him, nearly collapsing in his arms. "Help him!"

"The young Lord of Roanan is not in need," he growled.

"What?" Coquette asked, looking from Godfrey to where Valor stood, his foot pressed hard against Springhill's throat as the villain lay on the ground.

"You had better finish me if you have the courage, Lionhardt!" she heard Springhill shout. "For if you do not, I will yet kill you and take your lady for my—"

Coquette gasped, her hand covering her mouth as she watched Valor drive the blade of his sword through Springhill's chest.

"You will not harm her," Valor panted, "nor me."

"Valor!" Coquette cried, pushing past Godfrey and rushing to Valor. She did not pause to look at the dead villain at her champion's feet, only flung herself against him, weak and sobbing.

Valor withdrew his sword from Springhill's corpse, tossing it to the ground as he endeavored to embrace Coquette. Yet he was weak from battle, lack of rest, and the wound at his shoulder. As Godfrey reached them, Valor sunk to his knees, still labored in his breathing.

"Valor?" Coquette gasped.

"He is winded," Godfrey said.

"Winded?" Coquette asked. "He is far more than winded, Godfrey!" She was angry, furious, that Godfrey did not recognize the seriousness of Valor's condition.

"What is this?" Valor breathed then. "He has wounded you?"

Coquette looked to see his eyes fall to the wound at her side. Still kneeling, he reached out, tearing the cloth of her dress, exposing her side and the wound.

"Godfrey!" he shouted. "Send for the physician! At once!"

"It is only a scratch," Coquette said, knowing the wound at Valor's shoulder was far more severe.

"A scratch?" he shouted.

She gasped again as Valor spit on his hand, wiping at the wound of her side in order to better see the damaged flesh of it.

Godfrey too dropped to his knees to investigate Coquette's wound.

"It is not so deep, milord," Godfrey said.

"It is a frightful wound!" Valor growled, spitting on the wound itself and dabbing at it with the hem of her dress. "You will bring the physician! Make haste!"

"It is not so bad, sire," Coquette told him as she reached down and pulled aside the torn leather and fabric at his shoulder to reveal Valor's own wound. "Not near so severe as this," she added, looking to Godfrey.

"I will ride for the physician at once," Godfrey

said, nodding at Coquette with understanding. Coquette's wound gave her pain, yes, but it was not but a scratch compared with the wound at Valor's shoulder.

Rising to his feet, Valor laid a strong hand on Godfrey's shoulder. "And tell Richins Goliath is wounded. Tell Richins to tend to him when he returns to the stables."

"I will, milord," Godfrey said, placing a hand on Valor's shoulder briefly before turning to leave the gardens.

"Come," Valor said, and Coquette gasped as he unexpectedly lifted her into his arms. "We will see to this as best we can until the physician arrives."

"I am well enough to walk, milord," Coquette reminded him.

"I will say when you are well enough to walk," he growled as he strode toward the house.

Coquette was astounded that for his great fatigue and brutal wound, her weight in his arms seemed effortless enough for him. As he carried her, she looked over his shoulder to the body of Lord Noah Springhill lying motionless among the autumn leaf litter on the ground. He had meant to kill Valor, and she was glad he was dead.

Valor did not even wince as the needle pierced his flesh again and again in the physician's sewing

306

his wound. All he could think of was the danger Coquette had been in, the wound to her beautiful and tender flesh. He had demanded the physician tend Coquette first, for he could think of nothing but her well-being. Even still, after seeing her wound tended, knowing it was not a wound to threaten her life—even still he could not bear the thought of her having been wounded by Springhill's sword.

He trembled with fatigue, fear, and a sickness in his stomach and chest. Though he did not speak of it to Godfrey or the physician, he wondered if he would awaken in the morning to find himself among the angels instead of in the comfortable linens of his bed.

Valor felt he had somehow suffered a far deeper wound than the one at his shoulder. His chest hurt deep within, as if a hot steel blade had been thrust into his bosom. Perhaps it was the weight of killing three men in one day, but he doubted it. More, he thought, it was the wounded beast in him struggling to remain in power, battling to keep his heart and mind eternally encased in stone.

"You need rest, milord," the physician said more to Coquette and Godfrey than to Valor.

"Is she well enough to travel to Bostchelan?" Valor asked.

"Milord?" the physician asked.

"Milady. She is to attend her sister's wedding four days from this," Valor explained.

"She is full well enough to travel," the physician answered.

"I am not going to Bostchelan," Coquette said. "I am not leaving y—I am not leaving Roanan now!"

"Has the body been removed from my gardens?" Valor asked. His own voice sounded foreign to him; his mind seemed to swim in some thick fog.

"The villain's remains have been carried to Roanan, milord," Godfrey said. "The constable saw to it."

"I have fresh water, milord," Victoria said, arriving with a basin of steaming water and several small towels. "We will bathe your face and arms, your chest. You will sleep better for it." She set the basin on the floor next to the chair and plunged a small towel into the water it held.

"I am no infant!" Valor growled. Why did they insist on treating him as if he were ill or fatally wounded? He was merely fatigued from a long night's ride and strenuous battle.

"Your behavior would prove otherwise, milord," Coquette said, taking his face in her hands and forcing him to look up at her from his seat in a chair near the fire.

He nearly moaned aloud, so overcome was he suddenly by her sweet beauty, the bright moisture in her eyes. He was weakened, for there dwelt in him the wounded beast—wounded and weak—

and he had not the strength to summon its full character.

"Bathe him and put him to bed," the physician told Victoria. "I will return on the morrow to be certain no infection has set in the wound."

"Very well," Victoria said, wringing the water from the small cloth in her hand and handing it to Coquette.

Valor moved away when Coquette endeavored to bathe his face with the wet cloth.

"An infant or a man?" she said, her expression daring and determined. "Thank you, Mr. Dithers," Coquette said to the physician as he took his leave. Tenderly, she pressed the cloth to Valor's face.

"You are quite officious this morning, milady," Valor said as he gazed up at her. The warm moisture of the cloth on his skin was refreshing, soothing, and relaxing. He could feel the onset of sleep; his body and mind were fast giving into fatigue.

"Hush, milord," her soft voice whispered. "You must rest."

Working quickly, for she knew he was dangerously tired, Coquette assisted Victoria in the bathing of Valor's face, arms, hand, and torso. Then, with Godfrey's help, for Valor's strength was quickly leaving him, she led him to his bed and watched as he drifted into unconsciousness.

Still, her heart hammered with residual fear, with the knowledge he might have been killed—whether by the highwaymen set on him at Springhill's hand or by Springhill himself. And once she was certain he slept soundly, she buried her face in her hands and bitterly wept.

"He is well, milady," Godfrey said. "You need not fear for him any longer. It is only great fatigue overtaking him now."

"I nearly brought him death," Coquette whispered, her hands trembling with residual anxiety.

"That devil nearly brought him death, milady," Victoria said, "not you."

"But it was because of me . . . because of my father's promise to Lord Springhill . . ."

"Then with your own mouth you have spoken the blame is not yours," Godfrey growled. Instantly he frowned, bowed his head before Coquette, and said, "Forgive me, milady. I spoke—"

"You spoke only the truth, Godfrey," Coquette said. "And . . . and it is only grateful I can be that my father entered Roanan's gardens and stole a rose . . . else what might my fate have been?" And it was true! Had her father not stolen the Roanan rose, had Valor not sought vengeance because of it, would she indeed have found herself married to the demon who now lay dead at the gravedigger's feet? "Still, all of it nearly brought him to his death!" she cried in a whisper.

"But it did not," Victoria said, taking Coquette's face in her soft hands. "There he is, resting in his comfortable bed, breathing, living, and you should do the same."

"I should rest?" Coquette asked. It was true; she was overwhelmed with fatigue of mind.

"Yes, milady," Victoria said. "I will sit with him so you may rest as well."

"I cannot leave him," Coquette whispered, tears streaming over her cheeks. How could ever she leave him again? For the simplest tasks that must be done—even then, how could she ever leave him? "I cannot leave him," she repeated.

"There is no need that you should," Godfrey said then. " 'Tis big enough a bed for all of us."

And it was true. She was his wife! What necessity was there that she should leave him?

Coquette studied Valor's face for a long time. Certainly her eyes were heavy, her mind and body craving sleep. Yet simply to watch him breathe seemed a sudden necessity.

Godfrey and Victoria had left Coquette alone with Valor more than an hour past, and still she could not let her eyes close, could not release the vision of him lying next to her so battered and worn.

"Valor," she whispered, thinking how well the name fit the hero.

He moved, turned from his back to his side, facing her. Coquette could hear him breathing—sensed his breath on the ribbons at the bosom of her dress. So close was he, the warmth of his body warmed her own. He grimaced in his sleep, and she wondered what pained him most—the wound at his shoulder or the wounds in his soul, most of which were there at her own hand.

Her eyes felt dry, her eyelids heavy, and at last she did slumber—slumbered long until something drew her from her deep sleep. So greatly fatigued was she that, at first, Coquette could not raise herself from the depth of her sleep. At her side, near her wound, an odd sensation—pain mingled with a slight tickle—a sudden sense of cold there. Slowly, as she pulled herself to some breath of consciousness, she realized someone was touching her side, the flesh around her wound. Had the physician returned already? Had morning come so quickly?

She opened her eyes and looked down. Valor knelt at her side, his fingers gently caressing the flesh surrounding her wound through a tear in her dress. A dagger lay on the bed beside her, and she realized he had used it to cut into the cloth of her dress and expose the wound.

"So this is how my protection finds you," Valor mumbled.

"Alive is how your protection finds me," she whispered.

Valor looked at her then, his face weathered-looking, weary. Still he needed rest, and she wondered what had disturbed him. "You will go to Bostchelan," he mumbled. "You will go to Inez's wedding."

"I have no wish to go to Inez's wedding," she told him. How desperately she desired to reach out and weave her fingers through his brown mane, to feel the warmth of his face beneath her palm.

"But you do desire to see Elise," he mumbled, "and your father. Your desire is still to your father."

"In a manner," she said, anger welling within her. In truth, she did want to see her father—wanted to see his face when she told him it was Valor he had sent her to marry, wanted to witness his expression when she told him of Lord Springhill's revelation to her and of Valor's vanquishing him.

"For this," he said, lightly touching the wound at her side with his fingertips, "for this I will allow it. For this I will free you to go to your family."

"But I do not wish to—" she began.

He was instantly furious and rose to his feet as he growled, "You will go! You will go to your sister Elise . . . for I have sent her my word I would let you go!"

The beast was roaring. Valor had withdrawn,

it seemed, and the beast was baying at the moon once more.

"You wish to be rid of me?" she asked, unable to look at him, for she did not want to see the loathing that must be in his eyes.

"I wish to hold to my word to your sister," he growled. "I wish to hold to my word before you are sequestered here in anticipation of bearing my heir."

It was a lie, and Valor feared she would know it. He did not wish for her to return to Bostchelan. He did not wish her father to have any blessing of her company, for he did not deserve it. For in addition to all Antoine's evil lies and selfishness was Coquette's endurance of Springhill's—for had not Antoine allowed the monster to enter her presence in the first of it? Still, he knew she longed for her family, loved them without condition. The pain in his chest was forcing him to let her go.

"Then you mean to say," Coquette began, "that when I return you wish to . . . you wish to endeavor to have your heir?"

"I do," he growled.

Another lie, for in the dark of his day, in the deep regions of what had once been his heart and soul, he meant to release her. He had awakened in his bed, his wounded beauty at his side, bearing wounds of his making—wounds of heart, mind, and body—and he knew. He knew the beast was failing and he must release her. He would release her, for he loved her above all else in life—even above life itself. He would send her to Bostchelan for Inez's wedding, and Godfrey would inform her of her freedom when the time was right. She would stay in Bostchelan, and he would allow an annulment of their marriage. But for now, the lie of her return to Roanan afterward and his endeavor toward an heir would serve.

Coquette's eyes narrowed as she studied him. Something was strange in him. The amber of his eyes grew cool and unreadable. Yet to see Elise, to confront her father—perhaps it would serve.

"Then I will go, for I would not have your word held uncertain," she told him.

"You will leave on the morrow," he said. "Godfrey will accompany you in my stead."

"Godfrey is often in your stead, is he not, milord?" she asked.

A reminder of his brutality, cowardice, and unfeeling beast's heart—a reminder of his having sent Godfrey in his stead once before. Valor frowned, the beast in him rearing its vile head.

"He is, for he is my first-man and stands for me in situations of secondary importance," he growled. It was cruel, and he saw the pain in her eyes. Yet the beast was in him, and he must drive her away for her own well-being. He would not saddle her with the burden of such a beast.

He watched as she rose from his bed to take her leave.

"Rest well, milord," she told him, tears filling her eyes. "I must prepare for my journey."

He could not keep his hand from reaching out and catching hold of her arm. She turned to face him, tears already on her cheeks. He winced, hating himself all the more for being the cause of so much of her pain.

The beast was prowling, Coquette knew. Though she could not fathom his true reasons for sending her to Bostchelan, she knew there was more he was not telling her. Perhaps he wished for her to confront her father, to finally see Antoine de Bellamont's bad character proven. Further, she had not missed the pain in his eyes when he had implied their marriage was of such little importance that he had sent Godfrey to stand in his stead. He was lying, and she had begun to realize the beast could not mask his lies any longer. Hope still hung thick in her veins, no matter the facade of the beast.

"Milord?" she said, looking to his hand gripping her arm to stay her.

"Is it not tradition for the lady to bestow a gift, a token, upon her champion?" he asked. She sensed a battle in him, for the frown furrowing his brow was deep and uncertain. "I did battle for you this day, milady," he said. Again she sensed he was struggling for words, fighting for an excuse to give as to his having taken hold of her arm. Her heart swelled, as did her courage. It was time to test the beast—it was time to test Valor.

"Yes," she said, turning to him. "You are quite deserving of a gift, a token, milord." His frown deepened. He was unsettled by her agreeing with him. "What gift do you wish me to bestow upon you? This ribbon?" she asked, pulling the emerald ribbon from its place at the bodice of her dress.

"I-I . . ." he stammered. It was entirely unlike the beast to struggle for words so.

"My virtue perhaps?" she said.

"You mock me," he growled.

"As you mock me," she told him. Still, he remained unsettled as she placed her hands on his chest and gazed up into his eyes. "Yet you did fight the hero's battle today . . . and I am ever thankful and ever in your debt. Therefore," she said, pushing at his chest until he sat on the bed behind him, "therefore a token of my gratitude shall be yours. What token do you beg, milord? What gift of thanks this day?"

"I-I have no thought of what token to beg," he stumbled. Great fatigue was in his eyes. He was tired of battle, mind, body, and soul. The fight was gone from him. Valor had triumphed over the beast in that moment.

"None?" she whispered, leaning nearer to him, letting her face hover just above his.

"Your sweet mouth pressed to mine?" he mumbled. "If I beg a kiss as a token . . . if I beg a kiss, will you grant it?"

Warm delight drizzled through Coquette. Her heart swelled with triumph! The beast was wounded nearly to being vanquished. For a moment only perhaps—but a moment was a moment, and she kissed Valor ever so tenderly. Again she kissed him, allowing the soft kiss between them to linger. She kissed his upper lip, slowly—kissed his lower lip, letting her lips linger a moment before kissing him full on the mouth once more. She felt his arms go around her waist, sensed him rising to his feet as he pulled her against him. Her heart hammered with mad delight, for she knew he had grown impatient with her playful kisses, and in the next moment, his mouth captured her own in passion's flaming exchange. She was mindful of the wound at his shoulder, careful to embrace him and not cause pain. He, however, seemed entirely unaware of any wound, his or hers, as he crushed her body to his, drinking deeply of the moist warmth of her mouth.

For long minutes he held her thus, seeming to savor the feel and taste of their kisses. Suddenly, however, he broke from her, breathless and wholly disheveled and confused in appearance.

"I am worn, Kitty," he mumbled, placing a tight fist to his forehead as he staggered backward to sit on the bed once more. "I . . . I am not myself from it all. I do need rest."

Coquette could not help but smile. Kitty! He had, in consciousness, called her Kitty! "I understand, milord," she said. "I will leave you to your rest." Coquette knew it was best to leave him, to press the beast no further, lest he roar more furiously than ever before. "Rest well, milord," she said. He nodded and lay back on the bed. She left his chamber, closing the door behind her.

Inhaling deeply, she thought of her father—thought of the danger he had placed Valor in at Springhill's hand. Yes, she would go! Though she was loath to do it, though she was loath to leave Valor even for one moment, she would return to Bostchelan and face the truth—the truth of everything that blessedly found her at Roanan—the truth of all that had led her to Valor Lionhardt, her heart's only true necessity.

IN BOSTCHELAN

The landscape was beautiful indeed. Godfrey could smell the sea, though he could not yet see it. So far, the outer edges of Bostchelan boasted rolling hills of green, green grass as far as the eye could see. Even for autumn upon it, the grasses were yet green. He drew the lines of the team to one hand while the other reached into his coat pocket to ensure the documents were still there—documents he would just as soon toss into the sea as deliver. His master had misplaced his reason—sending milady to Bostchelan, somehow believing she preferred her insipid family to he who loved her best of any. Yet he knew his lady would not choose to stay, nor choose to sign the parchments cached in his coat pocket—the documents annulling the marriage of the Lord of Roanan, Valor Lionhardt, to Coquette de Bellamont.

Still, he had promised his master he would present them to milady when the moment was ripe. Very well. He would present them when he must, and milady would refuse. Godfrey assured himself of this, though doubt still pricked a bit at his mind.

320

"Godfrey?" Coquette asked as Godfrey opened the door that she might exit the coach. "Why have you stopped here?" The very sight of Lionhardt Manor caused both sweet and bitter melancholy to rise within her. Once she had loved Lionhardt Manor, for it had been the home of her beloved Valor. Yet still she loathed it, for he had quit it after her father's refusal of her hand. "Why have you brought me to—"

"Coquette! Coquette! My darling sister!" Elise exclaimed as she ran down the front steps of Lionhardt Manor, her arms flung wide in excited greeting. "You have come! He sent you just as he promised! I knew he would!" Elise threw her arms around Coquette's neck, hugging her with a near brutality, an odd sort of desperation. "I knew he would send you to me . . . to us," she breathed.

"Elise," Coquette sighed, smiling at the warm embrace of her sister. "Yes, he sent me," she said.

Elise pulled away, smiling at Coquette. "You look well," she said. "Rosy-cheeked and happy."

"Yes," Coquette said. "But . . . but why are you here? I thought Inez . . . I thought the ceremony would be at the church and the gathering afterward at Father's house."

Elise smiled, somewhat uncertainly, however. "It is what I did not want to tell you in my letters,

321

Coquette," she began. "But this is Father's house now. Lionhardt Manor. He acquired it shortly after you left us . . . shortly after the new ships arrived. It is strange, is it not? Us—living in such a home?"

Coquette felt a deep frown furrowing her brow as she turned and looked to Godfrey. "He sold his ancestral home to my father?" she asked.

Godfrey did not speak at first, but the narrowing of his eyes, the barely discernible nod he offered, answered in place of his voice. In the next moment, Godfrey uttered three words, causing Coquette's innards to tremble with conflicting emotion. "Gifted it, milady."

"Gifted it?" she whispered. "Without payment of any sort? Without . . ." Yet she paused, realizing there had been payment: she had been the payment.

"Who is this, Coquette?" Elise interrupted. "And what are you going on about?"

Having no wish to explain how their father had acquired Lionhardt Manor, having no wish to yet reveal it was Valor who was Lord of Roanan, Coquette answered quickly in order to distract her sister from further questions concerning her father's new estate.

"This is Godfrey, Elise," she said. "Va—the Lord of Roanan's first-man . . . and my friend."

"How pleasing is to meet you, sir," Elise said with a nod and a curtsy in Godfrey's direction.

"The pleasure is mine, miss," Godfrey said with a nod and a stiff bow.

"Coquette!" Inez exclaimed as she descended the stairs, Dominique close at her heels. "Coquette! You have come! How delighted I am that you are come to my wedding!"

Inez embraced Coquette loosely and with haste, all the while studying Godfrey and the coach.

As Dominique then embraced Coquette, Inez said, "How fine your coachman is dressed, Coquette. Blue velvet! And the coach . . . exquisite!"

Coquette glanced to Godfrey and then the coach. She had never before noticed the finery of either. To her, a coach was a conveyance—a means of getting from one place to the other. As for Godfrey, he was Valor's first-man, his friend, and her own. She saw only a strong and good man, not a servant dressed in finery.

"This is Godfrey," Coquette said.

"Is he come then too?" Inez asked, again looking past Coquette to the coach. "Has the Lord of Roanan come to my wedding as well?"

"He is not to attend," Godfrey answered. "Only milady has been sent."

Inez arched one eyebrow, her mouth tightening into a pinched pucker. "Your coachman speaks bold for a servant."

"Godfrey is my friend," Coquette said, "and

the Lord of Roanan's. He has been so kind as to accompany me in milord's absence."

"I must say, Coquette," Inez began, her mouth still pinched and puckered, "I feel I should take great offense at your husband's not attending."

"Was it your wish to see your sister again, Inez? To have her share in your special day?" Elise snapped. "Or would you have preferred her wealthy and titled husband attend, that his grand reputation might flatter you and your remaining guests?"

Coquette looked to Elise, surprised by her sudden burst of irritation and emotion. She watched as Elise frowned and put a hand to her temple. The battle of her two parts, the struggle she had mentioned in her letters, was plain on her countenance.

"Your frequent impertinence is beginning to wear on Dominique and me, Elise," Inez said.

"Yes," Dominique added. "For all your dramatics, one would think you were not happy for Inez and me—for father and his new acquisitions and heightened position in society."

Coquette turned to Godfrey. She wanted Valor—wanted nothing more than to return to Roanan, to see his beloved face, to linger in his company.

"Godfrey," she began. "I must—"

"Please take Coquette's coach and horses to the stables, man," Inez instructed. "We will prepare a place for you in the house."

"Milady?" Godfrey asked.

"Coquette, I thought I might die if you were not to come," Elise whispered, linking her arm through Coquette's.

"Godfrey?" Coquette whispered.

"Milord will be waiting at Roanan when we return, milady," Godfrey told her with a nod.

He understood, and Coquette smiled at him. Godfrey sensed her insecurities of separation from Valor. Yet he sensed Elise's need for her as well. With several days to himself to consider things, perhaps the beast would weaken further. Without Coquette present to vex the beast so often, perhaps Valor's nature would have the chance to dominate.

"Very well," Coquette finally decided. "Is John Billings's stable near here?" she asked.

The sudden light in Elise's eyes burst bright and radiant. "Why, yes!" she said. "Just there in Bostchelan," she said, pointing east. "Billings's Stables. He has done quite well for himself."

"Then would you shelter the coach and horses there, Godfrey? Instead of here?" Coquette asked. "Perhaps Elise would be willing to accompany you there. Would you be so kind, Elise, as to show my friend where Billings's Stables are located and then accompany him back?"

Elise's eyes widened with delight. "Oh, yes, Coquette!" she exclaimed. "I would love to!"

325

"Miss," Godfrey said, pulling the coach door open and offering a hand to Elise. She accepted his hand with a giggle of delight and settled herself into Valor's grand coach.

"Elise!" Inez scolded. "Father would want Coquette's coach at our stables."

"I assure you, Inez," Coquette began, "that my husband would want his coach stabled at Billings's."

Inez's mouth pinched tighter with angered indignation as Dominique's dropped open in astonishment. Coquette saw Godfrey's uncharacteristic grin as he witnessed Elise tauntingly stick out her tongue at Inez and Dominique when he closed the coach door.

Coquette tried to stifle the feelings of pride and triumph rising in her. Yet Inez was so arrogant, so assuming, Dominique so weak-willed and conforming. It vexed her terribly! It was time they had a lesson or two in humanity and humility. Further, Coquette, knowing of Elise's affection for John Billings, had seen the perfect opportunity to set her sister in the kind man's way.

"Thank you, Godfrey," Coquette said as Godfrey lifted her trunk down from the top of the coach, setting it at her feet. "I'm sure someone can help me with the trunk. Please give John Billings my thanks, and tell him I will visit soon."

"Yes, milady," Godfrey said.

Coquette watched the coach pull away, returning Elise's excited wave.

"My, my, my," Inez said once the coach was past the front gates of Lionhardt Manor. "Quite the lady, aren't we."

Coquette inhaled a calming breath, fortifying her patience before turning to face her sister once more. "These days are to be yours, Inez," Coquette said. "Your wedding. It is perhaps one reason my husband chose to remain in Roanan, for he knows you would not want anything or anyone distracting from you on your day." Coquette watched as Inez frowned. She knew her sister was considering on whether to be flattered or offended.

"How would your husband know what I would prefer?" Inez asked. "He does not know me."

"Doesn't he?" Coquette whispered.

"Come, Coquette," Dominique said then. "Wait until you see the surprise we have prepared, in the hope, however small, that you would attend."

Inez's eyes narrowed as she looked at Coquette, but Coquette simply smiled, feigning innocence.

"Elise," Inez grumbled as she followed Dominique and Coquette up the stairs. "The silly girl. She insisted on preparing a room for you just in case you were able to attend the wedding."

"And you will not believe the one she chose," Dominique said, pausing before a great oak door in the upper hallway of Lionhardt Manor.

Dominique pushed the door open to reveal an elegant bedchamber bedecked in red velvet and white linens. It was very similar to Valor's chambers at Roanan Manor House, and it struck her instantly—this room too had once belonged to Valor.

"It was Valor's," Inez said, though Coquette's heart already knew it to be true. "Silly goose that Elise is, she thought you might enjoy the reminiscence of your long-lost love."

"Oh, he was a handsome one, Valor Lionhardt," Dominique sighed. "How difficult it must've been for you, Coquette—abandoning the memory of Valor in order to marry some weathered old Lord of Roanan."

Coquette swallowed the need to burst, the need to reveal who the Lord of Roanan truly was. This was not the time. Let her sisters gloat over her, for she had her love. Perhaps he was not fully revealed yet, but she knew he would be. She knew Valor would be hers entirely—one day.

"The room is beautiful," Coquette said.

"When Father took possession of the house, we did dust in here and clean the linens, for it looked as if it had not been touched in years—since Valor's departure, I suppose," Inez said.

"Thank you," Coquette said. "If you would be so kind as to have someone bring up my trunk, I would like to change from my traveling clothes and perhaps rest for a few moments."

"Certainly," Dominique said. "However, there is much to do, and we would appreciate your help as soon as you are able."

"You may be the grand Lady of Roanan in Roanan, Coquette," Inez added. "But to us, you are simply our sister."

"I would have it no other way," Coquette said, forcing a smile. "However, may I ask . . . is Father at home?"

"Father is in Bostchelan," Inez said. "We received some disturbing news this morning. His good friend, Lord Noah Springhill . . . you remember him, do you not, Coquette?"

"It is well I remember him," Coquette said, anxious perspiration suddenly beading on her forehead. How would she ever forget the man who attempted to murder her husband?

"He has been killed!" Dominique exclaimed. "Run through, so we've heard."

"Indeed," Coquette said.

"Naturally Father is terribly upset," Inez began, "for Lord Springhill was a great collector of antiquities—a wealthy client of Father's."

"Father has gone into Bostchelan to acquire more details of his death," Dominique explained.

"And to post a bidding on his estate—being that Father knows of its worth in antiquities," Inez added.

"Lord Springhill was an animal," Coquette said. "It does Father's character no good to have been in league with such a man." Coquette's hand went to her side, to the healing wound dealt by Lord Springhill himself. Yet she smiled, for it was not the pain of the wound she felt there. Rather it was the exhilarating touch of Valor's fingers and hand. Even still she thrilled at the memory of his tender touch, his concern over her wound.

"What would you know of Lord Springhill?" Inez spat. "He bought many things from Father."

"And Father endeavored to sell many things to him," Coquette said.

"You are greatly changed, Coquette," Inez said, her mouth pinching into an indignant pucker.

"Do you mean in that I no longer turn this cheek and then the other to be slapped?" Coquette said.

"Slapped? Whoever slapped you?" Inez spat.

"Those I allowed to, I suppose," Coquette said then.

For it was true. In her despair over losing Valor, in her desire to remain kindhearted and good, she had allowed herself to be abused by her own father and family—used and taken advantage of. Since leaving Bostchelan and residing at Roanan with Valor, she had learned one could yet be kind and good and still own strength and self-worth.

"It's clear you require rest, Coquette," Inez said, "for you speak in riddles."

"We will have your trunk carried up to you, and then you may rest for a time before you attend to the duties we have for you," Dominique said.

"I will rest until I am well enough rested," Coquette said. "And please, send Godfrey to me as soon as he returns."

"Very well, milady," Inez said, sarcasm heavy in her voice.

"Thank you, Inez—Dominique," Coquette said, smiling.

They left then, in a bustle of annoyance and indignation. Coquette closed her eyes for a moment, inhaled deeply, and fought the urge to run from the room, seek out Godfrey, and beg him to take her back to Valor. Why had she allowed him to send her away? She worried the wound at his shoulder was paining him, worried he would somehow disappear while she was in Bostchelan for her sister's ridiculous wedding. She wanted to see him, to touch him, to know he was near to her. But he was not, and she must endure as best she could, for her own sake as well as Elise's. She sensed Elise was confused and wild with frustration. She must help her one good sister, her kindhearted sister who loved the man who was once her father's stableboy.

In an effort to distract herself, she began to look around the room. Smiling, she noted how similar this room was to Valor's chambers at Roanan. Crimson had ever been Valor's favorite color. She giggled, remembering how once, long ago, Valor had told her he wished she could wed him wearing a crimson wedding dress instead of white. "You draped in crimson, Kitty—it would be my utter undoing," he had said one cool winter's day long ago.

Moving to the wardrobe, Coquette opened it, gasping when she saw the clothing hanging within, recognized the blue velvet coat Valor had worn the day he'd come to ask her father for her hand. There were several sets of boots lining the wardrobe floor, other coats, shirts, and trousers hung within as well. Had he taken nothing when he'd abandoned Lionhardt Manor?

Suddenly overcome, she brushed the tears from her cheeks as she reached out and ran a hand over one sleeve of the blue velvet coat. What pain they had both known that day. And yet she loved the feel of the velvet on her palm, reveled in the memories of his arms through the very sleeves of it, the strength of them holding her close against the power of his body, his kiss—warm, delicious, loving.

How long she spent in sentimental exploration of Valor's discarded things, she knew not. Lost in her reveries, Coquette had no concept of time until Elise fairly burst in upon her.

"Oh, Coquette!" her sister exclaimed. "He grows more handsome each time I see him!"

"John Billings?" Coquette asked, smiling.

"Yes! Yes! Yes!" Elise said. "And Valor has sent him a note!"

"What?" Coquette gasped, so stunned by Elise's words she stumbled backward.

"Hush, Coquette," Elise warned, an index finger placed to her lips. Quickly she turned and closed the door to the chamber, bolting it behind her. Then turning back to Coquette and taking hold of her shoulders, she whispered, "I know it is Valor who is the Lord of Roanan, Coquette!"

"What?" Coquette breathed again in disbelief. How was it possible Elise knew of Valor?

"Oh, I am so happy for you! To belong to your true love at last!" Elise whispered with excitement. "Yet it is only several days I have known. I came upon the revelation by accident. Valor's signature . . . it appeared on a set of papers delivered to Father the week before last. I know everything, Coquette. Well, nearly everything," Elise said. "I know more than Father, for he is too lost in the joy of his riches to have even read the papers delivered to him. He yet does not know Valor is Lord of Roanan. And I must ask, though I fear you may be vexed with me in doing so, yet I must know. When did you realize Valor was he—the man you had been sent to marry?"

Coquette's mind reeled and spun with confusion. How could it be her sister knew of the Lord of Roanan's true identity and her father and other sisters did not? What papers were delivered?

"I-I did not know until we had been married—

until our wedding night," Coquette stammered. "It was, in fact, Godfrey who stood in Valor's place—as proxy in his stead at our wedding. And then . . . then at midnight . . . the Lord of Roanan appeared . . . and he was revealed to be Valor."

"Proxy?" Elise asked. "And why did not Valor reveal himself to Father? Why even now does he not reveal?"

Coquette shook her head. "This is . . . this is too overwhelming, Elise. I must tell you all of it, lest you will understand nothing."

"Then tell me, beloved sister, she only who knows me," Elise said, tugging at Coquette's hand until she sat down next to her on the bed. "How came this all to be?"

"I will tell you," Coquette said. "But I have one question first."

"Anything," Elise said.

"What papers were delivered to Father?" Coquette asked. "What papers were delivered that Valor had signed?"

Elise inhaled deeply. "I knew you knew nothing of it," she said. "I knew you did not!"

"Nothing of what?" The hair on the back of Coquette's neck tingled. She felt overly warm, feverish. Something of great importance was about to be revealed by her sister.

"The three new ships, all the cargo they carried, and this house," Elise whispered, "all were given to Father by the Lord of Roanan. The Lord of

Roanan, who signed his name in truth, Lord Valor Lionhardt, on the papers delivered here the week before this."

"What?" Coquette gasped.

"It is there! All of it, Coquette!" Elise exclaimed in a whisper. "I was going to write to you of it all, but . . . but I didn't know what to do. So I wrote to Valor, asked him to allow you to come to Inez's wedding. But not for Inez's sake . . . for mine! For I long for escape, and I wanted to see you, see your joy in finally being with your Valor."

"What was in the parchments, Elise?" Coquette asked. "Tell me—all of it."

Elise inhaled a deep breath and said, "Father is a coward, Coquette. Though I always suspected it, I am full assured now that he is a coward. The papers, though they do not state it, still they prove it—Father is the most cowardice of men."

"This I do know, Elise," Coquette whispered. "But pray, tell me what the papers reveal."

"They are worded by Valor's solicitor, no doubt, and at times are hard to comprehend. Yet from them—upon their meeting in Roanan, Father trespassed upon Valor's land, and the papers speak of his taking something . . . I assume this refers to the stolen rose. You remember the rose, yes?"

"Yes," Coquette said, the fragrance of Roanan

Manor's lavender roses suddenly fresh upon her senses.

"The papers state that rather than subject Father to the penalties of Roanan law—being imprisonment or the cutting off of one hand— rather than subjecting Father to the law, Valor, as Lord of Roanan, freed him and gave him a purse with one hundred seventy gold pieces, three ships laden with cargo, and this house in return for . . . in return for . . ."

"In return for me," Coquette finished.

"Yes," Elise admitted. "Yet I was curious. Three new ships? What of the old ones? Therefore, I myself wrote to Captain Calvert, Father's friend in Treehill, and he told me Father's original three ships were pirated, lost one week before he returned to us, claiming he had known success and sending you off to the Lord of Roanan to save his life," Elise said. "I am certain Valor never meant to kill Father, Coquette. Well, remembering Valor as I do . . . he may have threatened to kill him, but he would never have done it."

"All this he paid to a coward in order to . . . in order to . . ."

"In order to have you at last, Coquette," Elise said, smiling. "Have you ever heard such a romantic tale? To capture Father at his worst, play to his low character, with the intent of owning you? It is the stuff of fairy tales!"

"Fairy tales indeed," Coquette whispered, "for

it was much changed I found Valor to be when I first arrived. Cold, harsh, seemingly void of good emotion."

"But he is Valor still, is he not?" Elise asked.

"Deep within, yes. Deep inside him I know he is still my Valor. The beast he had become is weakening. Even his sending me here is proof of it," Coquette said, more to herself than to her sister.

"He is Valor," Elise said with such assurance Coquette was startled. "For it was Valor who sent a note to John Billings by way of your friend Godfrey! Only just now, Valor has sent John Billings a note, offering his support that we may elope!"

"What?" Coquette gasped, her heart pounding with excitement. Valor? The dark Lord of Roanan encouraging romance, elopement? "What do you mean, Elise? Do you mean to tell me that Valor—"

"Godfrey will run me through if he discovers I have told you, but how could I resist? My own joy fulfilled, Valor only further proving himself to be the man you know him to truly be?" Elise asked.

Coquette fairly leapt to her feet. "I must go, Elise," she said. "I cannot tarry here! My heart, body, and mind were loath to leave Valor, and with each moment I am apart from him I grow despairing somehow."

"I understand more than you know, Coquette," Elise said, rising to her own feet. "John has left it to me as to whether we should elope and when. I have chosen this very day. I will not waste another moment, nor risk anything interfering with my happiness as something did with yours when Father refused Valor."

"Good," Coquette said, smiling. "Go to John at once! Elope and be happy! I promise you, you will know your joy in choosing your love over all this."

Elise smiled. "Valor is Valor, Coquette. If he pretends to be this beast Lord of Roanan, you and I both know it is pretense indeed. Though I think there is one thing you should do before you leave."

"What?" Coquette asked. She was loath to linger one moment longer. Her intention was to summon Godfrey and return to Roanan as quickly as possible.

"Confront Father," Elise said. "For your sake, yes—but most of all for Valor's. Father should not live in ignorant bliss, having lied the way he has. I know he is distraught over the loss of his friend, Lord Springhill, but—"

"Valor has killed Lord Springhill," Coquette said.

Elise's eyes widened. "What? What do you know of Lord Springhill?"

"I know that Father's cowardice is far-reaching," she said. "Valor and I . . . we attended a dinner party this week last, given by a dear friend of Valor's. Springhill was there, and he frightened me."

"Frightened you? Why?" Elise asked.

"He once made advances toward me, Elise," Coquette explained. "Once, over a year ago, when he was here to deal with Father."

"Coquette!" Elise gasped, her hands covering her mouth.

"But there is more," Coquette told her. She hurried her story, for she suddenly cared for nothing, save it were to return to Valor. "He hired highwaymen to murder Valor."

"What?" Elise exclaimed.

"But they failed, of course," Coquette continued, "and Springhill rode to Roanan Manor, told me of Father's having promised my hand in marriage to him mere months ago. Lord Springhill was angry at Father for sending me to Roanan, and he meant to have Valor killed and wed me himself."

"Go on," Elise whispered when Coquette paused.

"Valor . . . Valor is strong, Elise," she continued, "I swear I do not think anything or anyone could vanquish him. He fought the highwaymen, survived, and rode to Roanan Manor to find me in danger from Lord Springhill. When Lord Springhill tried to kill Valor, Valor ran him through. It was Valor who killed Lord Springhill."

"Your hero indeed," Elise said. "As ever, it would seem."

"Yes," Coquette said. "And I cannot linger here. Yet I feel you are right. For Valor's sake, I should confront Father. He should know that I know of his . . . of his . . ."

"Of his cowardice treachery," Elise finished.

There was knock on the door.

"Who is it?" Elise called.

"It is Godfrey, milady," came Godfrey's answer.

Coquette went to the door at once, drawing the bolt and opening the door.

"The servants have brought your trunk, milady," Godfrey said.

"Godfrey," Coquette began, "I do not wish to upset you or to further put you to inconvenience, but . . . but . . ."

"Milady?" Godfrey asked.

"But I wish to return to Val—to Roanan Manor at once," Coquette said.

"At once, milady?" Godfrey asked, the hint of a smile spread across his face.

"At once," Coquette confirmed. "But after I have spoken with my father."

"Your father is returned, milady," Godfrey said. "I saw him downstairs only moments ago."

"You will take my trunk? Fetch the coach?" Coquette asked.

"I will, milady," Godfrey answered, the full dazzle of a pleased smile bright upon his face.

Coquette's eyes widened, for she had never seen Godfrey smile thus before. Coquette paused a moment. "In fact, leave the trunk, Godfrey," she said, "for I brought little and none of it important. I mean that you and I will walk to Billings's together when I have finished with my father."

"Yes, milady," Godfrey said, still smiling.

"You will visit?" Coquette asked, turning to Elise. "As soon as you and Billings are able?"

"Yes!" Elise said, embracing Coquette.

"Coquette! My darling!"

At the sound of her father's voice, Coquette released Elise and turned to face him. Inez and Dominique accompanied him and stood studying her with a thick air of superiority.

"Father," Coquette greeted as he embraced her.

"You have come for Inez and Henry's wedding? How wonderful! You look well enough," Antoine said.

"I am quite well," Coquette said.

"I am glad to hear it," Antoine said. "And what do you think of our new home? Does it not inspire you? Lionhardt Manor is ours."

"Have you written Valor your thanks for gifting it to you?" Coquette asked. "For he has not told me of your doing so."

341

"What?" Antoine said. "What do you mean, Coquette?"

"How could Father have written to Valor, Coquette?" Inez snapped. "No one knows where he is. And what do you speak of gifts for? Father bought Lionhardt Manor."

"Valor gave it to him, Inez," Coquette said. "This Father would know, had he taken the time to read the parchments Valor ordered delivered week before last."

"What parchments?" Antoine asked, frowning.

"The parchments Valor Lionhardt sent to you, Father," Elise said. "The papers with his signature . . . the ones officially deeding you this estate, the three new ships and cargo, and the gold pieces Valor paid to you for Coquette's hand."

"Valor Lionhardt?" Antoine asked. " 'Tis the Lord of Roanan who barters with me . . . the Lord of Roanan who threatened my life and who, I have only just discovered in Bostchelan this very morning, killed my dear friend Lord Springhill."

Coquette glared at her father, hurt, loathing, love, and an odd sympathy battling within her. "I arrived at Roanan Manor, Father—supposedly in saving your life—to find Valor Lionhardt is indeed the Lord of Roanan. I married him, became Lady Lionhardt, Lady of Roanan. Though you would not consent to our marriage three years past, you endeavored to marry me to a stranger who had allegedly threatened your life—

this after having promised my hand previously to a degenerate the likes of Lord Springhill!" Coquette brushed tears from her cheeks as she continued, "Lord Springhill, who endeavored to have my husband murdered by highwaymen and then, after wounding me with his sword, endeavored to kill Valor himself! But Valor Lionhardt was not vanquished at your loathsome friend's hand, Father. Lord Springhill *was* killed . . . run through by Valor's sword in defense of his life and mine!"

"You speak nonsense, Coquette!" Antoine exclaimed.

"Valor?" Inez breathed. "Valor is the Lord of Roanan? It was Valor who meant to kill Father?"

"Valor did not mean to kill Father. Did he, Father?" Coquette answered.

"Father?" Dominique asked. "You knew you sent Coquette to Valor?"

"Milady," Godfrey said. "May I?"

Coquette frowned. Godfrey wished to speak? She thought it odd. "Of course," she said.

"You remember me, do you not, merchant?" Godfrey asked.

"I do," Antoine said, swallowing hard.

"Then ask your father, milady," Godfrey instructed. "Ask you father, here in my presence . . . ask him if milord threatened his life. But first, I will give the merchant this: the Lord of Roanan remained ever in shadow when speaking to him. Your father did not know it was Valor Lionhardt with whom he bartered."

Coquette turned to her father and could see his fear as he looked at Godfrey. She realized then, Godfrey knew! Godfrey had always known the truth.

"Did Valor threaten to kill you, Father?" Coquette asked. "Before he gave you your new ships, this house, the gold in exchange for me—did he promise he would kill you?"

"He . . . he said the law gave him the right to kill me for trespassing," Antoine stammered.

"But did he say it? Did he promise he would kill you?" Coquette repeated.

"He said he would cut off one of my hands, Coquette! And how . . . how could I have continued, provided for my lovely daughters, with such a deformity? How can you expect me to have—"

"He did not tell you he would kill you, did he, Father?" Coquette interrupted.

"Would it have been any worse to die than to have lost everything?" Antoine asked.

Coquette swallowed, brushing a tear from her cheek. "Three years past, you refused Valor my hand, Father. You deemed him unworthy, at risk of becoming his own father's image. You broke my heart for your own purposes. Yet at the mere threat of physical harm to yourself, a threat that would never have seen fruition, at the temptation of wealth, you promised me to a stranger—a stranger you thought to be brutal and of cruel intention. Further, before this and for less gain, you promised my hand to a loathsome monster the like of Lord Springhill. Why? How could you, Father? How could you send me into such promised ruination?"

Coquette watched as her father's guilty frown disappeared. His face softened and then hardened into determination as he said, "I am a merchant, Coquette, and as a merchant, I know this: everything has value for gain. Especially a beautiful woman . . . even a daughter."

Coquette nodded. She felt sickened, hurt, yet somehow liberated. Valor! Valor had lied to her, yes. But for her own sake, not his! As much as he loathed her father, he did not want her in pain at knowing she meant so little to the man who had raised her. She suspected that, before that very moment, even her father—even Antoine de Bellamont—had not realized how little he valued his daughters. Anger at her father was suddenly gone from her soul, for she was free—free to love Valor, to be his, to peel away the flesh of the beast and belong to him!

"Elise will be marrying John Billings—a man whose worth and gifts were recognized by my husband, who encouraged him, and wisely, to quit you in favor of his own pursuits. You will not interfere, Father." Coquette looked to Inez and

Dominique. "I bid you farewell, sisters, though I pity you your lot in life." Turning to Elise, she smiled and embraced her sister. "Come at once to Roanan, Elise. You and John . . . as soon as you are able."

"We will," Elise said, brushing tears from her cheeks. Coquette could see the joy of liberation and love bright in her sister's eyes, and it warmed her.

"You cannot leave with such . . . with such accusations on your lips, Coquette," Antoine said suddenly. "You are my daughter!"

"Pardon me, milady," Godfrey said, stepping from behind Coquette. "But I believe milord would have me, once more, act in his stead."

Coquette gasped and Inez and Dominique screamed as the brutal force of Godfrey's fist met with her father's jaw, knocking him to the floor.

"You are a loathsome creature, merchant," Godfrey growled. "And I daresay, you are fortunate the Lord of Roanan was not near to hear you speak of your daughter, his lady, as if she were cargo on one of your insipid ships! His sword has vanquished one villain—rather, three villains—already in a week's time. Be thankful he was not here to vanquish another."

Coquette stood staring at Godfrey. He had acted in Valor's stay once more—this she knew with assurance.

"Milady," Godfrey said, taking hold of her arm

none too gently, "milord awaits your return."

At the mere thought of Valor, Coquette could not help but smile. Valor! Yes! She would race to him as fast as Godfrey, the horses, and coach could return her to Roanan.

"Goodbye, Father," she said. "I will gather a few cherished trinkets of Mother's and quit you. For all your ill character, yet I wish you whatever happiness you may find."

As Godfrey escorted her toward the stairs, Coquette looked back, calling, "As soon as you are able, Elise! As soon as you are able."

"Yes! Yes!" Elise called. "I will gather a few things and follow shortly. Tell John I will follow shortly."

Coquette nodded, sighing with delight. Elise too was free!

"Why did he keep the truth from me, Godfrey?" Coquette asked as she walked beside Godfrey, hastening to Billings's Stables. "Why did he not tell me of the truly despicable nature of my father's character? Why did he not tell me the truth—that he did not threaten to kill my father?"

"Man and beast battle within him, milady," Godfrey said. "The beast holds to bitterness, resentment, distrust, while the man . . ." he said, stopping to remove a set of parchments from his coat pocket and offer it to Coquette.

Coquette paused, frowning with puzzlement. She took the parchments Godfrey offered.

"While the man holds desperately to love," Godfrey said.

"What is this?" Coquette asked, her heart suddenly hammering with angst in her bosom.

"Parchments of Annulment," Godfrey answered. "His lordship instructed me to give them to you. He means to give you your freedom, milady."

"But I have only just won my freedom, Godfrey," Coquette said. "To be with Valor . . . 'tis heaven. Why would anyone want to be free of heaven?"

"It *is* a consideration of fools indeed," Godfrey said.

Coquette looked at the parchments in her hand. "The man holds to love," she said. "Are . . . are you certain, Godfrey?" she asked. She looked up to see him standing before her, smiling with triumph.

"As certain as your own heart, milady," he said.

Coquette smiled. Her heart swelled with rapture in the sudden inward confirmation that Valor loved her—had always loved her.

She looked to Bostchelan, to Billings's Stables and the blacksmith working at the fiery forge within. Lifting her skirts, she set out, running toward the stables. Quickly she tossed the parchments into the blacksmith's fire, watching with resplendent joy as they burned.

348

"Take me to Roanan Manor, Godfrey," she said. "Please, Godfrey—take me home."

Godfrey smiled. "At once, milady," he said. "At once."

TO BID THE BEAST FAREWELL

As the coach approached Roanan Manor, the warm pink of the sun's rise broke over the mountains to the east. Coquette's heart beat wildly with anticipation. Mere minutes! Mere moments and he would be near to her once more—Valor! It was hardly she could endure the wait to see him again, witness his handsome face, feel the soft nut-brown of his hair between her fingers.

Hurry, Godfrey! she thought. *Hurry me to my love!*

Richins was awake, grooming a large bay outside the stables as Godfrey pulled the coach to a halt.

"Milady?" Richins said as Coquette fairly fled from the coach.

"Good morning, Richins. William," Coquette greeted. She was frantic, desperate with mad desire, to see Valor.

"Is Valor about?" she asked. "Has he left the house or does he still rest?"

"He does not rest," Richins said. "The truth of it is, he has not rested since you left for Bostchelan yesterday morning, milady."

"What?" Coquette asked.

"He is mad with anxiety," Victoria said as she

approached from the direction of the house. She wore a worried expression unlike any Coquette had ever seen on her face. "Utterly distraught with despair and pain!" she added. "I . . . I have been fearful for his life. Milady, I fear he may simply expire from grief and hurt. When I saw the coach . . . oh, how I hoped you were here!"

"Surely," Coquette began, astonished at the revelations of Richins and Victoria, "surely he knew I would shortly return. After all, it was he who sent me."

"There is a change come over him, milady," Victoria said, taking Coquette's hands in her own. "H-he is weak. Weak of mind, body, and heart. He is poorly, milady, and we are all fearful for his well-being."

"Where is he?" Coquette asked, her heart hammering with fear and trepidation. Had the wound inflicted at his shoulder become infected? "Have you summoned the physician? His shoulder . . . has the wound at his shoulder—"

"It is not the wound at his shoulder that threatens him, milady," Godfrey said.

Coquette looked to him, bewildered.

"Rather he thinks you will not return. It is the wound to his heart that finds him ill and in danger."

"But surely he knew I would not accept the parchments," Coquette whispered.

"The beast was brutal, milady," Godfrey said.

"What beauty would choose such a beast?" Victoria whispered.

Coquette frowned a moment longer. However, her heart swelled once more, and her inward assurance Valor loved her stoked her courage.

Turning to Victoria, she asked, "Where is he?"

"At the garden pond," Victoria answered.

Coquette did not pause to thank those standing near. Rather, lifting her skirts, she made for the pond with great haste. Surely Valor did not believe she would accept the annulment parchments! Had the beast been conquered in the space of one day? Further, could it be Valor loved her with such a love as she loved him? She knew he did! As her heart hammered, her feet racing to carry her to the pond, Coquette knew—the beast had gone. The beast had abandoned Valor! And what then? After battling the most grueling conflict of his life, had Valor triumphed, only to think Coquette had abandoned him? She would not let him think it one moment longer!

Valor raised a weak hand to rub at his weary eyes. How they burned with fatigue and the dryness of too many spent tears, too much worry, too much pain. Why had he let her go, after all he had endured to own her? Still, he knew his reason— unfailing love, selfless love—the truest form of love.

Valor had watched the coach leave Roanan

Manor—watched it carry Coquette away—and he had not found one moment of rest or respite since. The moment the coach had passed the gates of Roanan Manor on its way to Bostchelan, the contents of Valor's stomach had left his body, emptied onto the floor. Fever had overtaken him and further retching until, after an hour of such miserable disease of mind and body, Valor had managed to make his way to the garden pond. There he had stayed—all through the day and into the night—his mind and body wracked with the pain and agony of loss and heartache and the battling of the beast lingering in him.

Victoria had come to him often, bringing drink and nourishment, begging him to return to the house. "You'll catch your death, milord," she had said.

And Valor cared not if he did catch it, for to lose Coquette—it seemed death became preferable to life.

The lurking beast in him argued, *Let the siren go! She has brought you nothing but further pain and agony!* But Valor had silenced the beast, weary and sickened of its presence in his mind and heart. He wanted nothing save Coquette—no other companion, no comfort—for all seemed senseless without her.

He would drop to the depths of despair and then rise on the fiery wings of anger at the thought of her there in Bostchelan—happy in the company of her insipid father and selfish sisters. How little they deserved her strong and good spirit, her loving heart. Yet Valor knew he deserved it less, and it haunted him, for the chance had been given him—the chance to win her, to own her—and he had allowed the beast to devastate such a chance.

Torn with pain, anger, and despair, Valor had been unable to rest—unwilling and unwanting to rest. He wanted nothing, save it were to see her face again, feel her tender cheek beneath his palm, taste the sweetness of her kiss. But she had gone. He had released her, and he must determine a venue of survival—a different venue than that of the beast who had overtaken him before. Yet what venue was left to him—death? It seemed the only path in the dark of the night, for how did a man twice lose such a dream as Coquette and survive?

Valor watched the fish swimming in the pond—blind to their soothing beauty though his tired eyes were wide enough open. He would watch the fish—linger forever at the pond—for what other course was left him?

"Milord?"

The voice did not startle him. It was only Victoria come to beg him to return to the house once more. Would she not leave him to his misery, his defeat, his despair?

"Milord? Are you well?"

Valor frowned. His mind, his sanity was leaving him, surely—for he fancied it was not Victoria's

354

voice speaking from behind him. Even it sounded as Coquette's, and he knew madness was at last upon him.

"I am well," he mumbled, "as I have assured you each time you have inquired of me."

"Still, you look worn, milord—tired—and I feel you must take to your bed and rest, else you will not—"

Valor stood—turned. As in a dream, there she stood—Coquette—his beautiful Kitty! He was certain in that moment his heart had failed him, stopped beating at last.

"Coquette?" he asked.

Oh, how worn he looked, how tired and defeated in that first moment. His appearance caused Coquette's hands to tremble, and she wanted nothing save it were to melt into his arms, confess her love, beg for his kiss.

"Are you . . . are you well, milord?" she asked. "For I fear you are not."

"Why are you here?" he asked, and she fancied there was moisture welling in his tired-looking eyes.

"I live here, milord. This is my home," she told him. "Have you so soon forgotten?" Was he truly so unwell?

"Why are you here?" he asked again. "Have you come back to bid the beast farewell?"

Coquette could see the sudden trembling that

overtook him, the fear in his eyes, and she knew—the beast was gone. In its place there was only Valor. Yet he feared she had only returned to bid him goodbye. He did not yet believe she loved him.

"I have," she said, moving toward him. "And I see he is no more. He is gone . . . but I am here. This is my home. *You* are my home."

Still he frowned, doubted, trembled.

She walked to him, stopping to stand directly before him. Looking up into his tortured expression, into his tired eyes, she reached forward, taking his hands in hers.

"He has hurt you, caused you pain," Valor whispered. "He has ill-treated you, lied to you, threatened you, and endeavored to thrust you away from me. He has—"

"Ssshhh," she whispered, reaching up to smooth the frown of his brow. "He is no more. The past is beyond us. We will not linger on it any longer."

She watched as his frown deepened, his body still trembling as he looked down at her. She could see the love he held for her manifest in the warm amber of his eyes.

"I must atone," he said. "You cannot simply say it is passed. Not with such scars carried as proof of it."

"Scars are but evidence of life," Coquette said, "evidence of choices to be learned from . . . evidence of wounds, wounds inflicted of mistakes, wounds we choose to allow the healing of. We likewise choose to see them, that we may not make the same mistakes again."

"For such wounds to heal, forgiveness is required," he said. "How can you forgive such wounds as I have—"

"Sshhh," she whispered again. She was silent for a moment, looking away from him as tears traveled down her cheeks. "Can *you* forgive *me?*" she asked in a whisper.

"What is there you could ask forgiveness for?" he asked.

"Can you forgive me for failing three years past?" she said. "For not taking your hand the moment my father refused you? Can you forgive me for not abandoning him for you?"

"But with your own words you prove there is nothing I can hope to forgive," he said. She looked to him, bewildered as he continued, "For I had not drunk of Victoria's tonic last you and I shared kisses before the fire in my chamber. Liar that I was . . . I was fully awake when you told me of leaving your father's home after he had refused my proposal. I was fully aware when you told me you sought me at Lionhardt Manor only to find it was I who had abandoned."

"You were . . . you were aware?" she asked. Suddenly her heart beat even more rapidly, with even more excitement. What delicious kisses they had shared that night! What blessed, loving endearments he had spoken when last he had administered the whispered kiss to her warm and wanting mouth!

"I was," he admitted. "Do you see what a liar your beast was?"

Coquette sighed, smiling up at him. "No more will we speak of the past, whether of your beast's ill deeds or of my own weakness. I love you, Valor! It is ever I have loved you and ever that I will."

She heard him draw a labored breath—gasped as he suddenly fell to one knee before her, clutching at his chest with one hand as if experiencing intense pain.

"Valor!" she cried.

Taking his face in her hands, she turned his face upward that she may see he still breathed, still lived.

She was breathless then, robbed of her every sense save awe, as she saw her true Valor before her—handsome and strong. A dazzling and very familiar smile spread across his face as he looked up at her. Valor Lionhardt had returned! Suddenly she felt shy, uncertain of herself. Instantly reminded of his uncanny attractiveness, his power and strength, Coquette began to tremble.

Still smiling at her, he rose to his feet, his piercing gaze never leaving hers.

"The past is beyond us," he said. "And I am Valor Lionhardt—who loves you more than life itself. I love you, my Kitty," he said.

Coquette struggled to breathe as his strong hands crushed the sleeves of her dress at the shoulders in powerful fists.

"Ever I have loved you . . . only you," he said.

Coquette's mouth began to water for want of his—for want of Valor's mouth to hers.

"And it is passed," he said, his hands moving to her waist as he pulled her nearer. "All of it . . . your father, mine. Lies, deception, hurt, pain—the beast and cause of it all. It is gone from us both, I can feel it."

"You will keep me then?" Coquette asked, her eyes transfixed on his smile, his mouth. "Will you keep me, Valor?"

"Keep you?" he breathed, taking her face in his hands. "Oh, I will most certainly keep you, Kitty. I will keep you here, at Roanan. I will keep you in my eyes as ever I have—as the lion standing sentinel over my bed has kept the portrait of you painted in his."

"What?" Coquette breathed, wanting only to kiss him. Still, the meaning of his words bewildered her.

He chuckled, delighted by her breathlessness.

"It is true," Valor said. "The lion in my chamber, the one you have seen looking down on you from my bed—you cannot see it from so far, but you are there . . . painted in his eyes as ever you have been from the day the artist put you there— replicating the miniature of you I have kept these years. Now I will keep your person as well."

"Valor," Coquette breathed, tears streaming down her face.

"Oh, how I will keep you, Kitty," he began again. "Keep you in my heart and in my eyes and in my arms." His smile changed to that of delighted mischief—the mischievous smile of Valor Lionhardt Coquette so long loved, so long missed until that moment when it was bestowed upon her again as he continued, "And I will keep you in my bed. Bedchambers of separation are for strangers, not lovers who are husband and wife."

"Keep me then, my Valor," Coquette whispered. "Keep me *ever* near to you! Never from you. Never again!"

Valor pulled her into his arms, crushing her against him. She endeavored to return his embrace with all the strength in her. Still, she desired to hold him tighter, breathe more deeply of the scent of his shirt and flesh.

"Kiss me, Kitty," he whispered. "Kiss me, and I will whisper to your mouth such promises of love and keeping as to find you helpless against any of my own amorous intentions."

"Oh, Valor! How I love you!" Coquette breathed as Valor's lips lightly touched her own.

"I love you," Valor whispered against her mouth. And the whispered kiss was spent, for their mouths melded—drenched in passion—filled with promise.

Beast: [beest]

-noun

A coarse, cruel, heartless, or otherwise beastlike
　　being

Thief: [theef]

-noun

One who steals, especially in secret

Merchant: [**Mer**-ch*uh* nt]

-noun

One who purchases and sells commodities for
　　profit

Valor: [**val**-er]

-noun

Heroic courage; bravery, especially in battle

Coquette: [koh-**ket**]

-noun

Enchantress

AUTHOR'S NOTE
(aka, Author's Ramblings Concerning Her
Personal Feelings for the Story)

Yes, truly one of my favorite fairy tales has always
been Beauty and the Beast. To me, the tale of
Beauty's beast whispers of so many aspects I love
about romance, as well as of life in general—the
idea that patience and love see beyond the battered
and broken, that the power of love brings change,
compassion, sympathy, courage, and triumph. It's
a wonderful lesson, a beautiful romance, and I
always wanted to write my own version of it.

And then there's the fact that, to my way of
thinking, Beauty and the Beast represents the
ultimate example of the "bad-boy syndrome"
so many of us girls secretly long for and utterly
understand . . .

I once had a conversation with a young man
of nineteen. This young man (we'll call him
Bob) explained to me that he had been what
he called a "late-bloomer." A bit chubby and
somewhat shy in his early teens, Bob had been
unable to capture the attention of any of the
girls he had experienced crushes on in those
early years. By the time he was nineteen, he had
certainly bloomed, as he put it, but he still didn't
understand the bad-boy syndrome.

He asked me, "Why do girls always want the bad boys? Why don't they see us good guys as attractive too?"

Well, *we* all know the answer to that question. It's the "Beauty and the Beast Principle," as I like to call it—the idea that the gorgeous, brooding, troubled bad boy will fall in love with one of us so completely that his entire life alters. In loving us so desperately, the Beast transforms into Prince Charming! Oh, certainly we girls want enough of the Beast to remain that it keeps things interesting, keeps our Prince Charming masculine, mischievous, and "perfectly imperfect." Yet to imagine a man could love us so thoroughly, so obsessively, that he entirely gives his heart over, now *that's* why so many of us are drawn to the bad boys in our youth. At least that's my theory.

I tried to explain my theory to Bob, but he just couldn't quite grasp it. And so he gave up, eventually telling my daughter (at the time she was fourteen), "Sandy, you are going to be a goddess! Total eye-candy! But do me a favor— don't overlook the plain guys and the good guys. When you're, like, eighteen and a goddess . . . give those guys a chance." He certainly had a point but had simultaneously given up on trying to understand my "Beauty and the Beast Principle." So off Bob went—off into life with his unanswered question.

Well, shortly after Bob left on his grand post–high school adventures, I watched the movie *A Walk to Remember*, based on the book by Nicholas Sparks. Voilà!

"That's it!" I told my husband. "That's what I was trying to explain to Bob!"

That story is such the perfect example of my own "Beauty and the Beast Principle"—good girl falls for bad boy and the bad boy falls so in love with the good girl so he completely alters his entire way of life—that it boggled my mind for a moment! As soon as the opportunity presented itself, I relayed my findings to Bob. I'm not certain Bob ever really grasped the concept, but it further solidified my own feelings on the matter.

Whether Bob ever really got it, I know *you* do. And in understanding my theory, you'll further understand why I love the story of Valor and Coquette—which began to imprint itself indelibly in my brain this past summer. A handsome hero, tormented, bitter, angry—for all appearances a beast—acquires a sweet, beautiful "good girl."

The story was blending and ripening in my mind one day when my friend Amanda was over for a visit. Of the many stories playing out in my mind, Amanda was inquiring as to which one I would finish next.

"Well," I began, "I'm a little nervous about it."

"Why?" she asked.

"Because . . . I'm thinking of doing another fairy tale retelling," I confessed.

You must understand this is a nerve-wracking thing for me. Whenever a story is playing out in my head, I'm always afraid my readers will hate it.

"Oh!" Amanda said. "Which one? I wish you would do Beauty and the Beast," she said. "It's my favorite!"

"Mine too!" I exclaimed, feeling a tiny wave of relief wash over me.

"Except I think the beast should be gorgeous instead of ugly. I think he should be really, really handsome, and his heart should be what's ugly," Amanda said.

"Exactly!" I replied, another wave of relief washing over me.

It was then I decided to let Valor and Coquette leap from my mind and onto a page. Amanda had given me the affirmation and courage I needed. (Thanks, Amanda!)

August was upon me, and I had written the prologue, first chapter, and first whispered kiss encounter between Valor and Coquette. Off I was to a book convention, my flash drive in tow. Valor and Coquette, however, needed liberation, and I couldn't get the story out of my mind. Therefore, one August night—as my good friend Marnie and I were sitting around in our pajamas in our hotel room listening to Bon Jovi and Harry Connick Jr.

and eating jerky and cookies—I asked Marnie if she would read the prologue and first chapter of the book I had entitled *The Whispered Kiss*.

As I sat on the bed in my Tinkerbell pajamas, Marnie read the prologue out loud. At one point, she paused and asked, "Where do you come up with this dialogue? How do you think of having them talk like this?" referring to the style of verbiage Valor used. I was momentarily bewildered. What did she mean? I didn't think of it—Valor talked that way!

"Well," I began, "that's the way he talks . . . in my head. When I hear his voice, that's how he speaks."

Marnie laughed, grabbed another cookie, and read on. It was then, however, that I realized something: I had to share my "Beauty and the Beast" story. I had to let Valor and Coquette out of my mind and into your hands.

I'm always nervous about a new book, fearful of disappointing friends, not entertaining to the fullest. And I will admit, releasing this story for all to read causes a certain amount of anxious trepidation to linger in my bosom. *The Whispered Kiss* is burned deep into my heart. I love its Beauty and the Beast flavor, its lessons of patience, love, understanding, and triumph. I love that it's a retelling of Amanda's favorite fairy tale, that Marnie ate cookies and read it out loud to me while wearing her pajamas one warm

August night. I love that my dear friend Amy called me up one day after reading over a few chapters and uttered two sentences that still make me laugh so hard I cry whenever I think of them! I love that my daughter realized the name of the city "Bostchelan" [bost-sha-**lan**] came from a blend of Boston (the intriguing and historically rich city) and Chelan (a beautiful blue lake in Washington state our family once visited). I love that my friend Kay-Ron found that I couldn't spell *Godfrey* the same way twice. I love that Valor has amber eyes and that Coquette is named after a line in a song sung by Bing Crosby in the Disney version of *The Legend of Sleepy Hollow*.

In the end, I love this beauty and her beast—this good girl and her bad boy—one of my favorite fairy tales, retold just for your heart and mine.

~Marcia Lynn McClure

Center Point Large Print
600 Brooks Road / PO Box 1
Thorndike, ME 04986-0001 USA

(207) 568-3717

US & Canada:
1 800 929-9108
www.centerpointlargeprint.com